Barely Breathing

A COLORADO HIGH COUNTRY NOVEL

by

Pamela Clare

BARELY BREATHING

A Colorado High Country Novel

Published by Pamela Clare, 2016

Cover Design by © Carrie Divine/Seductive Designs

Photo of couple by © dariyad/fotolia.com

Photo of mountain © avmedved (Andrei Medvedev)/
Depositphotos.com

Copyright © 2016 by Pamela Clare

ISBN-10: 0-9903771-6-4

ISBN-13: 978-0-9903771-6-0

Dedication

For Marie Force, who reached out to me in 2011 when I lost my newspaper job and encouraged me to self-publish — and then showed me how. From notes on a napkin at RWA13 to reality, here is the book we talked about.

Thanks for everything.

Acknowledgments

Many thanks to Michelle White, Jackie Turner, Shell Ryan, Pat Egan Fordyce, Debby Owens, and Ann Wainwright for their feedback as I worked on this novel.

Special thanks to Jeff Sparhawk, public information officer with Rocky Mountain Rescue Group™, who took the time to explain the complex work of alpine rescues so that I could present it to my readers. My admiration for RMRG never ceases. Any errors in this story are mine.

Additional thanks to Rick Hatfield, park ranger, for the ride-along and continued friendship; and to my younger son Benjamin Alexander for his insights as a county seasonal ranger. I couldn't have written this book without these two bunny-loving tree-huggers.

Thanks to author Julie James for giving me some insights into life in Chicago. I'll have to visit one day and try Lou Malnati's deep dish pizza.

And, finally, thanks to all my climbing heroes, those here and those who are gone, for living the dream: Lynn Hill, Alex Lowe, Conrad Anker, Gören Kropp, Dean Potter, Steph Davis, Alex Honnold, Ueli Steck, Chris Sharma, Sasha DiGiulian, and the Wideboyz… In my imagination, I'm touching the sky right beside you.

Glossary

Colorado and climbing lingo is listed here in order of appearance. I have included only those terms that were not specifically defined in the text. Many of these are probably self-explanatory, but I'm offering this reference just to be certain. I encourage you to watch climbing films on video to get a feel for this dynamic sport.

"At altitude" — A phrase Coloradans use to distinguish life and conditions in the mountains from life anywhere else.

Rock cut — A place where a rock has been cut or blasted away to make room for a road, usually leaving high rock walls on the uphill side but sometimes on both sides. Also, an overlook on Trail Ridge Road.

Knockers — Short for "tommyknockers," a mythical creature brought to Colorado and other states by miners from Cornwall and Devonshire. Some people believed they were the spirits of dead miners. Others believed they were supernatural. Most agreed that they played pranks on miners and protected them by warning them of impending cave-ins. Some, however, believed they were evil and caused the cave-ins. It was a tradition for miners to toss the crusts of their pasties to the knockers to keep them happy.

Evac — Short for evacuation, the term used for rescuing a stranded, lost, or wounded party from the wilderness. "Vertical evac," means more or less straight down (or sometimes up). "Scree evac" means following the fall line down over rocks and dirt. "Trail evac" means using an existing trail.

Free solo climbing — Climbing without ropes or other protection.

Sports climbing — Climbing with ropes using permanently fixed protection, such as bolts drilled into the rock.

Take a whipper — An especially hard fall, often with a pendulum motion that slams the climber into the rock. Often caused by unskilled belaying.

Belay — To provide security to a climber by letting out or taking in slack, often through a braking device, in order to limit the distance a climber might fall.

Rack — A term used to describe the collection of gear that they take with them on a climb. It's not on a rack, per se, but rather a loop of webbing that is often slipped over one shoulder and across the torso like a sash with the gear dangling by the hip where it can be easily reached. Yes, there are lots of "check out my rack" jokes.

Anchor — A configuration of gear, such as ropes, cams, and cables, used to secure belay ropes during an evacuation.

Anchor problem — Doing the mathematics to figure out how best to create the anchor to ensure it will hold the required weight. This includes how the anchor is set, where it is set and what is used to set it.

Lead climber — The climber who goes first and places protection on the rock as he or she goes, attaching the belay rope as they climb (traditional climbing) or clips the belay rope into preplaced equipment attached to bolts (sports climbing). They're responsible for picking the route and making sure that protection is set safely. This person is often a very experienced and skilled climber.

Down climb — To climb back down a climbing route.

Call number — The number assigned to an individual in law enforcement or search and rescue that identifies them to dispatchers on the radio. Different agencies have identifiable numbers. All sheriff's deputies might be 16-something, while all city police might be 12-something, for example.

SAR — Search & Rescue

Crack climbing — To ascend a rock face by climbing up a natural fissure in the rock.

Offwidth climbing — To climb a crack that is too big to manage using fingers and too small to climb by wedging your entire body ("chimney") into the rock. Expect to bleed.

Hand stack — Both hands pressed together, sometimes bent, to fill an offwidth crack.

Fist stack — Using fists side-by-side as an anchor in an offwidth crack.

Heel-toe cam — Using one's entire foot as an anchor in an offwidth crack.

Big Bro — The name of an expandable bolt used to create anchors in a rock face.

Cams — Expandable devices inserted into cracks as anchors. Camalots are a brand of cams.

Pitch — A section of a rock climb

Undercling — A type of hold where one latches onto a horizontal crack from the bottom

To "dirt" someone — To lower them down to the floor or the ground when you're on belay.

Dyno — An upward lunge during which both hands and feet completely leave the rock. Failing to "stick" the dyno means you fall. It's something of a show-off move in climbing.

Crimper — A tiny hold big enough only for the tips of one's fingers or toes.

Sloper — A handhold that is really just a bulge in the rock. There's no edge to hold onto, but friction from a flattened palm makes them useful (but tricky) as a handhold. I haven't defined the other holds because they're pretty self-explanatory.

Crux move — The toughest move of any given climb or pitch.

Rap down — "Rap" is short for rappelle, which is to descend a rock face or other near-vertical surface by using an anchored rope coiled around the body.

Emergency webbing harness — A harness made by wrapping nylon webbing (which isn't web-like at all, but is basically a thick nylon strap) around a person's body in a certain way.

Timberline — The elevation beyond which trees will not grow on a mountain. In Colorado, that's just above 10,000 feet elevation. Also called "tree line."

Chapter One

Lexi Jewell drove her silver Lexus IS convertible up Forest Canyon, top down, sunlight spilling from a clear Colorado sky. The late May breeze was warm in her hair, the air rich with the scent of ponderosa pine. Big Head Todd and the Monsters' "Broken Hearted Savior" blasted on her sound system, a nod to the fact that she'd spent last night in Boulder, the group's hometown.

She glanced in her rearview mirror, the blue SUV behind her riding her bumper hard. The driver must think he had superpowers and didn't need to worry about the speed limit, hairpin turns, sheer cliff walls, or steep drop-offs. But Lexi had grown up here and knew only too well how deadly these roads could be.

She saw a slow-vehicle turnout ahead and pulled over, letting the speed demons pass. An SUV with three mountain bikes in a carrier on the back. Another SUV, this one with two kayaks perched on top. A battered blue Ford carrying bales of hay, its dented bumper sporting a faded sticker that read, "Keep Scarlet Weird."

Well, no problem there. If "weird" were a country, Scarlet Springs would be its capital, its shining city upon the hill. And Lexi was moving back there.

No, she wasn't *moving* back. She would only be there for a few weeks. She'd brought only three suitcases—clothes, personal stuff, her computer— and a box of books she'd never gotten the time to read. Most of her things were still in storage in Chicago, where they would stay until she could regroup and get the situation with her father and stepmother under control.

Chicago, not Scarlet Springs, was her home now.

She hadn't been back to Scarlet since the Christmas before last. She'd been weeks away from making partner at Price & Crane, or so she'd believed.

Her sister, Britta, had come home, too, and the two of them had spent hours snuggled in front of the fireplace, getting to know each other again. They'd promised to spend their next Christmas together, just the two of them, either in Lexi's Bucktown condo or in Britta's apartment in San Diego. It was a promise Lexi hadn't been able to keep.

By her thirtieth birthday that following March, the life she'd built for herself had fallen apart, thanks to Mr. Crane of Price & Crane. Now, she was thirty-one and had no job, no condo—*and* she was on her way back to Scarlet, the town she'd spent her entire childhood wanting to escape.

How did big-city life work out for you, Lexi girl?

She could almost hear her father's voice.

None of this had been her fault. Her work had been outstanding, her initiative and work ethic excellent, her performance reviews stellar. She'd never broken a rule or violated a single corporate policy. No, none of it was her fault, but you wouldn't know that from the way people at the firm had treated her.

As soon as the news had leaked, her co-workers had started tip-toeing around her, giving her the side-eye in the hallway and the break room, whispering behind her back. People she'd thought of as close friends had suddenly stopped returning calls and quit inviting her out, afraid for their careers. Chris, her boyfriend and a junior partner at the firm, had blamed her for the whole thing and dumped her.

"Maybe if you didn't dress like you were looking for a fuck, Crane wouldn't have gotten the wrong message. You should never have reported him."

She couldn't help feeling like some pathetic stereotype of the small-town girl who'd gone off to the big city full of dreams only to be chewed up and spit out.

That pretty much describes what happened, doesn't it?

And now, as a bonus, the father she'd never been close to had apparently gone off the deep end since his wife, Kendra, had left him. He drank too much, neglected the inn, and, if Kendra hadn't exaggerated, had taken up shoplifting.

Shoplifting?

What a brilliant idea, Dad.

This was his way of showing Kendra how much he needed her, but turning into the world's biggest loser was not the way to win her back. If he didn't watch it, she'd divorce him. If that happened, either Lexi or Britta would have to move back home to help him run the inn, something neither of them had any interest in doing.

She turned up the music, trying to drown out her worries, the next curve sending her past the Mine Shaft, a little roadside pizza place that catered mostly to bikers and had been in business as long as she could remember. "World's Best Pizza" read the hand-painted wooden sign out front.

Not even close.

Though the pizza there was better than frozen, store-bought pizza, it was nothing compared to Lou Malnati's deep-dish pizza—her favorite.

A wave of homesickness washed through her, so many of the things she'd come to love now far behind her—the city lights reflecting off the Chicago River at night, walking on the beach in the summer, the culinary thrill of Taste of Chicago.

Victoria Woodley, her best friend and former college roommate, said she needed to look at the silver lining. "After all that stress, you're getting a long vacation at the expense of those bastards at Price and Crane. You'll have all the time you need to unwind, sort things out, and make new plans."

Lexi supposed that was true, but this was not the way she'd planned it, not the way she'd thought her life would go. And, God, she was going to miss Vic, too.

This is just temporary. Just temporary.

The canyon began to widen, the view opening up before her, the mountainsides dotted with barren heaps of yellowish rock, mine tailings left from the days when the gold and silver rushes had brought prospectors to Colorado's mountains.

She rounded the next curve, and her breath caught.

The Indian Peaks—South and North Arapahoe, Apache, Arikaree, Kiowa, Navajo, Ogalalla, and Pawnee. They ringed the valley that nestled Scarlet Springs, their white-capped summits jabbing toward the sky, jagged and awe-inspiring, remnants of a massive volcanic eruption that humanity had been fortunate enough to miss.

No matter how many times she saw that view, it never failed to amaze her. Some of the tension she'd been carrying lifted. She didn't hate everything about Scarlet Springs, after all. The mountains were beautiful, and the men ...

Austin Taylor.

It had been a long time since she'd thought about him.

Okay, not all that long. A few hours maybe.

Well over six feet tall with dark blond hair and the bluest eyes, he'd been her first serious boyfriend, her first lover, her first heartbreak. He'd lettered in football and had been the school's champion skier, taking state in both giant slalom and freeride—a big deal for a senior class with fewer than a hundred students. He was a park ranger and paramedic now, or so her father had said. It was the perfect job for him.

You're going to run into him.

Of course, she was going to run into him. Scarlet was a small town with a single grocery store. Everyone bumped into everyone all the time.

Not that it would be a big deal for either of them when it happened. They were now adults with busy lives, not high school seniors in the throes of their first sexual relationship. They had both moved on a long time ago.

Well, mostly.

She was on the outskirts of town now. Highway 119 intersected with a dirt road with a brown parks sign that read, "Moose Lake." A few yards down the road from that stood another that read, "Scarlet Springs Town Limit, Pop. 1,447, Elevation 8,936."

Well, here you are.

Yes, here she freaking was.

She'd reached the top of the hill that overlooked town when something off the side of the road caught her eye and had her pushing on the brake. At first, she thought it was a mountain goat hanging out on the rocky embankment, but it was too small. As she got closer, she realized it was a little white dog, and it seemed to be stranded.

She pulled onto the shoulder, parked, and got out of the car. "Hey, buddy, how'd you get up there?"

The dog stood on a rocky ledge about twenty feet off the ground on what was a steep rock cut. It wagged its little tail, barked, then whined, staring down at her. If it had climbed up there, it could surely climb down. Right?

She whistled, called to it, tried to encourage it, clapping her hands against her thighs in universal doggy sign language for "come here." "You can do it, boy. Or girl. From here, I can't tell. Sorry."

The dog gave a brave little wag of its tail, took a hesitant step, then stopped, whining again. The little guy was terrified, its body trembling.

A semi drove by in low gear, using its engine to break as it hurtled down the hill toward town, the roar making the dog even more afraid. It whimpered, dark eyes looking down at her as if she were its only hope for salvation.

"I can't come up after you, or we'll both be stuck up there."

The fire department.

They had trucks. They had ladders. If they got cats out of trees, couldn't they get a dog off a rock cut?

"Hold on, buddy." She drew out her cell phone, looked online for the fire department's non-emergency number, and dialed, giving her location to the dispatcher and explaining the situation.

"I'm alerting both the fire department and the Rocky Mountain Search and Rescue Team, ma'am," the dispatcher said. "You're right up the road from the fire department. They should be on the scene in a matter of minutes."

"Thanks." Lexi slid her phone back into her pocket and called up to the dog, trying to soothe it. "Hang in there, buddy. We'll save you."

The morning sun beat down on her, and she remembered too late how quickly her skin burned at altitude. Being a natural redhead had its downside. Wishing she'd remembered to bring a hat, she glanced down the hill, expecting to see an emergency-response vehicle headed her way. Apart from a couple of cars, the only other person on the road was a hiker in a red hat.

Above her, the dog whimpered and whined.

"You poor baby!" Where was the dog's owner? Lexi had no sympathy for people who neglected their pets. "Help is on its way. I promise. How long have you been stuck there? You're probably thirsty, aren't you?"

She glanced down the hill again. There was still no sign of either the fire department or any rescue team, but the hiker was moving quickly in her direction. He wore shorts and flip flops, his short-sleeved shirt unbuttoned, his red hat...

That wasn't a hat. It was a firefighter's helmet.

He was the fire department's response?

One man in shorts, an unbuttoned shirt, and flip flops.

Only in Scarlet.

He reached her in a matter of minutes, giving her a nod, only a little out of breath. He seemed to take in the situation at a glance, then stared at her, his face splitting in a wide grin. "Lexi Jewell. I sure didn't expect to find you here."

It took her a moment to recognize him, and when she did, she found herself smiling. "Eric? Eric Hawke?"

Oh. My. God.

What had happened to the skinny kid who'd blushed every time she'd looked at him? Eric Hawke had grown up to be … well, *ripped* was the first word that came to mind. *Hot* was the second.

There was stubble on his jaw, his skin tanned. A sprinkling of dark hair covered his chest, bisecting a six-pack and disappearing in a thin line behind the waistband of his shorts. Even his legs were tanned and muscular.

He reached for the hand mic clipped to his collar, and she saw he wore an earpiece. "Scarlet FD on the scene, made contact with the RP."

She willed herself to look into his eyes. "So, you're a firefighter now?"

Of course he's a firefighter! Why else would he wear a firefighter's helmet?

"I'm chief of Scarlet's fire department." His gaze shifted from her to the dog. "Looks like we've got a little problem here."

He took off his helmet and handed it to her, his dark hair damp with sweat. Then he walked around her car to the rock face and started to climb.

She didn't mean to tell him his business, but this hardly seemed safe. "Shouldn't you use a rope or a ladder or something?"

"Nah." His gaze was on the rock. "This is easy."

He'd gotten perhaps five feet off the ground when a white SUV with the words "Forest County Parks & Open Space" on the side pulled up behind her car, lights flashing. A tall man in an olive green ranger uniform and mirrored aviator sunglasses stepped out.

Lexi's pulse tripped.

Austin.

He was taller, his dark blond hair shorter, his body filled out, more muscular, but she would have recognized him anywhere—those cheekbones, that jaw, those lips.

She'd known she'd run into him sooner or later, but why did it have to be today?

She sucked in a breath and put a smile on her face. "Austin."

*A*ustin Taylor tried to ignore the fact that his heart had skipped a beat. He acknowledged Lexi with a nod, then turned his attention to Hawke. "You got this?"

"Yeah. No need to tone out the Team." Hawke drew himself up beside the dog, took it beneath his left arm, and started down climbing.

Austin reached for the hand mic of his radio, which he kept clipped to a loop on his uniform shirt. "Fifty-six-twenty."

"Fifty-six-twenty, go ahead."

"Disregard that last call for SAR. Scarlet FD has it under control."

"Ten-twenty-three," dispatch responded, noting the time for the official record.

Hawke dropped the last few feet to the ground, the dog under one arm. He scratched behind its ears. "How the hell did you get up there?"

Lexi hurried over to Eric, handed him his helmet and took the dog, a smile on her face. "I can't believe you climbed that in flip flops."

"It was nothing, really, but if you want to be impressed, go ahead." The grin on Hawke's face told Austin he was enjoying the attention.

Hawke had once had a serious crush on Lexi, calling her "Sexy Lexi." Okay, so Hawke hadn't been the only one to use that nickname. All of the boys, including Austin, had used it, too, because…

Damn.

She looked just like he remembered her—long hair a soft shade of red, high cheekbones, big, green eyes, a perfect mouth. Well, maybe she *had* changed a little. Her hair was longer, and the white tank top and denim skirt she wore clung to curves that were clearly fuller.

Holy hell.

She set the squirming dog on the ground, knelt beside it. "You're happy to be down, aren't you? Poor puppy."

The dog wagged its entire body, lavishing her face with kisses.

She laughed, looked up at Austin with those big eyes. "Do you have water? I think he's thirsty. He's been stuck up there for a while."

She didn't seem to have a leash, and she hadn't brought water either. What kind of dog owner was she?

"I've got some in the vehicle." Austin went to get it, returning with a bottle of water and a collapsible water bowl.

She gave him a bright smile that made his pulse skip again. "I guess you're prepared for everything."

Everything except seeing *her* again.

He knelt down beside her, close enough to catch the scent of her skin— clean and feminine and familiar. He lost his train of thought, his mouth struggling to find words. "I come across stray pets fairly often. Sometimes I work with rescue dogs."

The dog drank greedily.

"You were thirsty, weren't you?" He scratched behind the dog's ears, disappointed to see dirt, burrs, and tangles in its fur. He would have expected better of Lexi. She had always loved animals. "Do you have a leash?"

She shook her head.

"This is Forest County Open Space. Dog owners are required to keep their dogs on leash at all times. I'm going to have to issue you a ticket for—"

"A ticket?" Lexi gaped at him. "How can you ticket *me*?"

Her response surprised him, made his hackles rise. Did she think he would give her a break because they'd once had a connection?

"Aw, come on, man," Eric protested. "Cut her some slack. She just got here."

Austin's temper spiked. Hawke had spent five minutes with Lexi and already he wanted Austin to bend the rules for her? He was thinking with his balls—again. "That's not how it works."

Then Lexi's eyes went wide, her lips forming a little O, a look of comprehension on her face. She laughed, the sweet sound stirring memories.

What was so damned funny?

"It's not my dog."

"It's not your dog?" Austin repeated, stupidly.

Behind him, Hawke chuckled.

"I was just driving by when I saw the little guy up there and stopped to help."

And the pieces came together.

"Got it. Not your dog." He found himself laughing, too. "I guess that means no ticket. I'll grab a leash and take it to impound."

It was disappointing, really. He'd been working his way toward seriously disliking her—the woman who'd broken his teenage heart and didn't take care of her dog. But she'd stopped to help a stranded animal.

Damn.

He strode to his vehicle, grabbed a leash, and returned. He was about to fix it to the dog's collar, when a young woman in a crocheted halter top and ankle-length tie-dyed skirt clambered over the opposite embankment and ran across the highway on bare feet, blond dreadlocks hanging down her back.

She glared at Lexi, her hands making fists. "What are you doing with my dog?"

Austin hadn't seen her around here before and guessed she was with the group of transients that had camped out on Forest Service land over the weekend. Her tone and bearing had him instinctively stepping closer to Lexi.

Lexi started to answer her. "I—"

"Your dog was stuck up there." Hawke stepped in front of Lexi. "She stopped and called for help. I believe what you're trying to say is, 'Thank you.'"

The woman scooped the dog into her arms, still glaring at Lexi. "You didn't have to call no one. I'd have found him. I always find him."

Austin would have ticketed her, but he could see the woman wasn't carrying an ID with her. She probably didn't have a permanent address. There was no way to be certain she'd give him her real name and no mechanism to ensure that she paid the ticket. In other words, giving her a ticket would accomplish nada.

"Take this." He held out the leash. "Dogs must be kept leashed at all times on National Forest and county open-space land."

She glared at him. "Dogs gotta run."

Austin nodded. "Sure they do. Sometimes they run into packs of coyotes that tear them apart. Sometimes they run into skunks, porcupines, rabid foxes, bears. Sometimes they run across highways and get hit by cars. If you care about your dog, you'll want to do all you can to keep it safe. If I find it abandoned again, I'll take it to impound."

She jerked the leash from his hand, set the dog down, and attached the leash to its collar, muttering profanities.

Austin didn't give a damn if he made her angry. He pushed a little harder. "There's a low-cost pet clinic in town. If the dog isn't up on its vaccinations, take it in for a quick checkup. Rabies shots are free on the third Friday of every month."

"Whatever." She shot Lexi one last dirty look before crossing the highway again and disappearing down the embankment, the dog following behind her.

Lexi stared after her. "What did I do?"

"No good deed goes unpunished." Hawke shook his head. "You handled that well, ranger man."

"You both did," Lexi said. "Thanks for your help, guys."

"That's what we're here for." Hawke flashed that stupid grin of his.

Go ahead, buddy. Play it for all it's worth.

Austin kept his voice neutral, professional, irritated by the way some part of him had reacted to her praise. He was as bad as Hawke. "Thanks for calling it in. There aren't many rangers. We depend on people to be our eyes and ears."

"Are you here for a while or just a few days?" Hawke asked her.

Austin already knew the answer—or thought he knew.

"I came to help my father, but I won't be staying long."

Of course, she wouldn't.

Still, Austin knew she and her father had never been close, so he supposed it involved some genuine sacrifice for her to put her life in Chicago on hold to help the old man. "I'm sure he'll be glad you're back."

"I'm not." There was no emotion in her voice. It was just a statement of fact. "He wants his wife, but he's stuck with me for now."

Austin was about to ask Lexi what was going on between Bob and Kendra, but that was too personal a conversation to have with someone he hadn't spoken with for twelve years and, frankly, none of his business.

Instead, he bent down, dumped the leftover water out of the bowl, and shook it out before collapsing it again. He turned to Hawke. "You need a lift back to the station?"

"Nah, man, I'm good." Hawke grinned. "Though I wouldn't say no to a ride in Lexi's snazzy little convertible."

Lexi laughed. "Hop in."

Austin glanced at his watch, feeling the need to move on. He reached for his hand mic. "Fifty-six-twenty."

"Fifty-six-twenty, go ahead."

"Show me back in service."

"Fifty-six-twenty. Ten-thirty-two."

"I imagine I'll see you around town, Lexi." He turned toward his vehicle. "Hawke, I'll see you at Saturday's training, if not before."

Both of them were members of the Rocky Mountain Search & Rescue Team and never knew when they might get called out. It was rare during the warmer months for a week to go by without the Team getting tasked with multiple missions.

Hawke shouted after him. "Hey, you want to grab a burger and a brew at Knockers tonight? Timberline Mudbugs are playing."

That actually sounded good, though Austin might go for a scotch instead of beer. "Sure. I get off at seventeen-thirty. Meet you at nineteen-hundred."

"You'll join us, won't you, Lexi?"

Austin heard the trap Hawke had set for him snap shut.

You bastard.

Hawke just grinned.

Lexi looked from Hawke to Austin and back again, then shook her head. "Maybe some other time. I need to get settled at my dad's place tonight."

Austin tried not to let his relief show.

Chapter Two

Lexi put her car into gear and nosed back onto the highway, Austin disappearing up the road behind her in his service vehicle. "He didn't appreciate that, you know. He wouldn't have agreed to meet up with you if he'd known you were going to invite me."

She might not have seen Austin in twelve years, but she could still read him. She hadn't expected him to be excited about seeing her again, but she also hadn't expected him to be so … *cold.*

"Dude needs to lighten up." Eric took his helmet from his head, dropped it into his lap, the wind catching his hair. "It would have been good for him. He'd have had a few beers, gotten reacquainted with you, realized you're not an ogre."

"He thinks I'm an ogre?" She laughed but felt a twinge of hurt just the same.

Eric gave her a "duh" look. "You *did* break his heart."

"He broke *my* heart." She'd never cried so hard in her life as that night he'd dropped her off in front of the inn and driven away. He hadn't even said goodbye. "He's the one who ended it."

"Sure." Eric nodded, then looked over at her. "But only after you told him you thought the two of you should date other people. What did you expect?"

"That's *not* what I said." She ought to have known Eric would side with Austin. The two had been best friends since they were little.

"Okay, so you both played a role in screwing things up, but, hey, you were just kids. That's why I tried to get you together. I thought it would give you both a chance to let go of the past."

"I let go of all that when I left Scarlet."

"Uh-huh." The tone of Eric's voice told her she hadn't fooled him.

Months had gone by before the pain in her chest had dulled to something bearable. God, how she'd missed Austin. She'd missed him more than she'd known she could miss anyone. She'd missed his kisses, his sense of humor, the way he'd made her feel special. Everything had reminded her of him—a song on the radio, their favorite TV shows, a couple kissing in the park. It had been a solid year before she'd even considered dating again. To this day, she never saw a box of Junior Mints—his favorite movie theater candy—without thinking of him.

If only she'd kept her mouth busy kissing him that night instead of talking, that entire summer might have been very different. It's not like she'd truly *wanted* to date other guys. She'd been in love with Austin. Still, she'd known their lives were about to change and that they were headed in different directions. She'd thought she was being mature by forcing herself to face that fact, but he'd thought she didn't love him.

What she hadn't known, what she couldn't have known until she'd gotten settled in Illinois, was that she would have changed her plans—just to be with him. But by then it had been too late.

"If I were you, I wouldn't stir the pot." She turned into the parking lot behind the fire station. "You'll only make Austin angry."

"I think I've made *you* angry." He grinned, apparently untroubled by this. "Damn, it's good to see you again, Lexi."

She let go of her irritation. "It's good to see you, too. But, hey, if you ever actually fight a fire, you might want to, you know, wear something. I hear fires are hot and dangerous."

Which was also a great description of the man sitting beside her.

He chuckled. "I'll try to remember that."

"Good." If he dressed like this, the women and gay men of Scarlet from age nine to ninety might start setting their houses on fire just to stare at him.

"Hey, if you're looking for a date during the short time you're in town, I'm available." Eric rattled off his phone number, then opened the door and stepped out. "If you can't remember that, just dial 911."

She laughed. "How do you know I'm not already in a relationship?"

She hadn't been with anyone since Chris. Trust issues, Vic said.

Eric glanced at her hand. "No ring means there's nothing I need to take seriously."

"I don't recall you being this bold in high school."

The Eric she remembered had been shy.

He looked her straight in the eyes. "If I had been, Austin wouldn't have been the one to pop your cherry."

She gaped at him, unable to keep from laughing. "You're sure of that, are you?"

"See you around, Lexi." He gave her a devastating smile, then disappeared inside the fire station.

Still laughing at Eric's brashness, she left the fire station, passed St. Barbara's Catholic Church and Frank's Pump 'N' Go, and soon reached the town's biggest intersection—a roundabout where Highway 119 intersected with Second Street and Highway 72. She kept to the right, driving past the fossil store and the New Life Institute, where people paid thousands of dollars to have their heads cryogenically frozen after death so they could be brought back to life. Then she took a right turn onto West First Street. There, across from Rose's New Age Emporium, Izzy's Mountain Café, and a new marijuana shop called Nature's Meds, stood the Forest Creek Inn.

Yellow with white trim, it was an enormous three-story Victorian home, one of the town's oldest inhabited buildings and a registered historic landmark. The large yard had been landscaped over several generations with small clusters of aspens, tall blue spruce, two benches, dozens of flower beds, and a pond. The bed and breakfast was run out of the top two floors, while the family had four bedrooms, a bathroom, a family room, kitchen, and dining room on the ground floor.

Everyone assumed it must have been great fun to grow up in a stately, old house with so much history. They had no idea how much work it was to run a business out of one's home. They looked at the inn and saw its charm. She saw endless chores and lots of rules. Toilets to clean. Beds to make. Furniture to dust. No running. No jumping. No shouting. No friends coming for sleepovers.

She turned into the long, paved driveway and headed back to the parking area reserved for family. She'd no sooner parked the car and turned off the engine, when she caught sight of her father. He stood in the backyard watering one of the flower beds wearing nothing but his underwear.

Sweet Jesus, Mary, and Joseph!

He really *had* gone off the deep end.

Leaving her suitcases, she jumped out of the car and ran over to him. "Dad, what on earth are you doing? You're going to scare the guests away!"

He turned his head, looking much older than the last time she'd seen him, his jaw covered with gray stubble, his salt-and-pepper hair unwashed and uncombed. "So, one of the prodigal daughters has returned."

*A*ustin turned off the highway, drove the short distance to Moose Lake, and parked. He reached for his hand mic. "Fifty-six-twenty. Moose Lake on foot patrol."

"Fifty-six twenty," dispatch acknowledged. "Moose Lake. Eleven-oh-five."

So … Lexi Jewell, huh?

Damn.

He'd known she was coming back to Scarlet, had known his path would cross hers eventually, but running into her as the reporting party of a call had caught him off guard. What had surprised him most was his reaction.

Some part of him had actually felt *happy* to see her.

How he could feel anything for her—good or bad—was beyond him. Like cleats, ski racing, and homecoming floats, she was a part of his past, just a woman he used to know. They might as well be strangers.

Except that she hadn't felt like a stranger.

It had been twelve years since he'd seen her, twelve years since he'd kissed her, twelve years since he'd held her, but everything about her had felt familiar—the sound of her laughter, the way she smiled, the dimple in her left cheek. He'd felt drawn to her, as if some stupid part of him—probably the part attached at his groin—recognized her and wanted to stake some kind of claim.

Well, she wasn't his. She never had been.

She'd made that clear on July 4, 2004—a date he remembered only because it was a holiday. They'd gone up past the ghost town of Caribou—to watch the fireworks, he'd told her father—and fucked each other's brains out on a blow-up mattress he'd tossed in the back of his old Ford. Afterward, she'd lain naked on top of him, and they'd kissed. It had been perfect—until it imploded.

"I'm going to miss you so much, Austin."

"I'm going to miss you, too, but we'll see each other over break."

"I'm not coming back here."

"What? What do you mean you're not coming back?"

"Once I leave town, that's it. I'm not coming back to Scarlet—not for a very long time, anyway. I can't stand this place. You know that."

"When will we see each other?"

"I don't know. I suppose you could come to Champaign, and I could visit you in Fort Collins."

"You suppose*?"*

He had imagined them going to college, spending breaks together, and getting married after graduation. But she'd had a very different future in mind, one that hadn't seemed to include him. With a few words, she'd brought his world crashing down.

If he'd had half a brain in his eighteen-year-old head, he would have let it go and taken the summer to convince her that she couldn't live without him. Instead, he'd accused her of not loving him the way he loved her—which had been true—and had ended their relationship that night.

"I thought we'd stay together, spend our vacations in Scarlet, and maybe get married, depending on how things go."

"Get married? Austin, we're way too young even to think about that. We both need to see new places, try new things, meet other people. Maybe when we're older—"

"You want to date other guys?"

"That's not what I said. But the world is going to get bigger for both of us, and chances are we'll change a lot. Statistically speaking, the vast majority of high school relationships don't last."

"Is that what this is to you—just a high school relationship? Am I just a fun way to pass the summer till you leave for college and hook up with other guys?"

"Austin—"

"Get dressed. I'm taking you home, Lexi."

He'd been so angry, so hurt. They hadn't spoken a word to each other while he'd driven her home, fireworks exploding overhead, his heart in pieces.

In retrospect, they'd both been right. He truly had loved her more than she'd loved him, and she'd understood that they were far too young for serious commitment. She'd also known herself well enough to see that the life she wanted couldn't include him. He had to give her credit for that. But knowing all of this didn't take away the memory of heartbreak.

First love. Why did people romanticize it? It sucked.

True, none of the handful of relationships Austin had had with women since then had been able to match the intensity of that year with Lexi. The two of them had spent every spare minute thinking about sex, reading how-to manuals about sex, talking about sex, or having sex, practicing until they'd got it perfect for each other.

Had it really been *that* good, or was he remembering it through the rose-colored lenses of a teenager?

Hell, he didn't know.

He climbed out of his service vehicle, grabbed his pack, and slipped into it, fastening the waist belt and adjusting its weight on his back. He checked to make sure the trash had been collected then walked over to have a look at the restrooms. The women's room was out of toilet paper, and the men's room…

"Son of a … !"

This day was going downhill fast.

He let the door swing shut, reached for his hand mic. "Fifty-six-twenty."

He didn't understand how shit like this even happened—no pun intended.

"Fifty-six-twenty, go ahead."

"We need the water truck and high-pressure hoses up at Moose Lake. It's time for a Code Brown hose down of the men's room."

There was a hint of laughter in the dispatcher's voice when she answered. "Fifty-six-twenty, Code Brown hose down, Moose Lake. Eleven-oh-nine."

Well, shit.

Literally.

Lexi took advantage of her father's being in the shower to search the place for booze. She'd smelled it on his breath the moment he'd spoken and knew alcohol had to explain some of his strange behavior. She found *seven* half-empty bottles of rum and a couple of bottles of scotch, along with a few dozen mini bottles of every conceivable form of hard liquor known to humanity, carried them to the kitchen, and dumped them down the kitchen sink.

"Are you crazy, girl?" Her father's voice came from behind her. "What the *hell* are you doing?"

Lexi tried to ignore the way his raised voice made her tense. His shouting had always scared her when she was little. "Keep your voice down. We have guests upstairs."

"You're dumping my hard-earned money down the drain."

"Better down the drain than down you. No more drinking, Dad."

"You think you can show up when you like and then go through my things? My drinking is none of your damned business."

"When I find you standing drunk outside watering flowers in your underwear at eleven in the morning, it becomes my business."

He gave a snort. "Should I have waited till afternoon?"

She turned to face him, startled to see that he was wearing only a skimpy towel, his face clean-shaven, his hair wet. "Good grief, Dad! Put some clothes on."

"What's the matter?" He looked down at himself. "I'm decent."

"Only if you're alone with your wife." Seeing her father half naked had never been on her bucket list.

"You been talking to Kendra?"

"She called a few times. That's why I'm here."

"Figures." What he meant by that he didn't say.

"I want to help you win her back." She poured a little bottle of tequila down the drain, the odor of alcohol overpowering. "You can't do that if you're drunk."

He frowned. "That's why you're here?"

She nodded. "You can't run this place on your own. If she divorces you, you'll have to sell the inn, and then what will you do? Do you want to move into a cabin with no electricity and no running water and live off handouts like Bear?"

Bear had lived in a cabin somewhere above Scarlet for as long as anyone could remember. No one knew how old he was or where he'd come from or what had happened to make him the way he was. He'd just always been there, and the townsfolk had always accepted him. As big as a grizzly and gentle as a lamb, he came into town most days, Bible in hand, blessing those kind enough to donate change or buy him a meal.

Her father's eyes narrowed. "What's it matter to you? You don't care about your old man, and you don't give a damn about the inn. Are you doing this for me or for yourself and your sister?"

It sounded so harsh when he put it like that, and she felt an impulse to object, to tell him that she *did* care about him and the inn in her own way. But she couldn't bring herself to say it. "If you get Kendra back, does it matter?"

He seemed to consider this. "No. No, I guess it doesn't."

Then his eyes went wide. "Jesus, no, not the Glenmorangie. That's my Glenmorangie Signet."

Lexi looked at the label. "Not anymore."

Her father clapped both hands to his head, a look of genuine panic on his face. "You can't dump that! That's a two-hundred-dollar bottle of scotch!"

"Two hundred dollars?" She looked at the label, and an idea came to her. "Fine."

She turned and walked out of the house and across the street to Rose's place. She opened the door to the tinkling of bells, the cloying scent of patchouli hitting her in the face. She found Rose in the back doing a tarot reading. Dressed in a gauzy pink sundress, she hadn't changed one bit, her silver hair hanging down her back, crystals dangling from silver chains around her neck.

"A reverse card isn't necessarily a negative thing. It can also mean change, and change can be good." She looked up, saw Lexi. "Hey! I didn't know you were in town."

Lexi held out the scotch. "This is for you."

Rose took the bottle and looked at the label, her eyes going wide. "Oh! My goodness. Thank you!"

"You're welcome." Lexi willed herself to smile. "I didn't mean to interrupt. I'll see you later, I'm sure."

Now that Rose knew she was in town, Lexi wouldn't be able to avoid seeing her. Not that Lexi didn't like Rose. Rose was kind and caring and a very good listener, but she had a tendency to share everything she heard with the rest of the town. She also had a gift for turning what ought to be a ten-minute conversation into a three-hour visit, complete with tarot reading—whether a person wanted one or not.

Lexi turned and walked out the front door into the fresh air, Rose's voice and the reek of patchouli following her. "Come back a little later, and we'll get caught up. I'll read your cards!"

Across the street, her father stood in their front yard, still wearing only a towel. For a moment he stared at her open-mouthed, then he threw up his hands and walked back inside. "Son of a bitch!"

Hawke laughed as Austin recounted his day. "Oh, the glamorous life of a park ranger. Hose downs and garbage duty."

Knockers was doing good business for a Tuesday night. Then again, it was the only brewpub in town. With great beer, decent food, a climbing wall, pool tables, and live music, it was the center of Scarlet's nightlife.

Outsiders and tourists thought the pub's name was about boobs. They didn't stick around long enough to learn that it was a reference to tommyknockers—mythical spirits that dwelt in the mines, watching out for miners. Scarlet Springs had once been a Cornish mining camp, so knockers were just a part of the local history.

Which wasn't to say the pub's name had never made Austin think of boobs...

Bear was going from table to table asking for spare change, while Timberline Mudbugs was laying down a good zydeco beat up on the small stage. The music was loud enough that Austin had to shout to be heard across the table.

"If I'd known what I was getting myself into when I applied for this job..."

Hawke grinned, took a swig of his Glacier Stout. "Hell, I know you. You'd have signed on anyway. You'd go crazy sitting at a desk."

"You're right about that." Austin took a sip of scotch, felt some of the tension he'd carried with him all day ease.

They'd already polished off their burgers and fries. Neither of them had mentioned what had happened earlier with Lexi, and that was just fine with Austin. He wished everyone else would stop talking about her.

From the moment he'd finished his shift, every person he'd run into had asked him whether he knew she was back in town. Rose had seen her, and that meant the whole town knew. Twelve years had gone by, but apparently everyone still thought of them as a couple—or an ex-couple, which was even better. Even his mother had called. She'd pretended at first that she just wanted to talk about his younger sister, Cheyenne. Then she'd brought up the fact that Lexi was back in an oh-so-casual and utterly transparent way that might have made Austin laugh—if he hadn't already been so irritated.

"You ready for Saturday?" Hawke asked.

They would be practicing a standard vertical evac with a modified brake plate up on Redgarden Wall in Eldorado Canyon State Park.

Austin nodded. "Can't wait to see how Belcourt's new invention works out."

Son of a Lakota Sun Dance chief, Chaska Belcourt had come to Colorado to study engineering, had discovered rock climbing, and hadn't looked back. He'd joined the Team a few years back and had made it his personal mission to redesign the gear they used to make it safer and more versatile. He'd come up with a few useful modifications already, and his work was being replicated by rescue teams across the country.

"It tested well on the training tower last—"

Their pagers buzzed at the same time—not the emergency call-out tone, but a buzz. Austin drew his out of his jeans pocket, pushed the button to read the display. He looked up, met Hawke's gaze. "Megs?"

Eric nodded. "I wonder what she wants."

"She probably wants to chew us out for wasting resources again."

The Team had been having cash-flow problems for a while now, donations having taken a dip this past couple of years.

Maggie Hill, called Megs by her friends, was a climbing legend. One of the first women to jump into hardcore rock climbing with the boys back in the late 1960s, she'd helped start the Rocky Mountain Search & Rescue Team after a climbing accident had stranded one of her friends, leaving him to freeze to death. In her early sixties and still climbing, she now served as the Team's director.

"I guess we'd best pay the bill and find out. Whose turn is it this time?"

Hawke grinned. "I had one beer tonight, and you had a scotch. It must be yours."

"You're so full of shit." Austin motioned to Rain, their server.

She smiled, half-walking, half-dancing over to the table, her long blond hair tied up on her head with a red paisley scarf, tattoos of roses, ivy, and skulls twining their way up both forearms, a tiny silver ring in her right nostril.

Two years older than Austin, she'd dropped out of school when she was sixteen to follow her boyfriend's rock band. After he'd dumped her, she'd hitchhiked back to Scarlet, bringing with her a baby girl she'd named Lark. Caribou Joe, the pub's eccentric owner and bartender, had taken her and her daughter in and given her a job.

She crossed her arms over her chest, looked from Austin to Hawke. "Alright, boys. Who gets the damages?"

Hawke drew his wallet out of his pocket, feigning irritation. "Next time I'm paying, you drink beer."

"Yeah? Who had the rib eye last week?" Austin countered. "Cheap bastard."

Rain took Eric's debit card. "Hey, Lexi Jewell's back in town. Have you heard? I guess she came back to help her dad."

Eric met Austin's gaze, grinned. "Yeah, we heard."

Austin felt his teeth grind.

Chapter Three

Ten minutes later, Austin sat with Hawke and most of the other principal Team members in the ops room at The Cave, the group's headquarters. Coffee in hand, he waited with the others for Megs to make some kind of announcement. Her gray hair tied back in a ponytail, she worked her way through roll call, using both first and last names even though most of them had known each other for years and could probably recognize one another by smell.

With Megs, there was no cutting corners. It made her a pain in the ass to work with at times, but it had also saved lives.

"Mitch Ahearn. Chaska Belcourt. Harrison Conrad. Sasha Dillon. Dave Hatfield. Eric Hawke. Creed Herrera … is in Yosemite. Jesse Moretti?"

"Behind you getting coffee." Moretti, a former Army Ranger, had come to Colorado on a vacation to get his head straight after multiple deployments in Afghanistan and Iraq. He'd fallen in love with the mountains and stayed.

"Malachi O'Brien. Isaac Rogers. Gabe Rossiter … still on leave."

Rossiter wasn't really on leave. He'd had a catastrophic fall a few years back while saving his wife's life and had lost a leg. He still climbed, but his priority these days was his wife and their kids. One of the best free solo climbers in the world, he was a tenured member, which meant he had a spot on the Team whether he showed up for meetings or not.

"Jack Sullivan. Nicole Turner. Austin Taylor." Megs raised her head, looked at Austin. "Hey, did you know Lexi Jewell's back in town?"

Austin bit back a stream of profanity.

Eric answered for him. "She was the RP on a call we got this morning involving a stranded dog, so, yeah, he knows."

Megs pointed with her pen. "You all know Police Chief Jim McNalley."

"Hey." McNalley stood off to the side, coffee cup in hand.

His presence at the meeting wasn't unusual. Rocky Mountain SAR partnered with every law enforcement agency in the county. But the fact that no provisional or supporting Team members had been called in meant that something was up. Even so, when Megs finally spilled the beans, Austin was taken by surprise.

"Ted Breece has been stealing from us."

Silence.

"What do you mean 'stealing?'" Austin asked.

There were hundreds of thousands of dollars of gear in The Cave—climbing gear, search and rescue gear, medical supplies.

"I mean 'taking that which is not his.'" Megs always had to be a smartass. "He's been embezzling. We have John at the bank to thank for alerting us."

"How much did the bastard take?" Moretti asked.

Megs shrugged. "I honestly don't know. Twenty grand?"

Someone gave a little whistle.

"Holy shit." Austin met Hawke's gaze, shook his head.

"Well, that explains the cash-flow problems," Nicole said.

Twenty grand might be nothing to a bank or Wall Street investors, but for an independent, all-volunteer nonprofit like Rocky Mountain SAR, it was a damned fortune.

"I spent the weekend going over the books. You know I used to keep them myself. I tried to make sense of it, but he covered his tracks like a pro."

"You're going to need a forensic accountant, someone who knows all the tricks and can help build a case against him," said McNalley. "I've called in the FBI. We'll need their investigative muscle to find out what Breece did with the money. If I had to make a guess, I'd say it's gone. He has a gambling habit and owes a lot of money to the casinos in Blackhawk and Central City."

"Where is the son of a bitch now?" Conrad looked like he wanted to hunt the bastard down and break his neck, and he could do it, too. At six-foot-five, he was the tallest guy on the team and made of iron.

"I know this will come as a shock, but he's skipped town," Megs said.

McNalley drew out a chair and sat. "We just put a BOLO out on him and hope to bring him in for questioning."

"Are we broke? Is it time for bake sales?" At twenty-two, Sasha Dillon was the youngest member of the team—and the most famous. Blonde and petite, she looked fragile—until you watched her climb. She'd won two national sports climbing championships and had the corporate sponsorships to show for it.

"There's money in the bank, but not nearly as much as there should be." Megs let out a frustrated breath. "It's my fault. I should have stayed on top of it and not trusted him to manage it all by himself."

"Don't go blaming yourself." Ahearn had been with the Team longer than anyone other than Megs and was a climbing legend in his own right. He was also Megs' partner. "It's not fair to you and doesn't solve anything."

"Come on, Megs," Moretti said. "Cut yourself a break. How could you know the guy would turn out to be a lying bag of dicks?"

McNalley nodded. "The only person to blame here is Breece. An organization like yours depends on trust. You guys can't do the high-risk work you do if you don't trust one another. He knew that, and he took advantage of that trust."

Belcourt looked up from the brake plate in his hands. "I never did like that guy."

Enough wallowing already.

Austin wanted action. "Where do we go from here?"

"We need to find a forensic accountant willing to work his—or her—ass off for next to nothing," Megs answered. "I've already checked around town, and nobody has experience with this kind of thing."

For some reason, Megs kept looking at Austin. Was she volunteering him?

He was okay with that. "I'll make a few calls, contact some Denver CPA firms, see if any of them would like to earn some nice Rocky Mountain SAR T-shirts."

Everyone laughed.

Megs arched a brow. "What about Lexi Jewell? She's a CPA."

Austin had forgotten that.

"Feel free to ask her yourself." No way in hell was he going to ask Lexi for anything. "I'll check around, see what I can find in Boulder or Denver."

Kendra leaned in, tears in her cat-like eyes, which were a dazzling green tonight thanks to colored contact lenses. "You know how they say a leopard can't change its spots? Well, that man is going to have to change his spots before I come back—every last one of them."

If her father looked older, Kendra looked fantastic. Time off from being his wife had obviously done her some good, her shoulder-length brown hair sleek and shiny, her makeup impeccable, designer jeans and a V-neck tank top making the most of her figure. Lexi might have believed Kendra was better off alone except for one thing.

She'd never seen Kendra cry.

She took a sip of her pinot noir. "Have you told him that in those words?"

Kendra leaned back in the booth and looked away, wiping the tears from her cheeks, her fingertips smearing mascara beneath her eyes. "He knows why I left. We had a big fight one night over hiring someone to help clean. I packed and left. I'm tired of being treated like an employee. I've worked my fingers to the bone for him and that inn without so much as a 'thank you.'"

If anyone could understand that, it was Lexi.

"Sometimes I think he married me so he wouldn't have to pay someone to do your mom's share of the work—and so that you and Britta would have someone to take care of you. We all know how that worked out, don't we?"

Lexi wasn't used to this kind of honesty from Kendra, and for a moment she didn't know what to say, her stepmother's words hitting a tender spot inside her, stirring old resentments and hurts. She took another, deeper drink of wine. "My dad isn't good at showing his feelings."

"Oh, he's plenty good at showing emotion when he's pissed off. It's the other feelings he can't seem to handle."

Lexi knew that only too well. "Have you tried counseling?"

Kendra's head whipped around, her gaze sharp. "Do you really think your dad would sit down and share his feelings with a fricking therapist?"

"Stupid question."

Kendra took a drink of her beer, seeming to swallow her emotions along with the brew. "Enough about this. How are things in Chicago? You must have made partner at that big firm by now."

Lexi had rehearsed this moment in her mind. "I left Price and Crane. The organization had some serious ethical problems, so I quit."

Kendra seemed to measure her, her lips curving in a smile. "You didn't make partner after all."

Lexi had known Kendra would gloat. She'd always seemed to take pleasure in every mistake Lexi made, every slip, every disappointment. But this time, it hadn't been Lexi's fault. "I resigned."

"Huh." Kendra's smiled disappeared, her eyes narrowing to slits as if she were trying to see through Lexi. "I guess the other big firms must have thrown their doors wide open for a person with your skill and training. Where are you working now?"

"Right now, I'm weighing all my options."

Kendra's lips curved in a cold smile. "You don't even have a job."

Lexi smiled, too, keeping her voice cheerful. "I left with a great compensation package and am taking the time to make sure I end up with the right company. I'm considering opening a firm of my own."

It was the truth, though not the whole truth. But then she had never spoken in whole truths with Kendra.

"You got laid off?"

"What? No! I told you I *resigned*."

"They give nice compensation packages to people who *quit*?"

"They do when you take them to court." Lexi blurted out the words. She hadn't planned on going into the details, but she couldn't let Kendra walk away believing she'd been fired or laid off. She hadn't done anything wrong. None of it had been her fault.

Kendra's eyebrows rose. "You sued them. Why?"

She *would* have to ask.

"Sexual harassment. My case was rock solid, so they settled out of court."

For the first time since Lexi had known her, Kendra looked impressed by something she'd done. She raised her beer. "Good for you. Take the bastards for all they're worth. That's what I'll do to your father if he doesn't wise up."

"I'm really hoping it won't come to that."

"I put twenty-five years of my life into that inn." Kendra had left a lucrative marketing job with a ski resort to marry Lexi's father, something she'd never let any of them forget. "I'm not walking away from this marriage with nothing more than gray hair and wrinkles."

Lexi had spoken with a Denver divorce attorney this afternoon. Even without a prenup, Kendra wouldn't be able to take the property away from her father because he'd owned it outright before he'd married her. But she could argue in court that a fat piece of the inn's current worth as a business was a result of her contributions and hard work over twenty-five years. If her father couldn't come up with the money or make adequate payments, he might be forced to sell the inn.

Kendra smiled to herself, looked away. "So now you've come all this way to help your father and me when you could be hanging out on a Caribbean beach holding an umbrella drink. Why the sudden concern?"

Lexi side-stepped that thorny question. "You said Dad had been caught shoplifting. It seemed pretty serious."

Kendra took another drink. "He stole a pair of mittens and a can of chew from Food Mart. He had money in his wallet, but he took them anyway, stuffed them under his coat and tried to walk out the door. He didn't need them. He doesn't even use tobacco. Chief McNalley called me to come get him and let him off with a warning. I told your dad they could've thrown his bony butt in jail, but he didn't seem to care."

"I think it was a cry for help."

Kendra gave a snort. "It was a cry for help, all right, but not the kind that's going to do him any good. If he would just call me, tell me he misses me, say something nice, maybe we could talk."

"He hasn't called you?" Lexi wasn't sure why this surprised her.

He never called her or Britta, either.

"Oh, sure, he's called. The first time, he told me to quit messing around and get back home because we had four rooms to clean. I hung up on him. The second time, he called to say the dryer was broken and there were a bunch of wet sheets in the washer. I told him to call Dave's Repair Shop and gave him detailed directions to the clothesline in the backyard."

Lexi laughed despite herself. "I'm guessing he wasn't grateful."

"No." Kendra grinned, but then her face crumpled. "I miss him. Deep down beneath that thick hide of his, there's a good man. I've known him since before you were born. Something inside him died right along with your mother. I thought I could bring him back to life, and God knows I've tried. But he doesn't care about me anymore."

Lexi didn't want to talk about her mother's death and wasn't sure what she thought about the new, more vulnerable Kendra.

She changed the subject. "Where have you been staying?"

Lexi closed her bedroom door, stretched out on her bed, and called Vic. Chicago was an hour ahead of Colorado, but Vic wasn't the early-to-bed type and answered on the second ring.

"Hey, how does it feel to be home?"

"This *isn't* my home." Vic knew that. "But, yeah, it feels strange."

Lexi told Vic about her day starting with finding her dad watering flowers in his underwear. By the time she'd finished, she wondered if she'd been out of her mind. "I never should have come back."

"Isn't that what I said before you left? The next best thing to not having gone there in the first place is not staying. Feel free to drive home tomorrow. You can live with me until you've sorted everything out."

"Thanks, Vic, but I need to see this through. I need to get the two of them back together, or Britta and I are going to end up with a big mess on our hands. If my dad goes off the deep end like this over Kendra leaving, what will happen if she divorces him and he loses the inn?"

The joking tone left Vic's voice. "You sound genuinely worried."

She was. "My dad and I might not be close, but he's still my dad."

"What are you going to do?"

"I'm not sure." She talked through the possibilities with Vic, trying to decide whether she should just tell her father exactly what Kendra had told her or find some way to soften it for the sake of his pride. "I wish I could just bring them together and make them talk it out."

"With your dad acting bat-shit crazy and Kendra talking divorce? That has a high probability of turning into a disaster."

"The last thing I want to do is make things worse." There *was* a little good news.
"I spent a few hours after supper going over the books. The inn is in the black and doing well. There is no reason my father can't hire a housekeeper."

"That would make your stepmother happy. Will your dad do it?"

"I'm not going to ask him. I've already written up a classified ad for the Scarlet Gazette. I'll call the paper in the morning."

"Devious! I love it."

"I'm just looking ahead. Even if Kendra comes back, the two of them won't be able to handle this place on their own much longer. Kendra is sixty, and my father is seventy-two going on ninety. They need help."

Once her father understood Kendra wouldn't come back until this was resolved, he would get over himself. He'd damned well better.

"Hey, have you seen *him* yet?"

"Him who?" Lexi knew perfectly well whom Vic meant.

"The bastard who broke your heart."

"As it happens, he was the second person I ran into." She told Vic about finding the stranded dog and Austin showing up in full uniform.

"How was it seeing him again?"

"It was no big deal, really. He did his job and drove off. It's been a long time since high school."

"Hmm." Vic clearly didn't buy it.

They talked for a while about Vic's recent promotion and the hot date with her brother's rugby buddy that she had lined up for Friday night, then said goodnight.

As Lexi drifted off to sleep, her last thought wasn't about her father, Kendra or the inn, but Austin. He thought she was an ogre.

Jerk.

For Austin, Tuesdays marked the start of what was usually a three-day weekend—the upside of working four ten-hour days. He'd traded Thursday for Saturday so he could be part of Saturday's Team training, which meant he had only two consecutive days off this week.

Oh, the sacrifices he made.

He spent his morning cleaning his two-story log home, washing his uniforms, and shopping for groceries, then made himself a sandwich and sat down with his laptop and cell phone to call CPA firms.

His search led him to the Colorado Society of Certified Public Accountants, which gave him a few leads to firms that were known for doing pro-bono work for nonprofits. He called all of them. The first had closed its doors. He left a voice mail with the second. The CEO of the third took the time to speak with Austin but said his company was too small to take on an embezzlement case.

"The pro-bono work we've done in the past has been simple accounting, tax preparation, that sort of thing. You're talking about dozens of hours of forensic work, perhaps followed by testifying in court. I can't afford to devote a staff member to what could turn into weeks of non-billable hours."

The man had no recommendations for him either.

"There just aren't a lot of CPA firms around here that are willing to do forensic work pro bono," he said. "I hope it works out for you."

Frustrated, Austin clipped his pager to the waistband of his running pants, leashed Mack, his nine-month-old black lab puppy, and headed out for a five-mile trail run. "Come on, buddy."

The mountains had always been his church, his escape, his therapy, and he quickly fell into a rhythm, his lungs filling with fresh mountain air, Mack bounding enthusiastically along beside him. The sun shone from a cloudless sky, a cool breeze whispering through the pines and shaking the light green leaves of the aspen. A red-tailed hawk wheeled against a backdrop of blue, hunting for a meal. Golden banner, penstemon, and larkspur dotted the sun-warmed slopes with yellow, purple, and blue, patches of blue-and-white columbine blooming in the shade. Slowly, the tension that had been with him since yesterday began to fade.

By the time he reached home, he'd managed to convince himself that asking Lexi for help would be no big deal. He'd give her a call at the inn, explain the situation, and see if she could spare the time. If she could, Megs would take it from there. If not, then Austin would have done his part to help the Team resolve this crisis.

Either way, it was just a single phone call.

He brushed Mack, gave him a few treats, and had just refilled his bowl with fresh water when his pager went off. He scrolled through the emergency alert.

INJURED CLIMBER, CASTLE ROCK.

He yanked his sweaty T-shirt over his head and grabbed a clean, yellow Team T-shirt from his dryer, pulling it on as he made his way to his garage.

He climbed into his Chevy Tahoe and turned on his radio, switching it to FTAC1—Fire and Tactical Channel 1—listening in while he drove.

It didn't sound good.

The climber, a college kid, had taken a whipper on a route near the top of the wall and slammed into the side of the rock, hitting his head. He now dangled from his climbing harness more than a hundred feet in the air, upside down and unresponsive. The kid who had him on belay had shouted to hikers, who had called it in. He was still on belay and still high on the rock himself with no idea how to get his injured buddy down. Julia Marcs, a sheriff's deputy, was on the scene and acting as incident commander, while Megs managed Team ops from The Cave.

It took Austin less than fifteen minutes to reach the site, the massive citadel of stone that was Castle Rock coming into view on his right. Dave Hatfield, one of Austin's fellow rangers and a tenured Team member, was on duty today and had already closed off the access road to all but rescue vehicles. He lifted two orange cones and waved Austin through.

Austin drove along the dirt road until he came to Marcs' vehicle and parked behind her. Belcourt and Ahearn pulled in behind him in Rescue One, yellow overheads flashing. He grabbed his backpack and rack of climbing gear out of the back of his Tahoe, where he kept them always ready to go, then met Belcourt at the side of the truck. "Looks like you, Ahearn, and I are Hasty Team."

Belcourt tied his hair back in a ponytail. "Moretti isn't far behind us."

They'd done this dozens of times on similar rescues, and each of them knew what the others would do. Austin was one of the Team's lead climbers. He and Belcourt would climb past the kid who was still on belay with the fallen climber. If the victim was still alive, Austin would render first aid. If not, he'd tell dispatch to call the coroner. Either way, Belcourt would start working out the anchor problem for what was going to be a vertical evac, while Ahearn organized the rest of the team for the actual evacuation.

Austin and Belcourt geared up—climbing harnesses, helmets, radios, rope and other technical gear—then did a safety check and a radio check before heading over to the base of the climb.

High overhead, the fallen climber hung motionless.

Austin squinted through his sunglasses. "At least he's wearing a helmet."

Belcourt glanced up. "Let's hope that was enough to keep him alive."

Austin took a moment to pick out his route, then slipped into his climbing shoes and tied into the rope.

Austin moved up to the rock face, his gaze seeking out hand and footholds.

"On belay," Belcourt said.

"Climbing." Austin slipped his fingers into a good-sized crack.

"Climb on," came Belcourt's reply.

The route was tougher than it had looked from the ground. It took a good fifteen minutes for the two of them to reach the climber. He dangled before them, absolutely still. With Belcourt on belay, Austin moved along a narrow ledge to reach the kid, a sinking feeling in his chest. He pressed two fingers to the young man's carotid, relief rushing through him.

Thank God.

He reached for his hand mic and, using his Team call number, got out the good news. "Sixteen-twenty-five. I've reached the victim. He's got a pulse."

At the sound of Austin's voice, the kid's eyes fluttered open. "Am ... I ... dead?"

Austin grinned. "I'm only a paramedic, not a doctor, but I'm gonna guess no."

Chapter Four

Lexi got up early the next morning, showered, and dressed in jeans and a cream-colored sleeveless blouse, then went upstairs to help Sandrine, their French pastry chef, prepare the continental breakfast they served their guests. This was one part of running the inn that Lexi loved. Her mother had done this every morning, Lexi and Britta following after her, wanting to help as little kids always do. It was one of the few memories she had of her mother.

While Sandrine baked the morning's croissants, Lexi sliced fruit, made coffee, and set the tables in the dining room, the delicious scents of croissants, coffee, and pineapple making Lexi hungry. None of their guests had yet emerged, giving Sandrine a chance to vent her frustrations with Lexi's father—and to share her growing fear that the family would switch from croissants to bagels to save money.

Lexi bit back a smile, poured Sandrine a cup of coffee, handed it to her. "That's not going to happen. Your croissants are one of the reasons people come here. They're famous. My father knows that."

"Does he?" Sandrine met Lexi's gaze, took a sip of coffee. "You should have heard how he spoke to me last week."

Apparently, Lexi would have to add Sandrine to the long list of things she and her father needed to discuss.

She stayed upstairs to oversee the breakfast, making sure their guests had everything they needed, then went downstairs, two croissants and a bowl of fruit in hand, to get breakfast on the table for herself and her father. She found him sitting at the table, shirtless and wearing only his boxers. "Get dressed, Dad."

"Listen to you. You visit out of the blue and start giving orders."

"This isn't a visit, Dad. It's an intervention."

He glared at her, but got to his feet and shuffled back down the hallway, his shoulders bent under some unseen weight.

She made coffee, put two eggs on to boil, then set the table, running through what she would tell him and how. She'd just gotten the eggs out of their shells and on the table when he reappeared.

He was dressed, his hair combed, his face clean-shaven. The improvement was dramatic. When he wasn't unwashed and acting like a lunatic, her father was still a handsome man. "Better?"

"Much." She poured coffee into their mugs then took her seat, steeling herself against what she knew was coming. "I went over the books last night."

"Who said you could do that?" He didn't meet her gaze, his attention focused on buttering a croissant.

"I was happy to see you're in the black. Things are going well. You've got enough money to hire a full-time housekeeper, someone to handle—"

"I'm not hiring anyone."

"Yes, you are. I put an ad in the Gazette this morning." She let that sink in, her body tensing in anticipation of his reaction.

He froze, his expression turning angry. "What the hell? You can't do that."

"If you refuse to participate in the interviews, I'll have to choose the person myself, but I *am* hiring someone. You can offset the cost with a small increase in your rates. You haven't raised them in eight years."

"Jesus H. Christ!" He slammed his butter knife down on the table. "Who the *hell* do you think you are?"

She willed her voice to stay calm, refusing to let him intimidate her. "There are guests eating breakfast upstairs. Keep your voice down."

This time he whisper-shouted. "Don't tell me how to act in my own house, and don't tell me how to run this business. We are *not* hiring."

"Kendra won't come back unless you hire someone."

He balked. "She ... she said that?"

"She meant it, too." Lexi took a bite of her croissant, the buttery taste almost making her moan. "She also said she's sick of being treated like an employee. She says you never thank her for all the things she does around here."

"What the hell does she expect? She doesn't thank me when I mow the lawn or rake up the leaves or fix a leaky faucet."

Was he deliberately being obtuse?

"It's *your* business, Dad. You own all of it. She's worked here for the entire time you've been married without a salary. Doesn't that merit some gratitude?"

"She's my *wife!*"

"That *right there* proves her point, Dad. Just because she's your wife doesn't mean she has to work for *your* business unpaid seven days a week for the rest of her life."

He jabbed a finger at her. "You're taking her side."

"I'm not taking anyone's side. You want her to come home, right? I just told you what you need to do to make that happen." She took another sip of coffee. "I'll hire a full-time housekeeper. You need to stop drinking and acting pathetic and start showing her that you care about her. Give her a call. Talk with her."

"I *did* call her—twice. She hung up on me."

"You told her she needed to get back here to clean. Then you called to tell her the dryer was broken. Seriously, Dad? That's not romantic. That's you treating her like an employee, which is the problem. She won't come home until that changes."

He sprinkled salt on his egg, popped it into his mouth, and chewed, a sullen expression on his face.

Lexi took advantage of his silence. "She loves you."

"If that's true, why did she leave in the first place?" Beneath the anger in his voice, there was something Lexi hadn't noticed before—hurt.

Or maybe it was just wounded pride.

"I guess she just reached the end of her rope. It's time to pull yourself together and remind her why she fell in love with you."

"Sex?"

Oh, my God! Ew!

"Stop, Dad. Just stop. Now, about Sandrine …"

Austin was still on a post-rescue high the following day when he went for his morning run. The kid they'd brought down had a severe concussion and a lot of healing ahead of him, but he was going to make it. His buddy was okay, too. He'd been so shaken by his friend's fall that he'd lost his nerve and hadn't been able to down climb. They'd rescued him, as well, then called in Esri, the Team's victim's advocate, to give him some counseling on site.

Damn, but it felt good to win.

Austin got home and finished his workout with weights and fingertip pull-ups. Then he made and devoured a scramble—six egg whites, sweet potatoes, onion, ham, tomatoes, mushrooms, broccoli, spinach—and set out for The Cave to help wash, check, and repack the gear they'd used yesterday. He was about a dozen feet into one of the 200-foot ropes they'd used, watching for flat spots, bulges, frayed or fuzzy areas, and signs of discoloration, when Megs appeared at his shoulder.

"Any progress?"

"I got the name of a few firms that do pro-bono work. One is out of business. One turned us down outright. I haven't heard back from the other one yet. If we can't find someone in Denver, I could try bigger firms in New York or LA."

Megs glared at him but said nothing.

Ten minutes later, an executive assistant from the final firm called and told Austin that they didn't do forensic work.

Well, shit.

Megs overheard this, of course. "Are you going to call Lexi, or am I going to have to do it? She doesn't know me personally. I think you'd stand a better chance of winning her over than I would—unless you acted like an asshole and she hates your guts. I guess I hadn't thought about that."

"No, she doesn't hate me." Did she?

"You still haven't called Lexi?" Hawke walked up behind them, still wearing his turnout pants from a barn fire he and his crew had put out early this morning, a grin on his sooty face. "I'll call her. She doesn't hate me."

"*I'll* do it." The words came out so forcefully they surprised even Austin. He cleared his throat. "Just let me finish this."

Megs crossed her arms over her chest. "Was that jealousy?"

"Might've been." Hawke chuckled. "Well, Lexi and I *did* hit it off on Monday."

"Knock off the shit. Why would I be jealous because you hit it off with a woman I broke up with twelve years ago?"

Hawke shrugged. "You tell me."

Austin ignored that and started over, checking every inch of the newly washed-and-dried rope, coiling it, tagging it with the date and his Team call number, then carefully packing it away. When that was done, he slid his cell phone out of his pocket and walked out the open bay doors into the summer sunshine.

He didn't have to look up the number to the inn. After twelve years, he still knew it by heart. How pathetic was that?

She answered on the second ring. "Forest Creek Inn."

His heart gave a hard knock at the familiar sound of her voice, soft and feminine. "Hey, Lexi. It's Austin Taylor."

"Hey." If she was surprised to hear from him, she hid it well. "What's up?"

"Sorry to bother you, but I need a huge favor."

"A favor?" She gave a little laugh. "You treat me like a stranger, and then you want a favor."

"It's not for me." He needed to clear that up *right now*. "I'm asking on behalf of the Rocky Mountain Search and Rescue Team."

A pause.

"Okay. I'm listening."

"The guy who managed our books for the past few years has apparently stolen a lot of money from us. McNalley, the chief of police, said we need to find a forensic accountant to help us figure out how much was stolen. I've already called a few firms in Denver and gotten nowhere. We need to find someone willing to do this without pay—and fast."

"You want me to help you find a forensic accountant who will work pro-bono."

Austin winced at the poor choice of words that had led her to reach that conclusion. "Actually, we were hoping you could do it."

"Me? I'm not a forensic accountant. I've had some forensic training, but …"

He could tell by the tone of her voice that she was about to turn him down flat, and a part of him was relieved. He knew it left the Team in a bad situation, but he didn't want to spend the next few weeks running into her here at The Cave. "Hey, no worries. I know you're on vacation and dealing with family problems, so don't—"

"I'll do it."

It took a moment for her words to sink in. "You'll do it?"

What? *Shit.*

"Forensic accounting isn't my area of expertise, but I can do it. I'd love to help the Team in any way I can." Her voice softened. "They tried to save my mom."

"Oh, right." Austin had forgotten about that. To be fair, it had happened long before his time. He and Lexi had both been four years old. "Everyone's going to be happy to hear this."

"I can stop by this afternoon to get started if that works."

"I'll let Megs know."

"She's still around?"

"She runs the show. You'll be working with her."

"Tell her I'll stop by after lunch."

"I will. And, Lexi, thank you." He disconnected and turned to find Eric leaning against the brick wall behind him.

"That didn't hurt, did it?"

Austin walked past him. "Eat shit, Hawke."

"No thanks, buddy. I've already had breakfast."

A ustin wasn't there when Lexi arrived. Had she expected he would be? He was probably at work, which was fine. She wasn't here because of him. She was here because of her mother.

Megs, wearing a bright yellow Rocky Mountain Search & Rescue T-shirt, met her at the door. "Is this your first time at The Cave?"

"Yes, it is." She couldn't help but grin, the name evoking images of Batman and secret technology. "Can I get a tour?"

"Sure thing."

She listened, fascinated, while Megs showed her around.

"These are our two rescue vehicles—Rescue One and Rescue Two. We're super creative with names around here." Megs opened up the side of one to reveal a row of radios and hand mics in chargers, then pointed at a heavy electrical cord that plugged into an outlet on the side of the vehicle. "We keep the trucks plugged in when they're here in the garage to charge our radios and other electrical equipment. Everything is kept in a constant state of readiness."

She walked around to the rear and opened the tailgate to reveal a built-in shelving unit that slid out along a track. It held climbing gear, first aid supplies, helmets, and lots of things Lexi couldn't identify. "Most of this gear we make ourselves, including this shelving unit. Several of our members are engineers with their own machine shops. They get off on the high-stakes engineering challenge that rescues give them."

"Engineering challenge?" Lexi had always thought it was an issue of climbing skill and strength.

Megs grinned. "Bringing someone down the side of a cliff or the side of a mountain is kind of a big engineering problem in motion. You've got to know how much weight your anchor needs to hold and how best to rig cables and ropes. You can't screw up, or people die. That kind of pressure is exciting for some people. You can see them working out the equation in their heads when they arrive on the scene."

Lexi was grateful that no one's life depended on her math skills. As a CPA, she was good at basic math. Still, she used a 10-key for her calculations.

Megs turned and pointed to the walls. "The stuff you see here is either loaded on an as-needed basis or was recently used and is out for cleaning and inspection."

Litters and enormous bags that held ropes hung from one wall, together with skis and snowshoes, while a fortune in climbing gear hung from the other. Medical kits sat on shelves, their sides marked plainly with red crosses. In the far corner lay what looked like a naked crash-test dummy.

"That's Fred. Apparently, he lost his britches somewhere. We test our techniques and gear on him. We're taking him out on Saturday to try a new brake plate that one of those geeks I mentioned made for us."

Lexi bent down, lifted Fred's foot. "He's heavy."

"He weighs one-eighty. We need something to simulate the weight of a real person. Fred's a lot quieter than the average victim." Megs pushed through a door that led to an office area. "This is the operations room, or ops room. This is where we hold our meetings and manage search and rescue operations. That's the ops desk. We've got a little kitchen off that way. The bathroom is here to your left if you need it."

A large conference table sat in the center of the ops room, a floor-to-ceiling map of Colorado covering one entire wall. The ops desk—actually two desks pushed together—sat in one corner, their two police radios popping with static. Above the desks hung framed photos of the Team in action.

Lexi moved closer, her gaze passing over the images. Six men carrying a litter down a steep slope. A victim in a litter hanging over a raging river, Team members moving the person safely from one side to another. Rescuers standing beside the wreckage of a car in a ravine.

Her pulse skipped. Without thinking, she reached out, took the photo off the wall, and stared at it. Was this—?

"That's not your mother," Megs said from beside her.

Lexi handed her the photo. "Sorry. I shouldn't have—"

"Don't apologize." Megs set the photo down on the desk.

And then Lexi had to know. "Were you there?"

Megs nodded. "Ahearn and I were both there. That was a terrible night. You must have been pretty tiny when it happened."

"Four." She could still remember the look on her father's face when he'd told her and her sister that their mother would never be coming home.

It was the only time she'd seen him cry.

Megs patted her arm. "I'm sorry we couldn't help her."

Lexi swallowed the strange lump in her throat. "There's no reason to apologize. It wasn't your fault."

The blame belonged to the son of a bitch who'd driven up the canyon drunk.

Megs set a stack of folders holding computer print-outs down on the table—the Team's financial records for the past two and a half years. "I hope this makes more sense to you than it does to me."

Lexi willed herself to smile. "I've had a few classes on forensic accounting, so if I can't make sense of it, we're in trouble."

She listened while Megs went over the documents with her, then asked some basic questions. Who discovered the fraud? Who else was involved in managing the books? What source documents had they collected so far? Who created the budget?

By the time Megs had finished answering, Lexi understood how this Breece guy had been able to steal from them for so long. He'd handled both receivables and payables himself. In fact, he'd done everything himself—online donations, deposits, taxes. The only thing he hadn't handled was the budget.

"I'm going to need your annual budget for the current fiscal year and the two previous years. I'll make a list of the other documents I'll need when I put together an audit plan tonight."

"We'll get you whatever—"

Behind Megs, the radio gave off two loud notes.

"They're singing our song." Megs hurried over to the desk, listened.

"Rocky Mountain SAR, dispatch."

Megs lifted the mic to her lips. "SAR, go ahead."

"We've got a report of a missing child at Sun Valley Campground, break."

Megs grabbed a pad of paper and a pen. "Go ahead."

"The child is a male, three years old, brown hair, brown eyes. The RP is the child's mother. She said her son disappeared during a picnic at the campground. She's afraid he may have fallen into the creek. Sheriff's department is on the scene as incident commander and has requested swift-water rescue and search dog assistance."

Lexi's stomach sank. The creek that ran through Sun Valley was a torrent at this time of the year, swollen and wild with snowmelt. If the little boy had fallen in…

"SAR, copy."

"Tac channel is FTAC-2."

"SAR, copy. Switching to FTAC-2." Megs switched channels on the radio. "Sorry, Lexi. It looks like I'm going to be busy for a while. You can stay as long as you like. There are pens and paper and a calculator in these drawers."

While Megs spoke with Team members by radio, Lexi got a notepad and a pen out of one drawer and a calculator out of another. But no matter how she tried to focus, she couldn't get her mind on the work, her thoughts wrapped around a missing three-year-old boy.

Chapter Five

Austin had been in the middle of an oil change on his Tahoe when the Team got called out. He'd no sooner reached the staging area at Sun Valley Campground when Kenzie Morgan, the Team's search dog trainer, radioed in to say they'd found the child safe and alive. The boy had wandered off, curled up in the shade of a chokecherry bush, and fallen asleep. Cheers went up, the child's mother bursting into tears and holding her two other children close, while the father shook everyone's hands at least twice.

Ten minutes later, Kenzie walked out of the forest with Gizmo, a golden retriever, followed by Conrad, who was giving the little guy a ride on his shoulders.

"Is that your mommy?" Conrad asked the boy.

The child's face lit up. "You finded her!"

"You found *me*? Oh, Jason!" His mother laughed through her tears, reaching for her son. She held him tight, her husband wrapping his arms around both of them and resting his cheek on his wife's head.

"Thank God," Hawke muttered under his breath. "There's nothing I hate more than seeing parents lose a kid."

"Yeah." It left a sickness in the soul that stayed.

The Team had mobilized quickly for this one, everyone fearing the worst. This time, they'd gotten lucky. If the boy had fallen into the creek, there would have been nothing they could have done for him beyond retrieving his body so his parents could bury him.

Conrad and Kenzie walked toward Rescue One, sharing a smile. Austin knew just what they were feeling. When they reached the truck, they exchanged high-fives with Austin, Hawke, and the others who'd arrived—O'Brien, Rogers, and Sullivan.

Austin squatted down, gave Gizmo a scratch behind his silky ears. "You did all the work this time, didn't you, buddy?"

Kenzie smiled, gave Gizmo another treat. "He went right to him."

"Hey, everyone, it's Kenzie's birthday," Conrad called out. "Today, she hit the big three-oh. What do you say we all meet at Knockers at eighteen-hundred hours to celebrate?"

Kenzie glared at him. "What part of 'don't tell anyone' confused you?"

Conrad grinned. "I wasn't confused. I broke my promise."

Kenzie laughed. "Thanks for clearing that up."

"Don't take it personally, Kenzie." Austin lowered his voice, as if sharing a secret. "All that time in the Death Zone on Everest damaged his brain."

Even Conrad laughed at this, his tanned face split by a wide grin.

Austin climbed into his Tahoe and headed back to The Cave, where those who'd been part of the search would celebrate and have a short debriefing, and where he and Belcourt were meeting to plan out the details of Saturday's training. He rolled his windows down and turned on his radio, singing along to Brett Eldredge and savoring the sweet spring air.

The little boy was safe, and life was good.

He parked and walked through the open bay doors toward the ops room. He'd forgotten Lexi was meeting with Megs—until he opened the door and saw her.

She looked up from a stack of papers, her lips curving in a smile that hit him right in the chest. "Congratulations. I'm so relieved that you found him."

"The dog found him. I wasn't involved." He walked into the kitchen and grabbed a bottle of water out of the fridge.

What the hell is wrong with you, man?

God, he didn't know. Something about that smile fucked his equilibrium all to hell, knocked his brain out of working order, turned him into a mindless idiot.

He cracked open the bottle, drank.

Megs walked in, closed the door. "Way to be an asshole."

"I told her the truth. I wasn't involved in this one."

Megs looked at him like he was an idiot. "You were rude, and you know it."

"You're overreacting."

"So Lexi broke your poor little teenage heart. Boo-fucking-hoo-hoo. Get over it."

He opened his mouth to object, but she cut him off.

"This isn't like you. You're one of the good guys. If you can't treat her with the same respect you'd show any other person who's donating thousands of dollars' worth of pro-bono hours to the Team, you need to stay away for a few weeks."

When she put it like that...

"You're right." He took a deep breath, tried to sort out the tangle of emotions inside him. "Sorry. I'm not sure what got into me."

Oh, he knew, alright. He was just working overtime not to admit it to himself.

After all these years, he still had feelings for Lexi.

"I've spent my entire adult life working and climbing side-by-side with men, so trust me when I say that most male stupidity is a result of one of two things. It's either their egos, or it's that junk in their pants."

She turned and walked out of the kitchen, leaving him to stare after her.

*L*exi slipped the notes she'd made into her handbag and was on her way out the door when Megs stopped her. "Don't take off yet. Let me introduce you to some of our members. Most of them moved to Scarlet after you left for college."

Not wanting to seem rude or let on how much Austin's cold rebuff had hurt her, she smiled. "Thanks. I'd appreciate that."

She, at least, would act like an adult.

Megs led her through the door to the garage area, where Rescue One had just backed in. The driver's side door opened, and a mountain of a man stepped out, his skin brown from the sun, his dark hair windblown.

"This is Harrison Conrad," Megs said. "This is Lexi Jewell, the CPA who's helping us out. Unlike most of us, she was born here."

He grinned, held out a big hand, his grip gentle as they shook. "Nice to meet you. Thanks so much for your help."

"Conrad moved here from Alaska. He's our lead alpinist. If it's a mountain, he has probably climbed it. He summited Everest last year."

Lexi was impressed. "I bet that was an experience."

"Do you climb?" he asked.

She smiled. "Not if I can help it. And, no, I don't ski either."

"And you're a *native*?" He laughed, the robust sound filling the bay.

A petite woman with a long dark ponytail walked in, a golden retriever at her heel. Like the others, she wore a bright yellow T-shirt with her last name on the back that identified her as a member of Rocky Mountain SAR.

"There's the hero of the day." Megs bent down to pet the dog. "This is Gizmo, and the woman holding his leash is Kenzie Morgan. She trains rescue dogs."

Lexi shook Kenzie's hand. "I'm so happy you found that little boy."

Kenzie smiled. "Gizmo gets all the credit for that, don't you, boy?"

Gizmo wagged his tail, barked.

Then Lexi remembered. "Oh, happy birthday. I heard on the radio."

"Thanks." Kenzie smiled, then her eyes narrowed. "I'm going to kill Harrison."

A tall man with long dark hair and brown skin walked up to Megs. A white T-shirt stretched across his broad chest, the words Oglala Lakota College printed in black above what must have been the school's logo. "You seen Taylor?"

"He was in the kitchen a few minutes ago. Before you disappear, there's someone I want you to meet. This is Lexi Jewell. Lexi, this is Chaska Belcourt, one of those engineers I mentioned."

Chaska Belcourt was one of the most handsome men Lexi had ever seen. With his high cheekbones and full lips, he could easily have been a model—or a movie star. He didn't make eye contact, but took her hand and shook it. "What you're doing means a lot to us. We're all grateful."

"The Team tried to rescue my mother when I was a little girl. I'm happy to help."

His brow furrowed, his gaze meeting hers. "I take it that they failed. I'm sorry to hear that. Thanks again."

He turned and disappeared into the ops room.

"You're staring," Megs whispered.

Lexi cleared her throat. "Sorry."

"Don't feel bad. Most women do—some men, too."

Over the next ten minutes or so, Megs introduced Lexi to Mitch Ahearn, her partner, and Malachi O'Brien, who walked in shirtless in a pair of shorts, his muscular chest more than a little distracting. Names began to blur together. By the end, Lexi was certain of one thing: Rocky Mountain Search & Rescue Team had more than its fair share of physically fit, good-looking men—and women.

"If you're desperate to raise money, you could always make a Rocky Mountain Search and Rescue calendar," she said, letting her ovaries think out loud.

Megs laughed. "Don't let them hear you say that, or it will go to their heads. Are you going to join us at Knockers tonight? I think everyone is meeting there at six."

A part of Lexi wanted to go, but she didn't want to deal with Austin's arctic attitude. There was also her father to think about. She'd said a lot of things this morning that had upset him. She didn't want him losing his marbles and running naked down the middle of the street or something.

"Thanks for the invitation, but I need to get home."

Megs studied her for a moment. "Does this need to get home have anything to do with Austin?"

"Austin?" Lexi shook her head as if he were the furthest thing from her mind. "No. It's my father. He's going through a rough time lately. I need to pick some things up at the store and get home to help with dinner."

Megs raised an eyebrow, doubt in her eyes, but she didn't push. "Okay, then."

"I'll make up my audit plan tonight, along with the list of the source documents I'll need. I'll stop by tomorrow."

"Perfect." Megs smiled. "Thanks so much for doing this."

"You're welcome." As Lexi walked back to the inn, she wondered what she'd done to make Austin despise her so much.

*A*ustin was into his second beer when Hawke, who'd gotten tied up at the fire station and had been late to the party, moved down the bench to join him. Ahearn and Megs were taking turns on a 5.11c route on the rock wall at the other end of the pub, but almost everyone else had gone home.

"I hear you were an asshole to Lexi today." Hawke wasn't smiling.

Was Megs still going on about that?

"I was a little gruff. I didn't mean to be. It just came out that way." How could he explain what seeing Lexi did to him without sounding pathetic?

"In case you missed it, Lexi is doing the Team a huge favor."

"Jesus." Austin fought not to lose his temper. "Like I said, I didn't mean for it to come out that way."

"You going to apologize?"

"It wasn't *that* big of a deal."

"No? Megs said Lexi was visibly hurt and that she didn't join us tonight because of you. I guess it was a bigger deal than you think."

Well, hell. He hadn't meant to hurt her. "Okay, fine. I'll apologize."

"Good." Hawke took a drink of his beer. "Back in high school when I had such a crush on Lexi, my mom warned me that she and her sister were going to grow up to be heartbreakers."

"Your mom is a wise woman."

"She says that when their mother was killed, their father lost it. He and his wife had been crazy about each other, apparently, and losing her crushed him. He never really recovered. After the funeral, he disappeared inside himself, got more and more distant from everyone—his friends, his family, even his two little girls. She thinks it was hard for him even to look at them because they looked so much like their mother."

Austin had seen photos of Lexi's mother. The resemblance was uncanny, especially where Lexi was concerned—the same red hair, the same big eyes, the same heart-shaped face. "You'd think he would try to set his grief aside for their sake."

Hawke took another drink, then went on. "He married Kendra a year later and dumped his daughters in her lap. Kendra had no idea what she was doing and had never planned to be a mother, so the girls were left to deal with the loss of their mom by themselves. As soon as they were old enough to use a dust rag, their father had them helping at the inn. My mother says

Lexi didn't grow up with love, so she doesn't know how to love, but she does know how to work hard."

Austin knew that Lexi had never been close to her father or her stepmother and that she'd been made to work a lot more than most teenagers. He'd resented that for his own selfish reasons. There had always been *one more thing* her father wanted her to do before she was allowed to go out. But he'd never realized there'd been more to her frustration with her parents than that. "How does your mother know all this?"

"She was best friends with Lexi's mom. She babysat Lexi and Britta until their dad married Kendra." Hawke's eyes narrowed, his gaze pinning Austin. "How is it you dated Lexi for a year and you *don't* know all this? Let me guess. You spent more time fucking her than you did talking with her."

It was the truth. They'd been each other's first, crossing that threshold into sex together. Seventeen at the start and horny as hell, they'd barely been able to keep their hands off each other. Was he supposed to feel bad about that?

"She never mentioned her mom." The topic had always been off-limits. It was only after Austin asked his parents that he'd learned how her mother had died. "Why did you bring this up?"

A cheer went up from the bar as Megs reached the top of the wall.

Hawke shrugged. "No reason. Hey, want to show those two geezers what climbing looks like?"

Austin laughed at the absurdity of that idea. Megs and Ahearn were rock gods. There was nothing they didn't know. "Sure, but you're first on belay."

"Bastard." Hawke tossed back the last of his beer. "I should've known you were going to say that."

They took turns being each other's belay slave, going for big moves and speed, Megs and Ahearn and the chorus of regulars at the bar alternately cheering them on and taunting them. It was almost an hour later, his muscles pumped, when Austin called it a night. He had an early shift the next day and needed to get some sleep.

He thought about what Hawke had told him on the drive home. He thought about it when he took Mack for a quick nighttime walk. He thought about it when he brushed his teeth and climbed into bed. He thought about it as he lay awake in the dark, a vague sense of guilt following him into an uneasy sleep.

*L*exi sat at the breakfast table, put her napkin in her lap. "I've already gotten two applications for the housekeeping position."

Her father said nothing, glowering at her over the top of his coffee cup. At least he'd taken time to shower and dress before coming into the kitchen. That was something.

"One is from a woman in Boulder who has housekeeping experience with a hotel chain and says she's willing to make the drive up the canyon."

Her father shook his head. "That's what she says when it's summer. What's she going to say when it snows?"

"I agree. I don't see that working out." She tore a piece off her croissant, dipped it in her coffee. "The other is from Rain. She wants a second job so she can save up money to put Lark through college."

"Rain?" Her dad tore his croissant in half. "What happens when her kid gets sick or she's too tired because she worked late at Knockers?"

"Those are some of the things I'm going to discuss with her at her interview this morning." She waited for his reaction. "You and I still need to talk about that rate increase. I think raising the price of the rooms by twenty dollars a night should cover the extra budget. Your rates will still be lower than the B-and-Bs in Boulder."

He bit his croissant and chewed, but said nothing, his gaze hard and sullen.

She knew he was furious with her for interfering and worried about spending an extra thirty-thousand on a new employee. It was a sign of how badly he wanted Kendra back that he wasn't shouting down the house.

"Have you told Kendra that we're hiring a housekeeper?"

He shook his head. "I thought you would do that."

"Kendra doesn't want to hear from me, Dad. She wants to hear from you."

"She'll just hang up on me."

"Only if you say something stupid or try to make her work."

For a time, they ate together in tense silence, footsteps upstairs telling them their guests were up and about. They'd had a full house last night, which meant eight rooms needed to be cleaned this morning. It would be great if Rain could start today. If not, her father would have to clean them all—by himself. Lexi had cleaned her last room the day she'd left for college, and she wasn't about to go back to that. She'd help with the books, but barring a life-or-limb emergency, that was it.

"I'm going to be spending a lot of time over at The Cave this week helping the Rocky Mountain Search and Rescue Team sort out its books."

He gave a snort. "Megs roped you in, did she?"

"She asked politely, and I said 'yes.' The Team *did* try to save Mom."

His gaze shot to hers. "They did *nothing.*"

She stared at him for a moment. He hadn't spoken of her mother or how she'd died since, well … ever. Lexi and Britta had been forced to go to the library to look through old newspapers to find out exactly what had happened to her.

"There was nothing they could do, Dad. She was gone before they got there."

A knock came at the back door.

Her father threw his napkin onto the table, got to his feet, and strode over to answer it. "Well, I'll be damned."

"Good morning, Bob. Is Lexi home?"

Lexi's pulse skipped. She recognized that voice.

Austin.

Chapter Six

Austin waited outside the screen door. Why the hell had he decided he needed to apologize in person? A phone call would have been just as good. He was on duty and in uniform. He had no business taking time out for personal matters.

Lexi opened the door, stepped outside. "Here on Team business?"

He heard her question, but his brain seemed to have a short. "Yeah. Um ... no."

She looked good enough to eat, her white summer dress revealing sweet skin, her red hair braided and hanging over one exposed shoulder. If that wasn't bad enough, he could smell her—the floral scent of her shampoo, the soft, clean scent of her skin. And damned if his mouth didn't water.

"Was that yes or no?"

Get a grip, dumbass!

"I came to apologize."

She crossed her arms over her chest, arched a slender red brow. "Did Megs put you up to this?"

"No." Okay, so she and Hawke had gotten on his case, but they weren't the reason he was standing here. "Give me a little credit."

From inside, came a shout. "Hey, the coffee's all gone!"

"You know how to make coffee, Dad." She shook her head, clearly irritated with the old man. "Come on."

She led him to that little white bench that sat in the small grove of aspen some distance from the house. He sat beside her, shifting his duty belt so gear wouldn't stab him in the back. It was like slipping back in time. How often had they sat here together as teens, whispering, flirting, sneaking kisses?

Get to the point.

"I was out of line yesterday, and I'm sorry. I've had a lot on my mind."

Okay, that last part was bullshit. The only thing he'd had on his mind lately was Lexi and his inexplicable reaction to her, but *no way* could he tell her that.

"Apology accepted." She looked up at the mountains. "I'm sorry if my being here in Scarlet has resurrected bad memories or made you feel uncomfortable."

"Oh, no, nothing like that," he lied. "Not at all. I just... Yeah. I've had a lot on my mind—this crisis with the Team and all."

She looked up at him, shade dappling the features of her face—her little nose, her Cupid's bow mouth, the tiny freckles on her cheeks. "It's been a long time, hasn't it?"

"Yeah, a long time." And yet not long enough for him to have forgotten what it felt like to kiss her, to hold her, to be inside her.

"I know I hurt you, but you hurt me, too." She looked down at her hands, which were now clasped in her lap. Was she nervous? "I was hoping we could put that all behind us and be friends."

Friends.

Could it be that easy? Was it possible for him to be *friends* with the woman who had turned his teenage heart inside out? Hell, he didn't know. Then again, why not? All of that had happened twelve years ago. That was almost half of their lifetimes.

Hawke was right. It was time to let it go.

"Yeah, sure, Lexi. Friends."

Her face lit up—that smile again. "Good. I'm so glad."

Austin found it hard to breathe.

Shit.

He got to his feet, needing distance.

"Do you need to go already? Have you had breakfast?"

She wanted him to stick around? *Jesus!* Twelve years of silence, and today she was trying to feed him. He wasn't sure what amazed him more—the fact that she had gone from zero to breakfast in under a minute or the fact that a part of him was tempted to take her up on the offer. But he'd already eaten, and he needed to get back to work.

He glanced at his watch. "Thanks, but I've got to get going."

She stood, smiled. "I'll be over at The Cave later. I've got an audit plan and a list of source documents for Megs. Maybe I'll see you there."

"Maybe." He started to go, but then his brain must have shorted out again. That's the only explanation for what came out of his mouth next. "If you ever want to do a ride-along and see what being a ranger entails, let me know."

What the hell?

What had he just said?

She smiled again. "I'd like that."

"I'll clear it with my supervisor." He glanced at his watch, then reached for his hand mic. "Fifty-six-twenty, show me back in service."

"Fifty-six-twenty, eight-thirteen."

As Austin walked back to his service vehicle, he wondered what the hell he'd just done to himself.

Lexi resumed her seat at the breakfast table, spread her napkin in her lap, unable to keep the smile off her face.

"What did *he* want?"

"Team business." She wasn't going to explain.

Her dad had never liked Austin.

"Figures he'd come around the moment you arrived."

"I've been here for three days, Dad."

She ate her breakfast, running every word of her short conversation with Austin through her mind, remembering the changing expressions on his face. He'd been nervous. So had she. But he had apologized. Despite that cool exterior, he was still the Austin she remembered, the Austin she'd kissed under those aspens long ago—except that he was now a man. And every part of her appreciated that difference.

She'd never have imagined she'd be the kind of woman who'd get excited about a man in uniform, but, *damn*, it looked good on him.

Lexi fought to get her mind off Austin and back on the day's work. She finished breakfast, then met Rain upstairs for her interview, running through a list of questions. She was so satisfied and impressed with Rain's attitude and enthusiasm that she hired her on the spot. Her father took the news better than Lexi had expected, even promising he wouldn't bite Rain's head off.

"Don't worry," Rain said, smiling. "I've worked at bars since before I could legally drink. I can handle grumpy, old men."

With that situation under control, Lexi headed off to Food Mart, where she bought groceries for the next few days. On her way to check out, she stopped to peruse titles on the shelves and grabbed two romance novels. Then she remembered she'd brought a box of unread books. She set the books back on the shelf—only to grab them and put them in her cart again.

"Do you read vampires?" came a voice from behind her.

Rose.

She was looking very Stevie Nicks today in tiers of black lace and silver bangles.

"Sometimes."

"There's something deeply alluring about all that danger and dark male energy. It balances with the life-giving goddess energy of women."

"I suppose so." Lexi gave her a polite smile and moved on.

Rose followed. "Thanks for the scotch."

"You're welcome. I hope you enjoy it."

"How's your father?"

Not wanting to be rude, Lexi stopped. "He's doing better."

She left it at that, knowing that whatever she told Rose would be around town in a matter of hours. Then again ... "He just hired a full-time housekeeper, so he's busy training her today."

Maybe Lexi could make Rose's gossip mill work on her behalf.

Rose looked both surprised and pleased. "That will make Kendra happy."

With any luck, Kendra would be getting the news within the hour.

"I'm sure it will." Lexi glanced at her watch. "I'd love to chat, but I need to run. I've got to make lunch and then get some work done."

"You're helping the Team with that embezzlement case."

Rose knew about that, too. Had the news been made public?

"I can't talk about it—client confidentiality. Nice to run into you. See you later."

She went home first and made a quick salad.

"Salad? That's it?" her father asked. "Do I look like a damned rabbit?"

"Feel free to get off your butt, cross the street, and grab a sandwich from Izzy's if you don't like it, Dad. I'm off to The Cave."

She walked the short distance, the day bright and warm, a cool breeze blowing down from the snowcapped summits of the Indian Peaks. She took a different way this time, heading down First to Valley View, passing the old Victorian house she and Britta used to throw rocks at because they believed it was haunted. The place had a For Sale sign in the yard, but it looked more haunted than ever, the windows broken, the lawn overgrown with weeds. Who in their right mind would buy that?

At Third, she caught a glimpse of Bear preaching on his corner near the roundabout, his gray hair and beard shaggy and long, his buckskin jacket and blue jeans more appropriate for winter than summer. She turned left and made a detour down to the corner just to say hello.

Bear might not know how to drive or how to use a phone, but he sure did know his Bible. "For I was hungry, and you gave me food. I was thirsty, and you gave me drink. I was a stranger, and you welcomed me. I was naked, and you clothed me. I was sick, and you visited me, I was in prison, and you came to me."

It was a somewhat self-serving verse, she supposed, given that he had a sign up asking for spare change, but that was Bear.

"Hey, Bear." She reached into her handbag, found a couple of dollars, and dropped them into the battered cowboy hat that lay at his feet. "Good to see you."

"Lexi Jewell! May the Almighty bless you and keep you, and may this return to you seven-fold." Bear made the sign of the cross for her, then went back to preaching. "Whoever is generous to the poor lends to the Lord, and He will repay her for the deed."

Lexi found herself smiling.

She turned around and walked back down Third Street. A few minutes later, she entered The Cave to find Rescue One gone. Something had happened. In the ops room, Megs was listening to the radio.

"Fifty-six-twenty."

Was that Austin?

"Fifty-six-twenty, go ahead."

"Code Black. We're going to need the ME. Get Rocky Mountain SAR started to my location to evac the body, break."

"Go ahead with your traffic," came the reply from dispatch.

"We're going to need a victim's advocate for the hikers who found the body."

"Fifty-six-twenty, copy. SAR is already en route. Toning medical examiner." "Ahearn, please page Esri." Megs looked over, saw Lexi. "A suicide."

"Oh, God." Lexi sat, a chill passing through her.

Out there somewhere was a family that would be getting devastating news.

Lexi organized the source documents Megs had given her while Megs printed more, both of them listening to the radio as the evacuation of the body progressed.

Megs handed Lexi a folder. "Here's the file he kept of all the donations we received through our website."

Lexi glanced through it. "Is there any way to get fresh printouts from the website? There's always a chance he altered these."

Megs frowned. "You think he might have stolen our donations?"

"Your actuals from donations are significantly lower than you projected in your budget. If he were skimming from your donations, that would certainly explain why."

"Bastard." Megs sat at the computer and called up their website to print out the reports. "It's my fault for not keeping a closer eye on him."

A burst of static.

"Belay is off."

"The next rope length should bring us to the road."

They were almost down with the body.

Lexi willed her mind to focus. "Moving forward, you're going to need at least two people to handle accounts—one for accounts receivable and one for accounts payable. It helps prevent situations like this. When one person has control of the entire operation, it creates both temptation and opportunity. But we can go over that more after I'm done with the audit."

Another burst of static.

"Brakes, is belay back on?"

"Litter, belay is on."

"Rock! Rock!"

Lexi's pulse spiked.

More static.

"Is anyone hurt?"

"No. We're good to go."

Lexi let out the breath she'd been holding. "Does anyone ever get hurt doing a rescue like this?"

"We get scratches and bruises, but we've never had a serious injury. That's why we put so much time into training. We don't want to lose a Team member trying to save someone else."

By the time Lexi had all of the source documents, Rescue One was backing into the bay. Compared to yesterday, the mood was somber as gear was set aside for cleaning and inspection and the truck was made ready to head out again.

Ahearn came into the office, his hair and yellow Team T-shirt stained with sweat, and he and Megs hugged. "That's the second one this spring."

Sasha poked her head through the office door. Her eyes were red and puffy. Had she been crying? "I'm going to take the truck into town and gas up."

"You going to be okay?" Megs held out a credit card. "Maybe you should talk with Esri."

"I'm good." Sasha took the card, then disappeared.

Focus on your job, girl.

Lexi began comparing the fresh reports that Megs had just printed for her to the reports Breece had left in the file and immediately saw that he had been altering the printouts. In less than five minutes, she documented more than thirty instances in which Breece had deleted donations from the official report. She didn't have to guess to know what that meant.

She showed Megs, who stared in disbelief at the page. "I'm not a computer whiz, so I'm not exactly sure how he managed to alter the reports, but you can clearly see that there are many times—I've counted more than thirty already—in which a donation is reported but is missing from the documents he left in your file."

"That son of a bitch. How much is that?"

"That's almost ten thousand—and that's just from this year so far. It certainly accounts for the difference between your budget projections and your actuals. If we go by the unaltered printouts, donations are actually up."

"I guess that's good news."

Behind them, the radio blared out what Lexi now recognized as the Team's emergency call-out tone.

"Rocky Mountain SAR, dispatch."

Megs got to her feet, reached for the mic. "SAR, go ahead."

"We've got a report of a lost and injured hiker somewhere off the Buchanan Lake Trail in Indian Peaks Wilderness."

While Megs and the others scrambled to respond, Lexi found herself wanting to find this Breece guy and kick his butt. Only a heartless jerk could steal money from an organization that worked to save human lives.

Austin went home after his shift, exhausted. He took Mack for a short walk, then got into the shower. He was too damned beat to cook tonight, so he hopped in his truck and drove five minutes to Knockers. Not in the mood for music, he asked for a seat on the rooftop deck where he'd be able to watch the sun set over the mountains.

Already, the sky had turned pink, the sun behind a bank of clouds. He sat, took a deep breath, willed himself to relax.

Rain took his order—a deluxe burrito with guac and an Indian Peaks Ale—then returned with the beer. "Why are you lookin' so down in the mouth? Rough day?"

"You could say that." He took a drink. "We had a suicide west of town. A guy shot himself in the head."

The man had been a combat veteran with a wife and two kids. He'd ended his pain, but heaped grief and suffering on his family.

Rain winced. "I'm so sorry. I don't know how you deal with that stuff. It must be so hard to see. I think I'd throw up."

"The gore doesn't get to me." It was the emotional side of it that tore Austin up.

Tonight, a wife was grieving, and children were going to bed without their father.

Rain looked toward the stairs. "Someone else is alone tonight."

Austin's gaze followed Rain's, and he saw Lexi. She was wearing a white summer dress, though she'd put a denim jacket over it to keep off the evening chill.

She saw him, smiled.

"Should I bring her over?"

What could Austin say? "Sure."

"Hey." Lexi sat across from him. "I'll have a taco salad and a margarita with salt and ice. Thanks, Rain."

"I'll be right back with your drink."

Lexi's gaze was turned toward the sunset. "It's beautiful up here."

"Yeah, beautiful." But Austin's gaze was fixed on her.

One minute in her company, and he was already losing his mind. Megs was right. The junk in his pants was making him stupid.

"Needed to get out of the house for a while?"

She nodded. "Kendra heard that we'd hired a full-time housekeeper. She and my dad are in the kitchen talking. I figured they didn't need me hanging around."

"That's good news—isn't it?"

"Very good news. I hope they work it out. If not, she'll probably divorce him, and Britta and I will have to find some way of taking care of him. Since neither of us wants to live here..."

Her words were like a gust of frigid air.

"Right."

She doesn't plan on staying here, and don't you forget it.

"You all had a rough day today."

"Yeah—a tough one."

"I don't know how you deal with something like that afterward—knowing that someone has lost the person they love."

Unlike Rain, Lexi had cut right to the heart of it—the emotional toll.

"Yeah. That part really sucks."

"Megs said the man today was a father."

Austin nodded. "He had two little kids and a wife."

She looked down at the table. "Their lives are never going to be the same."

"You know how hard that can be, don't you?" Without thinking, he reached out, placed his hand over hers.

Awareness arced between them, unexpected and hot.

Jesus.

"Yeah." She drew her hand away and took a drink of water, clearly struggling with her emotions. "The Team tried to save my mom, but by the time they reached her, she was gone. There was nothing they could do. But they stayed with her all night, helped recover her body, and brought her back to Scarlet."

He felt a tug in his chest. "That's what I heard."

"What I'm trying to say is that even if you couldn't save this guy, you still did what you could to help his family. You brought him back." She turned those big green eyes on him. "I think you're all incredibly brave. I was listening today."

"You were at The Cave. How's the audit going?"

"I discovered that he was skimming from your online donations."

"That son of a bitch."

"Donations to the Team are actually up this year."

And then Rain was there with Lexi's margarita.

"Thanks." Lexi took a sip, smiled. "Mmm. Perfect."

Her little moan of pleasure sent a jolt of heat through him, a memory of going down on her flashing through his mind. She'd said those exact words.

Mmm, perfect.

Blood surged to his groin, his jeans suddenly tight.

Oh, he was in *so* much trouble.

Chapter Seven

Of anyone had told her a week ago that she would be sitting on the rooftop of Knockers having dinner with Austin Taylor, Lexi would have thought they were out of their mind. But here she was. And here *he* was, those kissable lips curved in a lop-sided grin, his blue eyes warm.

She couldn't remember the last time she'd felt so alive, aware of everything around her—the breeze on her skin, the tang of the margarita on her tongue, the delicious scents of food, the hot man who sat across from her. He listened while she tried to explain the audit process, being close to him like this making it hard to think.

What would it be like to kiss him again?

No, she'd better not think about that.

"How long do you think it will take you?" he asked.

What were they talking about? Oh, yeah, the audit.

"If I work four hours a day, I can probably finish in a couple of weeks."

He frowned. "I hate to think of you using your vacation to help us with our mess."

She started to tell him the truth but stopped herself. There was no reason anyone else had to know. The more people who knew, the greater the chance that someone would twist her story. Word would get around, and then everyone in Scarlet would blame her.

Then again, why should she give a damn what anyone thought? Besides, she'd already told Kendra. Why shouldn't Austin know? She didn't want him or anyone else on the Team feeling guilty.

"I'm ... I'm not on vacation. I don't have a job right now."

Rain arrived with their plates. "Can I get you anything else?"

"I'm good, thanks."

"Thanks, Rain." Lexi unfolded her napkin, smoothed it on her lap. "How did it go with my dad today?"

"Great. Don't worry about me. Your dad reminds me of my grandfather—all bark and no bite." Rain gave her a bright smile and hurried off.

"Well, that's a relief." Lexi picked up her fork, poked at her salad.

Austin dumped salsa on his burrito. "You don't have a job?"

So he'd heard her.

"I left Price and Crane with a big settlement after filing a sexual harassment suit."

While they ate, Lexi told him how Mr. Crane had acted as her mentor when she'd first joined the firm. She'd thought of him as a father figure, but he'd had different ideas. He'd invited her to attend a conference in New York, then showed up in her room and made it clear he expected her to have sex with him. She'd had to take his hand off her ass and push him away—hard—to make it clear that her answer was no.

"Even if I'd found him attractive—which I did not—he was married. I was upset and angry, but I kept it to myself because I didn't want to cause trouble." That had turned out to be a mistake. "A month later, his vote kept me from making partner."

She told Austin how she'd gone to human resources and reported what had happened. "He denied it and told them I'd come onto him. He made up some story about how I'd repeatedly tried to seduce him to persuade him to make me a partner. Some people believed him."

Austin's gaze had gone hard. "Tell me he paid for this."

"Not really." She told him how she'd hired an attorney and spent the next several months being deposed, answering all kinds of extremely personal questions, and having her work as a CPA criticized by the same people who'd once praised her. "That wasn't the worst of it. People I'd thought of as friends stopped returning my texts and calls. They avoided me at work, and I could tell they were talking about me. My boyfriend, Chris, who'd made junior partner two years before, called me an idiot and told me I'd brought it on myself because of how I dressed. He broke it off."

"Asshole."

She set her fork aside and took a drink of her margarita, her hands shaking. Talking about this was harder than she'd imagined, her anger and hurt still sharp. "In the end, I was given three years' salary."

One of his big hands closed over hers, held it fast. "So you came home."

Home.

No, Chicago was her home.

But then she lifted her gaze to his and saw the concern in his eyes, and it seemed that he was right—she *had* come home. "I guess I did."

A ustin listened while Lexi told him what she'd loved about living in Chicago, but inside he was seething. If he could, he'd hunt that fucker Crane down and make him eat his own balls. As for her ex-boyfriend, he'd done her a favor by dumping her. Still, if the bastard ever showed up in Scarlet, Austin would take him apart.

Lexi was now on her second margarita, her cheeks flushed, the distress he'd seen in her eyes earlier replaced by laughter. As she spoke, his anger began to fade, his blood growing warm.

Shit.

He wanted her.

Back off, buddy. You do not want to go there.

"When it snows, they shovel out their own parking spots and put a lawn chair there so that no one can take the space while they're away."

Austin laughed. "You're kidding me."

She shook her head, a smile on her beautiful face. "I still have a lawn chair stashed in my trunk."

"If anyone did that here, people would just drive over the lawn chair."

She laughed. "They'd key the *hell* out of your car—or slash your tires. You do *not* mess with the lawn chair."

"They're a tough bunch."

Rain walked up to the table, picked up their empty plates. "Do you want me to split the check?"

Austin cut off Lexi before she could answer. "Dinner is my treat."

She looked like she was about to argue with him, then smiled. "Thank you."

The conversation drifted after that with Austin catching her up on the news about people they knew from high school. Randy and Stephen, the gay couple they'd elected as prom king and queen their senior year of high school, had finally gotten married and were living in Denver. Mrs. Beech, their English teacher, had recently lost her husband. Dan Meeks, who'd been on the football team with Austin, had been killed in combat in Iraq. His wife, Ellen, had given birth to twins six months later.

"That's so sad." She took a drink, down to ice now. "So much has happened."

"You've been gone for a long time." Austin glanced at his watch, stunned to see that another two hours had gone by. "Did you drive?"

He was pretty sure she was over the legal limit.

Knockers made a mean margarita.

She shook her head, smiled. "Nope. I planned ahead. I walked."

He didn't like the idea of her walking home alone in the dark, not while she was tipsy. Scarlet wasn't a dangerous town compared to Boulder or Denver, but bad things happened—especially when alcohol was involved.

"If you don't mind swinging past my place so I can let Mack out, I'll take you home." He was *so* full of shit. Mack would be fine for another hour or so. Besides, the inn was only a two-minute drive from Knockers, while Austin's place was on the other side of town. Austin could easily drop her off on his way home.

You just don't want to say goodnight.

Who could blame him?

"Who is Mack?"

"He's my black lab puppy."

Lexi's face lit up. "A puppy?"

God.

That smile. It got him every time.

"He flunked out of the selection process for rescue training. I didn't want him to end up in a shelter, so I adopted him."

"Oh, can I meet him?"

"Sure." Austin paid, left Rain a good tip, then led Lexi to his Tahoe, opening the passenger-side door for her.

She climbed in. "This is a lot fancier than that old, beat-up Ford."

He walked around to the driver's side and climbed in.

"Hey, I loved that truck." He and Lexi had certainly made the most of its long bed. "This is more practical. I keep the back loaded with Team gear—ropes, my pack, my rack of climbing gear, first-aid supplies."

"You've got a radio, too."

He started the engine. "I like to stay in the loop."

He drove out of the parking lot, an awkward silence replacing conversation as they headed down Hot Springs Drive toward First. It was one thing to sit together in a crowded restaurant. It was another for two people with their intimate history to be alone together in the confined space of a vehicle.

Lexi broke the silence. "Where do you live now?"

"I bought a log house west of town. Some out-of-staters built it as their retirement home, then decided the snow and altitude didn't suit them and moved to Florida."

"Why would anyone build in Colorado if they can't tolerate snow?"

"Your guess is as good as mine. It's not exactly a secret that we get a lot of snow up here. As it turns out, their lack of foresight was good for me."

They talked about the weather for the next few minutes until he turned onto the dirt road that served as his driveway.

Lexi's jaw dropped. "*This* is your house? Wow."

"Home sweet home." He parked in the garage.

She hopped out before he could open her door, then followed him inside.

Mack launched himself at Austin, tail wagging.

Austin gave the pup a good scratch. "Behave yourself, buddy. We have a guest."

Lexi knelt down. "Hey, boy. Oh, you're so cute!"

And just like that, Mack forgot all about Austin. He slathered Lexi with sloppy puppy kisses, his tail wagging wildly.

That's when Austin noticed the bag of dried dog food Mack had ripped open, scattering kibble across the pantry floor and into the kitchen. He grabbed the broom. "That cuteness? It's a survival strategy."

"Have you been naughty?" Lexi crooned.

"Always," Austin muttered, sweeping up the mess.

When the kibble was cleaned up, Austin handed Lexi the dog's leash, and they took Mack for a short walk on the property, a great horned owl keeping them company with low hoots, the night alive with the chirping of crickets. It felt natural to talk with her, to walk beside her like this. More than once, he felt an impulse to reach for her hand.

When they got back to the house, Austin gave Lexi a quick tour.

"It's amazing, but…"

"But what?"

She shrugged. "Maybe you should get some furniture."

He supposed she *did* have a point. Apart from his brass bedstead and chest of drawers in his bedroom, the table and chairs in the kitchen, and the sofa and TV in the living room, the place was mostly empty. "I figured I'd grow into it."

For a moment, neither of them spoke, both of them looking out onto the lights of Scarlet through the living room's floor-to-ceiling windows.

"I'd offer you a drink, but I've got an early shift again tomorrow." He turned toward her, toward the door.

She smiled up at him. "I should probably head home anyway and find out whether Kendra and my dad have made up."

There was a moment of clumsy silence as if this were a first date and the two of them were trying to figure out how to say goodbye and whether or not they should kiss. Except that it *wasn't* a first date. It wasn't a date at all. Neither of them had any intention of getting physical.

He cleared his throat. "Let's get you home."

"Right."

But then she was in his arms, his mouth coming down hard on hers, her arms going around his neck, drawing him closer. Some part of him knew kissing her was stupid—*really* stupid, catastrophically stupid. But then she pressed her body hard against his, and he decided stupid could go fuck itself.

O *h, God, yes.*

Lexi had spent the evening fantasizing about this, but the fantasy was nothing compared to the reality. The familiar scent of his skin told her this was Austin, but the man who kissed her now was more aggressive than the teenage boy she'd loved, his body changed—harder, stronger, broader.

His lips moved insistently over hers, his tongue teasing hers with slick strokes. One of his big hands cradled the back of her head, the other sliding slowly up her spine, molding her against him, strong arms holding her tight.

She fisted her hands in his hair, answered the force of his kiss with demands of her own, heat flaring inside her as their tongues curled together. Instinct took over, her hips pressing impatiently against him, finding the hard ridge of his erection. And the heat inside her became an ache.

"*Lexi.*" He whispered her name, grasped her ass with both hands, and lifted her off her feet, his lips moving to her throat.

She wrapped her legs around his waist and held on, her head falling back as his mouth found the sensitive skin beneath her ear.

And then they were moving, Austin carrying her. Across the living room. Up the stairs. Down the hall to the darkness of his bedroom.

They sprawled across his bed, Lexi savoring the burn of Austin's stubble as he kissed and bit her throat. His lips and teeth made her skin tingle. One big hand moved to cup her breast through the cloth of her dress.

She tugged up his T-shirt, slid her palms over the shifting muscles of his belly and chest, the feel of him turning her on—the rasp of his chest hair, the hardness of his muscles, the softness of his skin.

He shifted onto his side, rucked her dress up to her hips, and pulled the crotch of her panties aside to cup her, his fingers parting her, teasing her, testing her.

Oh, it felt good.

She yanked his jeans open, freed his erection, and stroked his length, the feel of his cock making her hungry to taste him. But before she got that chance, he lifted himself away from her. For a moment, she believed it was over.

Disappointment lanced through her. Oh, she had *so* wanted this.

He flicked on the light on his nightstand and took something out of a drawer.

A condom.

Oh, thank God.

She started to tell him that she was protected. She'd gotten an IUD when she and Chris had started dating. But she and Austin had both been with other people these past 12 years, and right now she didn't feel like talking about their sexual histories.

She didn't feel like talking at all.

He tore the wrapper open with his teeth, then sat back on his knees and rolled the condom down the length of his erection, watching her as she wriggled out of her panties.

Still wearing her dress and bra, she smiled up at him, bent her knees, and let her thighs fall open.

His gaze went right where she knew it would, his blue eyes going dark, the breath leaving his lungs in a rush. *"Jesus, Lexi."*

He settled himself between her thighs, his mouth reclaiming hers as he nudged himself slowly into her.

She moaned against his lips, lifting her hips to meet him, impatient to have all of him inside her. *"Oh! My. God."*

She'd forgotten how perfectly he filled her.

And then he began to move.

There was nothing in the world like this sensation—the slick glide, the precious stretch, the piercing sweetness. Hungry for the feel of him, she slid her hands under his shirt, over the muscles of his back, and down to his bare ass, mounds of muscle bunching beneath her palms as he fucked her. No other man had ever done for her what Austin did. He knew just what she liked, and, *oh, Christ alive*, he didn't miss a beat, moving up and down against her, his pubic bone and the base of his cock rubbing her aching clit, making her crazy, frantic, desperate.

She came with a cry, the sweet shock of orgasm singing through her.

He stayed with her, whispering her name, pressing kisses to her face until the quaking inside her began to fade.

She opened her eyes, looked up at him, a strange ache in her chest. "Austin."

His pupils were dilated, a strained expression on his face, the muscles of his neck and shoulders tense. Without breaking eye contact, he shifted his weight, adjusted the angle of his hips, and let himself go, thrusting into her.

He went slowly at first, his eyes drifting shut as he picked up the pace, driving into her hard and fast, his deep strokes sending her headlong toward a second climax. When she came this time, he was right behind her, moaning out his pleasure against her cheek as he shook apart in her arms.

Unwilling to rush, Austin stayed where he was, pressing kisses to Lexi's face, his pulse still pounding, his body floating. Her eyes were closed, a slight smile on her lips, her fingers tracing the length of his spine beneath his T-shirt.

He ought to be angry at himself. This shouldn't have happened. It would be a big mistake to get mixed up with Lexi Jewell again. And yet he couldn't seem to muster any real regret, because, well …

God in heaven.

He'd spent years telling himself that his memories of her were blown out of proportion by teenage hormones and breakup angst. She'd been his first serious relationship, his first lover, his first heartbreak. There's no way that sex with her could have been *that* good.

Well, he'd been right—sort of.

Sex with Lexi wasn't good. It was incendiary.

He couldn't remember the last time an orgasm had taken him apart like that, and he was fairly certain she'd left claw marks on his ass.

"Am I heavy?" He must outweigh her by a good seventy pounds now.

"No." Her voice was soft, sexy, sleepy.

He felt something thudding against the mattress and glanced over his shoulder to see Mack sitting at the foot of the bed near his feet, tail wagging.

Lexi laughed. "You didn't tell me your puppy was a voyeur."

"For God's sake, Mack. Can't I get any privacy?" Austin lifted his weight off Lexi, tossed the condom in the trash, and cleaned himself up with a tissue. "It's bad enough that he follows me to the bathroom. You hungry?"

She sat up, smiled. "Starving."

They walked downstairs to the kitchen, Mack at their heels.

Austin settled the puppy in his crate for the night, then searched the fridge, grabbing bread, sliced cheese, a tomato, and butter. "How does a grilled cheese sandwich sound?"

"Yum." She looked through his cupboards, found a skillet. "I suppose we should talk about what just happened."

"Why? I don't regret it. Do you?"

Her lips curved in a shy smile. "God, no."

"Then what is there to talk about? We're both adults."

She watched him, seemed to consider this. "I'm going back to Chicago."

The words sliced through him. "I know. When?"

"I'm not sure. It depends on the situation with my dad and Kendra. Also, I need to decide whether to start my own firm or look for a job. I'm guessing I'll be here for a few more weeks—long enough to finish the audit, if that's what you're wondering."

"I wasn't thinking about the audit. I was thinking about us."

"Eric says you think I'm an ogre."

"A ... what?" He made a mental note to kick Hawke's ass.

"Ha! That is *not* a denial."

Austin sliced the tomato. "I don't recall ever saying you were an ogre. A bitch, sure, but not an ogre."

She glared at him. "Oh, well, I'm glad we got that cleared up."

"Hey, I was eighteen and heartbroken."

"I never meant to hurt you, you know. I didn't even want us to break up. I spent the rest of that summer crying."

This wasn't news.

Everyone in town had seemed hell-bent on making sure he understood how upset Lexi was. After all, it was an unofficial rule of high school dating that when a girl broke up with her boyfriend, she was making good life choices, empowering herself, moving ahead, while a boy who broke up with his girlfriend was just an asshole.

He set the knife down and turned to face her. "Let's not ruin tonight by dredging all of that up. That was *twelve years* ago. We both made mistakes. As for tonight, we both know it can't go anywhere. I'm staying. You're leaving.

Same old, same old. So let's just enjoy each other's company—no expectations, no strings."

Her lips curved in a slow smile. "Are you saying you want to be friends with benefits?"

"If that's what you want to call it." He'd never been into casual sex, and some part of him knew he'd pay a high price for getting involved with Lexi again. But damn if he could walk away from this.

He was a freaking idiot but, for the moment, a happy one.

She leaned back against the counter, looked up at him from beneath her dark lashes. "What kind of benefits exactly?"

He closed the distance between them in a single step and reached beneath her wrinkled dress to cup her through her panties—only to discover she hadn't bothered to put her panties back on. "Holy fuck, Lexi."

He rucked up Lexi's dress, lifted her off her feet, and settled her on the edge of the counter, then dropped to his knees before her.

Chapter Eight

Lexi fought to balance herself on the edge of the counter, her gasp of surprise becoming a moan as Austin went to work on her with his mouth.

Somewhere nearby, her cell phone rang, the sound barely registering.

"God, I love your pussy." His words sent a bolt of pure lust sheering through her, even as his tongue began to stroke her.

"Mmm." She slid the fingers of one hand into his hair, the palm of her other hand splayed on the countertop. "*Perfect.*"

Whatever he was doing—it was better than perfect, his lips and tongue bringing her to full arousal in a heartbeat. He'd always been good with his mouth, better than any man she'd dated. How did he do this to her?

She willed herself to open her eyes and find out, only to discover him looking up at her, watching her. The intensity in his blue eyes made her pulse skip, the sight of his mouth covering her clit almost making her come right then. Then the corners of his eyes turned up as if he were smiling—and he slowly drew back, his lips gliding over the swollen nub, tugging on her clit, catching and stretching one sensitive inner lip.

"*Austin.*" She moaned, her head falling back, her hand fisting in his hair, the sensations almost too good to be real.

And then she understood.

Austin was better at this than other guys because he truly *enjoyed* going down on her. He wasn't just doing it so that she'd go down on him. He loved tasting her.

He gave a little groan, then took her into his mouth again, penetrating her with his fingers, caressing that sensitive spot inside her.

It felt so good, so good. She wanted it to last forever. She wanted to stay right here with his mouth on her forever.

"*Don't. Stop.*" Barely able to breathe, she got the words out somehow.

But he clearly had no intention of stopping, his lips and tongue and fingers relentless, coaxing her to the brink and holding her there.

OhGod! OhGod! OhGod!

She couldn't say whether she'd said it aloud or just thought it, the pleasure almost unbearable, need driving her out of her mind. Up and up and up she went, until she was flying. She heard herself cry out, climax exploding through her, bright and beautiful, carrying her out of this world and leaving her to drift.

Awestruck, she opened her eyes, found Austin still watching her, his pupils dark, his wet lips pressing soft kisses against her sensitive inner thighs.

He rose slowly, his gaze never leaving hers, one hand jerking down his zipper, while the other drew a condom from his pocket.

She took the packet, tore it open with her teeth, then slid the condom over the length of his erection, aching to have him inside her. "How do you want me?"

"Choices, choices." His words were humorous, but his voice was deep, husky.

He drew her off the counter and against him, kissed her hard, her own musky taste flooding her mouth. Then he released her and turned her to face away from him, one hand sliding beneath her dress, lifting it high above her hips.

She bent over the counter, arched her lower back, and spread her legs for him.

"Oh, hell, yeah." His hands caressed the bare skin of her ass and teased the entrance to her vagina, and she knew he was savoring the view.

She wiggled her bottom impatiently. "Fuck me, Austin."

"In a hurry?" He slowly nudged himself into her, filling her completely, the thick, hard feel of him making her moan. "*Lexi.*"

He whispered her name, gave a few slow and easy thrusts, then let himself go, driving into her harder and faster, his breath going ragged.

Lexi held fast to the counter, the power of his thrusts almost lifting her feet off the floor, his cock striking the sweet spot inside her. Then he reached around and caught her clit between two of his fingers, squeezing, tugging, teasing.

The world shattered around her as she came, Austin a split second behind her, their moans mingling as pleasure flooded them both.

A ustin withdrew from Lexi, holding fast to the condom, tossed it in the trash, and cleaned himself up with a wet paper towel. He turned to find Lexi leaning against the counter as if she didn't quite trust her legs to support her, her cheeks still flushed, her dress tugged back into place. She was adorably disheveled, her long hair tangled, one lacy white bra strap having slipped down her arm, her dress now hopelessly wrinkled. She looked like a woman who'd just gotten thoroughly laid.

Their gazes met, and he couldn't help but laugh.

"What?" she asked, smiling.

"We've had sex twice, and we haven't undressed yet."

She laughed, her cheeks getting pinker. "That sounds like us."

It sure did. Except that there was no "us." Not really.

Friends with benefits.

That's all this was. That's all it could be.

He resisted the impulse to pull her into his arms and kiss her, ignored the strange tenderness that had blossomed behind his breastbone, turning his attention instead to the stove. "Okay, where were we before you distracted me with your private parts?"

He couldn't afford to let his emotions get tangled in this. She'd be gone in a few weeks, running away from Scarlet and back to the city that had been so cruel to her. There was nothing he could do to change that, so he needed to enjoy this for what it was and not get caught up in her.

What if it's already too late?

He ignored that voice, focused on making grilled cheese, kept the conversation light as they ate, washing their late-night post-sex snack down with a couple of beers. And then it was time to drive her home.

She said goodbye to Mack, who whined in his crate as she walked away, then they climbed into Austin's SUV and backed out of the driveway.

"I got the okay to have you ride along." He'd forgotten to tell her. "Just let me know when you'd like to go."

"How about Monday?"

"Monday it is."

They talked about little things after that—how clear the sky was, the stars, the forecast for the rest of the week. How strange it felt and how familiar—driving through the dark with her beside him, pulling up in front of the inn, opening the door of his vehicle for her.

She hopped to the ground, a frown on her face. "Kendra's truck isn't here."

"You were hoping she'd move back in tonight?"

Lexi nodded, clearly disappointed. "Maybe it was too late when she left, and she'll move back in tomorrow."

"Give it time."

Lexi looked up at him, smiled. "Tonight was wonderful. Thanks."

"My pleasure." It was on the tip of his tongue to tell her he cared about her, that he'd never stopped caring about her, that he'd been an idiot to end things the way he had, but he bit back those words. "See you Monday—if not sooner."

He ducked down to give her a light kiss on the lips, but she caught his face between her palms and kissed him hard.

"You were always the best," she whispered.

Then she turned and walked away, looking back over her shoulder at him, her lips curved in a little smile.

Austin stood there as if his feet had grown roots, watching until she was safely inside, the scent of her still on his skin. When the kitchen light came on, he climbed back into his Tahoe and drove home, feeling strangely contented—and a little worried that he'd lost his ever-loving mind.

Still smiling, Lexi stepped inside the kitchen, flicked on the light—and froze.

Her dad sat there in his underwear, a bottle of whisky on the table in front of him. He spoke with slurred words, his tone sharp with anger. "Where the hell've you been?"

Her stomach sank. Clearly, things hadn't gone well. "You're drunk."

"You damned well better believe I'm drunk."

She pointed to the bottle. "Where did you get that?"

"I told Rose you stole it from me. She gave it back."

Wasn't that wonderful?

Now Lexi would have to apologize to Rose.

She crossed the room, reached for the bottle, but her father yanked it away and staggered to his feet, cradling it against his chest, amber liquid sloshing.

"Nope, girl. Nope. You're not takin' this from me again. It's my Glen... my Glenm'rangie."

"What happened with Kendra?"

"Your little plan didn't work. When she found out *you* hired Rain and not me, she got up and stomped out that door." He made a sweeping motion toward the door, then sat again and took another drink.

Lexi slid into a chair, buried her face in her hands. "No, Dad."

How could her father be so completely inept with his wife?

"Man, she was pissed. You shoulda seen her."

Lexi looked up. "What exactly did you say?"

He frowned as if struggling to remember. "She told me she was glad I'd changed my mind about hiring someone, and I told her I hadn't changed my mind at all. I told her you'd done all of it without my permi... permission. S'the truth, isn't it?"

Yes, it was the truth—and the best way Lexi could imagine for her father to ensure that Kendra divorced him.

Lexi grabbed the bottle from her father, walked to the sink, and dumped the whisky down the drain, her father apparently too drunk to realize what she was doing.

"You know what you've done, Dad? You've wrecked everything. All you had to do was tell her how much you miss her and how much she means to you, and she'd have come back. Instead, you might as well have told her you want a divorce."

"But I don't want a divorce. Why would she think that?"

Lexi would have to call Kendra in the morning and try to smooth things over. She could only hope it wasn't too late.

Her dad still didn't understand. "The woman got what she wanted, didn't she? Why does it matter who hired Rain?"

"It matters. Trust me, Dad. It matters."

Lexi dropped the empty whisky bottle into the recycling bin and turned toward the hallway, certain that anything she said to her father now would be forgotten by morning. She needed to wait until he was sober again. And then she would explain it all in language even he could understand.

"Where are you going?"

"I'm going to bed, and so are you. It's late."

She'd taken a few steps when he bellowed after her, his voice surely disturbing their guests upstairs. "Where the hell's my Glenm'rangie?"

She didn't bother answering, but shut and locked her bedroom door behind her.

*L*exi and her father didn't speak at the breakfast table. She was furious with him for blowing his opportunity to make amends with Kendra last night, and he had a hangover and was still upset over the wasted whisky. She did the breakfast dishes, then went outside, sat on the bench, and called Britta.

That's when she discovered Eric's voice mail.

"Hey, Lexi, I'd like to take you out for dinner Saturday night, if you're free. Give me a call."

Drat.

What was she going to do about that? If she and Austin hadn't reconnected last night—and it had been amazing—she'd have called Eric back in a heartbeat. But she didn't think she could spend time with another man, no matter how hot he was, as long as she was sleeping with Austin.

She set the problem from her mind for now, saved the message, and called her sister. San Diego was an hour behind Colorado, so she caught Britta just getting out of the shower.

"You'll have to make it quick. I've got a meeting with a client in an hour."

Lexi gave her sister the bullet points on the situation with their father and Kendra. "How did Dad ever meet and marry Mom, much less Kendra? He is such an idiot when it comes to women."

"He's not an idiot," Britta said. "He's just being stubborn."

"What do you mean?"

"If he were to let Kendra believe he changed his mind and hired Rain, then she would think she'd won their argument. You know how Dad hates to lose a fight."

Lexi hadn't thought about it like that, but Britta was right. Their father hated to lose an argument—especially when he was wrong.

"I have no idea what I'm going to say to Kendra."

"I can't help you there."

Lexi felt a quick stab of resentment. Her sister was in San Diego running her graphic design company, while Lexi was stuck here in Scarlet dealing with their father by herself. "I could really use some moral support, you know. If Kendra divorces Dad, it's going to affect both of us."

"It won't affect me." Britta's tone of voice was firm. "If she divorces him, it will be his problem. Let him sell the inn and move into a cabin. I don't care. It's nice of you to try to help out, but if he's determined to destroy what's left of his life, maybe you should let him."

Oh, the idea was tempting—so tempting that Lexi almost felt guilty. But she couldn't leave, not yet. She needed to complete the forensic audit for Megs and the Team. And then there was Austin. She had no idea what she'd gotten herself into where he was concerned, but she certainly intended to find out.

"I guess I'll call Kendra, invite her to lunch, and see what happens."

"I hate to hang up. I can tell you really want to talk this through, but I can't show up at this meeting naked. I'm trying to land a logo redesign project for a major pharmaceutical company."

"I had sex with Austin last night."

"Okay, great. I'll give you a call when ... *What?*"

"Hope your meeting goes well." With that, Lexi ended the call, certain Britta would call her back tonight.

Austin watched EMTs load the hiker into an ambulance. The man, a fit guy in his fifties, had gotten short of breath jogging around Moose Lake and called 911, afraid he was having a heart attack. Austin, who'd been patrolling, had been the first on the scene. He'd given the man oxygen and done what he could to keep him comfortable until Scarlet FD, the ambulance, and the Team arrived.

After the EMTs had hooked the hiker up to a heart monitor and started IV fluids—it looked like the guy was dehydrated, not having a heart attack—Austin, Hawke, Belcourt, Ahearn, O'Brien, and Sullivan had packed him into a litter, attached an ATV wheel to the bottom, and trailed him back to the parking lot.

Austin was about to call in and tell dispatch to show him back in service when Hawke walked up to him.

"So I guess you and Lexi patched things up."

How did he know about that?

Rain.

She'd been their server. She must have run into him and said something.

"I apologized for being a jerk, and we agreed to move on."

Hawke glared at him through the blue, mirrored lenses of his Revos. "How, exactly, does the two of you sleeping together constitute moving on?"

Austin stared at him. "Who told you we were sleeping together?"

"Your face just now. Jesus!" Hawke rubbed a hand over his jaw. "When Rose said she saw the two of you kissing outside the inn late last night, I thought she was just trying to get me riled up, but she was telling the truth."

Rose.

Shit.

What did that woman do when she wasn't sticking her nose into other people's private lives?

"We didn't plan it. It just happened. Lexi and I…" How could he explain what he and Lexi did to each other when he didn't understand it himself? "We're just friends. It's nothing serious. She's leaving in a few weeks. Until then…"

Hawke shook his head. "You and Lexi—just fuck buddies? If you believe that, you're even dumber than I thought."

Austin knew what was going on here—and it pissed him off. "You *are* jealous. You wanted to hook up with her while she was here. That's what this is about."

Hawke turned and stomped back to Rescue One, cursing.

Austin followed him. "You want to go out with her? Fine. Call her. Ask her out. We haven't made each other any promises. She's free to do what she wants."

Even as he spoke the words, Austin felt pretty sure he'd punch his best friend in the face if he caught the two of them in bed.

Hawke opened the door and climbed into the driver's seat. "I called her last night, but she didn't call me back. Now I know why."

"You called Lexi?" Austin stopped short.

Well, shit.

"You just stepped into a minefield, buddy, but this time you're on your own. I won't be there to help you pick up the pieces when she leaves."

With that, Hawke threw the vehicle into reverse, backed out, and followed the ambulance out of the gravel parking lot.

Lexi stood, leaned across the table. "Look at me, Dad. If you do not stop being a thoughtless, stubborn idiot, Kendra will divorce you. She will *divorce* you! Got that?"

Her father glared at her through bloodshot eyes. "Do you have to shout?"

"I don't know. Are my words making it through your ears to your brain?"

"Yes! Quiet down!"

"Did you read these?" Lexi pointed to the list she'd printed out—a comprehensive list of behaviors her father had to eliminate if he wanted his wife back. Guessing he hadn't, she read them aloud. "No drinking."

"You owe me two hundred bucks for the Glenmorangie."

Lexi ignored that and kept reading. "No treating your wife as if she were an employee. No saying anything to her that isn't kind and caring. No more pathetic attention-seeking behavior—walking around unshaven in your underwear, shoplifting, calling her about problems at the inn, etc. Is that clear enough, or do you need a comprehensive list of what constitutes 'pathetic attention-seeking behavior'?"

He didn't answer, his mouth a hard line.

She slid a second sheet of paper under his nose. "In place of those behaviors, which guarantee that Kendra will *divorce* you, you may choose behaviors from this list. They include calling her to tell her you love and miss her, calling her to apologize for your previous incidents of pathetic attention-seeking behavior, sending her flowers with sweet cards, asking her out to—"

"I'm just supposed to swallow my pride and give that woman every damn thing she wants?"

Lexi remembered her conversation with Britta. "I know how you hate to lose an argument, Dad, but if you insist on winning this fight, you'll lose your wife. Got that?"

"You think living with her for all these years has been easy?"

Lexi knew it had been difficult—and not just for her father. "The two of you need to see a marriage counselor. Kendra would probably appreciate—"

"Oh, no." He shook his head, his mouth set in an angry frown. "No way am I going to any damned head-shrinker. This is a private matter between my wife and me."

"You think everyone in town isn't talking about it? You turned this into a topic of public gossip when you stole chew from Food Mart. Do you know how embarrassing that was for Kendra—and for Britta and me?"

He shifted in his chair, his brow furrowed.

She pressed on. "You need to get your act together. I'm not going to help you if you refuse to help yourself. I'll fly back to Chicago and leave you to your own mess."

He shrugged, a mask of indifference on his face. "Go ahead. I sure as hell didn't ask for your help."

His words struck her hard, little barbs to the heart, but she fought back her reaction. "It's shit like this that makes Kendra sorry she spent the last twenty-five years of her life with you. You don't care about anyone but yourself. If she divorces you, you'll have done everything you can to deserve it."

"Where do you get off talking to your father like that?"

She laughed—a hard, angry sound. "Oh, so now you remember you're my father? That's rich. For most of my life, you seemed entirely unaware of that fact."

She turned and left the kitchen, refusing to let him see the tears in her eyes.

Chapter Nine

Austin finished his foot patrol of Caribou Open Space, ate his lunch at the picnic area nearby, and then moved up the highway to Russey Ranch, one of the county's more remote properties. He veered off the trail, heading toward the wildlife closure area, hoping to hike off his bad mood. Despite the high altitude and the exertion, he couldn't get the argument he'd had with Hawke out of his mind. That explains why the guy with the rifle saw him first.

Bam! Bam!

Two shots rang out, whizzing past his ear, striking a large boulder behind him.

On a surge of adrenaline, he dropped to the ground and drew his firearm from its holster, his gaze searching the mountainside. He spotted the shooter about thirty feet uphill from him. The man fled west through the trees, dropping something as he ran.

Austin reached for his hand mic. "Fifty-six-twenty. Code Ten. Emergent."

"Fifty-six-twenty, go ahead."

"Shots fired at Russey Ranch. Requesting backup. Break."

"Go ahead."

"I'm about a mile west of the Russey trailhead near the Pinnacles wildlife closure area. Break."

"Go ahead."

"Shooter was a white male. He was armed with a rifle. He took off headed west. I no longer have a visual."

"Fifty-six-twenty, copy. Do you need medical?"

It was then he noticed the trickling sensation on the side of his neck. He reached over and wiped whatever it was away, only to find blood on his fingertips.

Shit.

One of the bullets must have fragmented when it hit the rock and nicked him with a bit of shrapnel. Or maybe a piece of rock had sprayed up and gotten him. Either way, there didn't seem to be anything embedded in his neck. Still, if he kept this from dispatch, Rick Sutherland, his boss, would have his ass.

"Affirm. I got nicked by shrapnel. Send medical non-emergent."

"Fifty-six-twenty, I'm toning out medical, non-emergent."

"Copy that. I'm going to evacuate to the parking lot. I'll close the trail. Break."

"Go ahead."

"All units responding switch to FTAC2. I'll be switching as well and going as Russey Command."

"All units responding switch to FTAC2." Dispatch came back with the time. "Thirteen-thirty-six."

Austin reached down and switched his radio to the tactical channel, listening in as unit after unit responded. It sounded like every ranger and deputy in the county was en route. Then again, everyone loved a call that involved something more exciting than car accidents or unruly drunks. No one would want to miss out on the action.

His senses heightened by adrenaline, Austin tuned out the chatter in his earpiece and got into a crouch, semi-auto still in his hand. Whoever the shooter was, he was probably long gone, but Austin wasn't willing to bet his life on that. The bastard might be sitting somewhere watching through a scope, waiting for a clear shot.

Watching for any movement on the mountainside, Austin quickly took cover behind the boulder and then moved off downhill. He worked his way back to the trail, stopping a couple of hikers who were on their way up, then closing the trail when he reached the trailhead. There were a dozen or so cars in the parking lot, which meant there were still hikers up there.

That's just great.

Son of a bitch!

He told himself they'd be safe as long as they stuck to the trail. Whoever the shooter was, he'd headed west, away from the trail and picnic areas. Still, Austin couldn't shake a sense of urgency. They had a shooter running around on public land, and someone needed to stop him.

He glanced at his watch. "Come on, guys. Hurry the fuck up."

With every minute that passed, this asshole was getting farther away.

Lexi stared at the silent police scanner, pulse thrumming. Some bastard had just fired a gun at Austin. "Why isn't anyone saying anything?"

"He's okay, Lexi." Megs patted her arm. "You heard him say so himself. When the sheriff's deputies and medical arrive on the scene, there will be a lot of radio traffic. Until then, they'll status check him every five minutes or so."

Lexi looked at the stack of printouts in front of her, the numbers on the page no longer making sense. Her train of thought had shattered the moment she'd heard Austin say that someone had shot at him. "Does this kind of thing happen often?"

Megs seemed to study her. "I take it you and Austin have mended your fences."

"Well, yes." What did that have to do with anything? "Even if I hated him, I wouldn't want people shooting at him."

Megs lips curved in a slight smile. "Sadly, it happens more often than most people think. They forget that park rangers are law enforcement. A few years back, Larimer County lost a ranger when he came across an escaped fugitive in the backcountry."

Lexi didn't find this reassuring. "Will Austin go after the guy?"

"By himself?" Megs shook her head. "He's not that stupid."

A burst of static on the radio made Lexi jump. She listened as two sheriff's deputies announced their arrival on the scene, followed by EMTs. Ten minutes later the EMTs announced they were finished and back in service.

"See?" Megs said. "He's fine."

Lexi did her best to focus on her work, making her way line by line through the budget and comparing it to actuals. Still, every time traffic came over the radio, she stopped—and listened. She heard when Austin led deputies to a backpack the shooter had dropped. She heard when helicopters and police dogs joined in the search. She heard when dogs lost the man's trail at a nearby creek.

Even distracted as she was, she found several more incidents where Breece had apparently stolen money, this time by paying bills more than once. "Does your bank keep records of canceled checks?"

"Why?"

"I think he might have been writing checks to himself. He paid your liability insurance twice this quarter." She pointed to the entries Breece had made in the accounts. "He also paid your March and April utility bills twice."

Megs examined the documents. "Jesus fried chicken! That son of a bitch."

"If the bank still has those checks, we could confirm whether or not the money went to these organizations—or whether he put it in his pocket."

"I'm on it." Megs reached for the phone and called the bank.

Lexi took the moment to get a bottle of water from the fridge—and to call Kendra again. She'd already left two messages for her stepmother. When her call went to voice mail again, she disconnected.

So Kendra didn't feel like talking to her. Fine.

Back in the ops room, she found Megs on the phone with the bank, a look of rage on her face.

"We'll get the bastard somehow. Thanks, John." Megs hung up the phone, her gaze meeting Lexi's. "You were right. He was writing checks for cash and taking them to Food Mart, then recording the check as something else. How the hell did I miss this?"

"He took advantage of your trust, and he knew how to hide what he was doing." Lexi sat and went back to work, one ear still listening to the radio. "You really shouldn't blame yourself. I've heard of big corporations being embezzled, companies that had annual audits and all the right checks and balances. When someone is determined to steal, they can usually find a way."

Megs listened, but Lexi could tell she wasn't going to let herself off the hook.

Austin reached the parking lot, four frightened young women following closely behind him—the last of the hikers to be evacuated from the Russey Ranch property. They'd been skinny dipping in the wildlife closure area when deputies emerged from the scrub, rifles raised, and scared the hell out of them.

Austin wrote them each a ticket for violating the closure, explaining the ticket to them and the fine—a stiff hundred bucks. "You can pay online with a credit card or mail a check to the address on the back within twenty days from today's date. If you choose to contest the citation, you can appear in court on this date. Here's the address. Failure to pay the fine or appear in court will result in a warrant being issued for your arrest."

Instead of objecting or making excuses, they sheepishly accepted their tickets, one of them even thanking him. Then they climbed into a red BMW X5 and sped away.

Sutherland, the boss man, appeared at Austin's shoulder. "Good work today, Taylor. You're an hour past the end of your shift. Time to head home."

Austin started to object, but Sutherland cut him off. "You had one hell of a day out there. I should've sent you home when medical cleared you. I let you stay on because I thought it would help you work off some of the adrenaline. You've done more than your share today. Go home. That's an order."

Shit.

Austin reached for his hand mic. "Fifty-six-twenty, end of watch. Goodnight."

"Fifty-six-twenty. Good job today. Glad you're safe. Eighteen-oh-seven."

Sutherland slapped him on the shoulder. "Get some rest this weekend."

"Yeah." Austin glanced around, feeling strangely disoriented.

Where the hell had he parked?

He spotted his service vehicle on the other side of the blue portable latrine that served as the property's only restroom. He walked to the truck, stashed his gear in the back, then climbed inside and started the engine, listening in his earpiece as one of the sheriff's deputies took over as Russey Command.

It was over. He was going home in one piece.

"Goddammit!" He slammed a fist against the steering wheel, rage that had been on slow burn inside him all afternoon exploding.

The bastard was going to get away. Whoever he was, he was going to get away. Unless the CSI unit found prints on that backpack that just happened to be in the system, they wouldn't even know who he was. He'd be free to shoot at the next person in a uniform who crossed his path.

"Son of a bitch!"

Austin closed his eyes, drew a few deep breaths, then drove back to the Parks and Open Space office, where he checked in his vehicle and filled out an incident report.

"Good work, Taylor."

"It's good to see you in one piece, man."

Feeling on edge, he dropped the report on Sutherland's desk, then walked outside. He found Hawke leaning against his Tahoe, waiting for him.

"I hear someone took shots at you. I just wanted you to know it wasn't me."

Austin met Hawke's gaze, chuckled. "You wouldn't have missed."

"Damned straight." Hawke stepped forward and crushed Austin against him in a bear hug, slapping his back for good measure. "Goddamn, buddy. I'm glad you're okay."

"Yeah. Me, too." Some of the tension inside Austin eased away.

At least Hawke was over the Lexi thing.

Hawke released him, stepped back, cleared his throat. "Lexi called."

Or maybe not.

"Yeah?" Austin opened his SUV, tossed his backpack in the back.

"You two really can't keep your hands off each other, can you?"

Jesus! How much had Lexi told him?

Still, it was the truth.

"I didn't go to Knockers that night with a plan to hook up with her if that's what you were wondering."

"That's what she said. Shitty timing on my part—again."

"I guess so." Austin peeled off his duty belt.

"Also, sorry about what I said. No matter how much you mess up your life, I've got your back."

"I know."

"So how's this?" Hawke motioned to the bandage on Austin's neck.

"Fine. Just a nick." Austin yanked off the bandage, crumpled it, tossed it into the backseat.

Hawke leaned in, looked at the graze. "Shit. That's nothing. You've gotten worse injuries climbing at the gym."

"That's what I said." Still, the EMTs had insisted on treating him and checking him for shock.

"Let me buy you a drink at Knockers."

Austin didn't feel like hanging out, but he didn't say so. "A drink?"

"Let's celebrate. My best friend didn't get his damned head shot off today."

Austin grinned. "I'll follow you into town."

Lexi took Megs up on the invitation to join her and the rest of the Team at Knockers. When Austin walked in, Eric beside him, cheers went up throughout the pub. He shook his head, an embarrassed grin on his handsome face.

Lexi couldn't stop herself. She jumped to her feet, ran to him, and wrapped her arms around him, realizing at the last moment that he might not be up for a public display. She started to draw back, but his arms surrounded her, held her tight.

He pressed a kiss to her hair. "God, it's good to see you."

"I'm so glad you're okay." Her gaze dropped to the wound beneath his ear, a deep scratch about two inches long, her stomach twisting.

He'd come close to being shot and killed today.

She and Eric shared a glance, and she saw a flash of emotion—regret?—in his eyes before he looked away.

Then Rain came up behind them. "Joe says your money isn't good here tonight, Taylor. Your drinks are on us. What will it be?"

"That's awfully nice of him. Thanks. Scotch, straight up."

"How does Macallan sound?" Rain asked.

Austin grinned. "The good stuff? I won't say no."

His fellow Team members laughed, but Rain's expression went serious. "We take care of our own around here."

For some reason, her words put a lump in Lexi's throat. Her friends in Chicago had never said anything like that. When she'd needed them to stand beside her, everyone but Vic had abandoned her.

Austin slid his arm around her shoulder, and the two of them sat in a spot near the center of the tables that Team members had pushed together.

"Heard the bastard almost got you." Mitch got to his feet and leaned in to look at the wound on Austin's neck. "Hell, that's nothing. You got more beat up than that on our last training mission."

More laughter.

Lexi ordered a glass of chardonnay and a salad, listening while Team members expressed their relief that Austin was okay, the women coming right out and saying it, the men ribbing him as if the whole thing were a joke.

"Can't believe you didn't shit your pants."

"You do realize you had a firearm, too, don't you?"

"That will teach you to waste time watching pretty birdies on duty."

Austin laughed with them, but there was something forced in his smile. When Conrad challenged him to a little competition on the rock wall, he declined. "Sorry, but I'm wiped."

Couldn't they see the shadows in his eyes or the tight lines on his face?

Lexi waited till he'd finished his burger, then took his hand beneath the table and gave it a squeeze, whispering in his ear. "Let's get out of here."

He squeezed her hand back, dropped a five on the table as a tip for Rain, and got to his feet. "I'm headed home. Thanks, everyone."

Megs followed them toward the front door. "Don't worry about tomorrow's training. Take the day to yourself, and let me know if you want to set up an appointment with Esri. I'm sure—"

"I'm fine, Megs. I don't need a day off, and I don't need to talk to Esri."

"I knew you'd say that." Megs frowned. "Listen. Someone took a shot at you today. That can fuck with a person's mind. We can't afford to have you on lead if your head isn't a hundred percent in the game."

"I'm fine."

Megs nodded. "Okay. Show up tomorrow, but if you seem distracted, I'll pull you from the exercise."

Austin nodded, but Lexi could tell he was irritated. "Fair enough."

"Get some rest. We'll see you in the morning." With that, Megs turned and walked back to the table.

As they stepped out the front door into the cool night air, Austin swore under his breath. "Sometimes she drives me crazy."

"Sorry, but I'm with Megs on this one."

Austin grinned down at her. "Traitor."

A ustin left Lexi playing with Mack in the kitchen and made his way upstairs to the shower, weariness beating through him with every step. He knew it for what it was—an adrenaline hangover. He'd felt like this a few times after Team missions that had failed. It was nothing that a hot shower and a good night's sleep couldn't fix.

He stripped out of his uniform, stopping in front of the bathroom mirror to examine the graze on his neck. Ahearn was right. It was nothing.

He turned on the water, stepped under the spray, and closed his eyes.

Bam! Bam!

Rifle shots echoed through his mind, made his pulse spike.

Get a grip, man.

He willed himself to relax, washing the sweat off his body, shampooing his hair, then reaching for a razor and shaving. He wrapped his towel around his hips and walked back to his bedroom, where he found Lexi waiting for him, stretched out on his bed in nothing but black lacy panties.

"I put Mack in his crate." She got to her feet, closed the distance between them, then took hold of the towel and gave a yank. "I'm a firm believer in sex therapy."

Blood surged into his cock. "Yeah?"

He hadn't been expecting this.

"In cases like this, fellatio is particularly effective."

Holy shit. "Is that so?"

"Definitely." She pushed him onto his back on the bed, then straddled him, bringing his thoughts to a standstill with a kiss.

He let her take the lead, palming her naked breasts, the feel of them heavy in his hands, their soft pink nipples pebbling at his touch.

"I was so afraid for you." Her lips were hot against his, her voice a whisper. "God, Austin."

He slid a hand into her hair, drew her head back, looked into her eyes. "Hey, it's okay. I'm okay."

"Thank God." When her mouth took his again, there was an urgency to the kiss that surprised him, a raw current of emotion shuddering through her.

He took everything she gave, then turned the tables and demanded more, nipping her lower lip with his teeth, then soothing it with his tongue.

Damn, she tasted good.

She pushed off his chest, her wet and swollen lips curving into a smile that melted him down to the marrow, one hand closing around his cock.

God. This might be worth getting shot at.

She ducked down again, kissing her way down his chest and belly, her fingers stroking him slowly, root to tip.

He gathered up her red hair and drew it to the side so that he could watch, his abdominal muscles jerking when she teased his obliques with her tongue. They were her favorite muscles. Still, a man could only take so much of this. The anticipation was killing him, his cock aching to be inside her.

Mouth. Pussy. Either one would be *really* good.

Now.

She finally gave him what he wanted, taking him into the heat of her mouth, licking his cock from the base to the aching head.

His hips gave an involuntary buck, one of his hands fisting in her hair, the other clutching the sheets. "*Jesus!*"

At first, she teased him, circling the tip with her tongue, licking the underside as if he were a lollipop, the sensations a kind of torment. "God, I love your cock."

She was echoing the words he'd said to her last night, and, damn it was sexy, the heat in her eyes making his pulse skip.

She seemed to mean what she said, moaning as she moved up and down his length, her hand and mouth working together, stroking and twisting, the pressure just right. And, God, what she was doing with her tongue…

Fuck!

He fought to hold still, not wanting to force himself deeper into her mouth than she was prepared to handle. But, damn, she wasn't making it easy, his balls already drawing tight, the first hint of climax building in his groin.

She seemed to realize he was near the edge. She stopped, blew breath across his wet cock, her lips tracing kisses over his obliques again.

"Have mercy, woman." He was out of breath, his heart thrumming in his chest.

"Good orgasms come to those who wait." Her gaze met and held his as she took him into her mouth once more.

Again she took him to the edge, and again she stopped, pressing kisses to his thighs, his belly, his balls, making him moan with frustration.

"Third time's a charm."

Somehow he managed to speak. "Promises, promises."

This time, she took him hard and fast to the edge, fucking him with her mouth, her tongue, her lips, and her hand synched together in a rhythm that drove him out of his mind. Orgasm crashed in on him, a shockwave of blinding pleasure washing through him as she finished him with her hand.

He lay there, spent, his head empty, his body weightless, while she wiped the cum off his abdomen with a tissue then snuggled beside him.

"Good God, Lexi. You are…" What word could describe what she'd just done to him? "You are *incredible*."

She kissed him, soft kisses on his cheeks and lips, her fingers curling through his hair. "Thanks for not getting killed today."

He took her into his arms and held her.

Chapter Ten

Lexi awoke to find herself intensely aroused, Austin's big hand caressing her breast from behind, his thumb making slow circles over her nipple.

He nuzzled her ear, his voice deep and sleepy. "Good morning, beautiful."

The first hint of daylight shone through his open bedroom window, fresh mountain air carrying the scent of pine.

"Morning. Mmm." She gave a little moan as he tugged on her erect nipple then teased the very tip with his palm, the sensation heightening her desire, making her ache.

Last night, he'd fallen into an exhausted sleep almost immediately—something he'd never done before—and she suspected he was making up for that now. Not that Lexi had cared. He'd had one hell of a day. She'd done what she'd done to help him relax, not because she expected anything in return. Still, this was nice payback.

Delayed gratification was worth the wait when Austin was involved.

"Do you have any idea how much you turn me on?" He pressed his erection against her bottom, his hand leaving her breast to cup her, his fingers finding and teasing her clit. "You're already wet."

Pleasure shivered through her—but it wasn't enough. "Now."

He chuckled, nipped her shoulder with sharp teeth. "Patience, woman."

He kept up his assault, his hand busy between her thighs, his lips caressing the sensitive skin of her nape with little butterfly kisses. She lifted her leg, tried to drape it over his, but her ankles were caught in the sheets.

He kicked the covers away, nudged his knee between her thighs, enabling her to open herself to his touch. "Yeah, that's right. Let me in."

She moaned as he teased the entrance to her vagina—and then slipped a finger inside her. "Fuck me, damn it!"

"You give head with that dirty mouth?" he teased, withdrawing his hand and starting to turn away. "I need to grab a condom."

She held onto his wrist. "It's okay. I've got an IUD."

"Are you sure you're okay with this? We've never—"

"Yes. *Now!*"

He entered her with one slow thrust, his exhale becoming a moan. "Jesus, Lexi."

They'd never had sex without a condom before. Lexi had been so afraid of getting pregnant as a teenager that they'd always used condoms *and* the pill. But she wasn't a teen now. And, God, neither was Austin.

Did this feel as good for him as it did for her?

He adjusted the angle of her thigh where it draped over his, spreading her legs farther apart, moving in sweet slow strokes that already promised her heaven. Then he went back to work on her clit, flicking and teasing her.

One of her hands fisted in the sheets, the other grabbing onto Austin's arm, her face turned into her pillow as he fucked her from behind. He was driving into her now, hard and fast, and she was moaning like a porn star. Why, oh, why didn't they spend every spare moment fucking? When it felt *this* good …

"Austin!" Orgasm sang through her, bright and beautiful as the rising sun.

But he was there, too.

He thrust into her hard once, twice, three times, his breath hot against her nape as he came inside her.

For a moment, they lay there in silence. His cock was still inside her, his heart beating hard against her back.

Her heart was pounding, too, little ripples of pleasure still washing through her. "We should spend all our time having sex."

He chuckled, kissed her hair. "Isn't that what we've been doing?"

She thought about that for a moment, laughed. "I guess so."

He gave a little thrust with his hips, his erection beginning to fade. "It felt incredible to be inside you without a condom. I didn't think I'd last."

"I enjoyed it, too."

"Shit." He kissed her, withdrew, reached for a box of tissues, handing her one. "Time for breakfast. I've got an hour and a half to get all the way to Eldorado Canyon State Park."

She sat. "Are you sure you're up for it?"

"Are you kidding me?" He leaned in, kissed her, his gaze soft. "I could take on the world right now."

The warmth in his eyes left no doubt as to why.

Her heart seemed to trip.

"Hey, you should come with me."

"Can I do that?"

"Sure." He got out of bed, walked naked toward the bathroom.

The sight of his body sent a flutter through her belly because—*my gentle Jesus!*—he was glorious. He really ought to be bronzed. Or carved into marble. Or dragged back into bed.

"You can hang back and watch."

She *was* watching. Wait—what was he saying?

Oh, yeah. Today's training.

"You're part of the Team now, aren't you?"

Lexi liked the way that sounded. "I guess so."

She reached for her phone, saw that Britta had left a message sometime last night. She'd have to call her back later. But Kendra still hadn't gotten back to her, and her father didn't seem to want her around. Why shouldn't she hang with the Team today?

She got to her feet. "I'll have to go home first to shower and change."

"You can shower here. I've got a spare toothbrush." His gaze raked over her. "We'll find something for you to wear."

She found herself smiling. "Thanks. I'd love that."

Austin pulled into the main parking lot, which was closed off to everyone but Team members. Rescue One and Two were already here, along with a dozen other vehicles he recognized. He pointed through the windshield to the massive red buttress of rock that jutted toward the sky. "That's Redgarden Wall."

Lexi looked out through the window. "You're climbing *that*? You're crazy."

She looked adorable, her hair in a ponytail, one of his old Team T-shirts tied off at her waist, her ass doing things for his jeans he couldn't have imagined. She'd had to roll up the pant legs to make them work for her, but he thought that was cute, too.

He climbed out, went round to the back of his SUV, and grabbed his backpack, swinging its weight onto his back and fastening the waist strap. Then he grabbed his rack of gear. "Come on."

They headed for the bridge, Austin sharing a little of the history of Eldorado Canyon State Park with her, the glory days of rock climbing, when the generation known as the Stone Masters, which included Megs and Ahearn, had put up countless routes on Redgarden Wall, amazing the world.

"So this is famous?"

He grinned. "World-class climbing. We do a lot of rescues here."

"I bet." She glanced over the edge of the bridge at the rushing water below.

"This creek is the *biggest* pain in the ass. If the victim is far up the creek, it's safer and much faster to cross the water rather than bringing them over land to the bridge. Most of the year the creek is low, and we cross it on foot hauling a litter. But when the water's high in the spring and summer, which is when most people climb, we have to evacuate people via Tyrolean traverse— stringing ropes across the water and moving the victim to the other side."

"They just dangle above the creek?"

He couldn't help but laugh at her horrified expression. "They're in a litter, and they have rescuers with them."

They'd be practicing on Doub-Griffith, a 5.11c route that started on a ledge that was a good one hundred fifty feet off the ground. It would demand the best of him and everyone else on the Team. He held Lexi's hand, her fingers warm against his, and led her toward the trail that would take them to the base of the route.

The sun was still low on the horizon, the sky a bright Colorado blue, the ponderosa pines buzzing with broad-tailed humming birds. It felt right being here with Lexi, her presence making this place—and Austin—feel complete. He didn't realize he was smiling until they reached the base of the route.

Megs walked over to him. "It looks like someone got laid—or is that satisfied smile on your face for me?"

Lexi's cheeks turned flaming pink.

Austin laughed. "You know I adore you, Megs."

Eric came up behind them, carrying the dummy over his shoulder. "Fred, you heavy son of a bitch, we need to put you on a diet."

"You found his pants." Megs laughed. "Good. I don't want someone calling the cops to report a naked man on the Wall."

Then Hawke spotted Austin and Lexi. "You're looking good. Lexi, nice to see you here. Uh … cute outfit."

He shook his head and passed them without another word.

"Looks like everyone is here. Let's move." Megs reached into a pile of gear and tossed Lexi a helmet. "You'll need this."

Lexi stared at it. "Oh! Oh, well, I'm not climbing."

Megs fought back a grin. "There's a lot of falling rock on this wall. We'd like to keep your brains inside your pretty head, if that's okay with you."

Austin took the helmet from Lexi and put it on her, then helped her adjust the chin strap. "Don't worry. It's going to be fine."

It was time to get to work.

The first job involved stranding poor Fred high on the route's third pitch. Conrad and Creed Herrera, who was finally back from climbing El Cap, had volunteered to hike up the East Slabs—the reverse side of Redgarden Wall—and set up the haul system that would enable the team to hoist Fred up.

While they finished getting the system set up, Belcourt gave the rest of the Team a refresher on how to use the new brake plate. They'd all tried it out on the tower already, but in this business, there was no such thing as too much practice.

The new brake plate was an ingenious piece of metal with three sets of loops angled down the sides. It promised to simplify rescues. Rather than needing a separate brake plate and brakeman for each rope or cable, they'd be able to manage up to four ropes with just one person.

Belcourt had just finished his demonstration when Hawke began to snicker. He pointed up at the rock face. And there came Fred's pants, falling to the earth, the dummy's plastic ass gleaming beige in the sun.

Megs shook her head. "Oh, for fuck's sake. I hope the rest of you can keep your pants on for the duration of this exercise."

Everyone burst into laughter.

"Hasty Team—Taylor, Hawke, Belcourt," Ahearn called out. "You're on."

Austin geared up—harness, radio, hand mic, climbing shoes, harness, helmet, chalk, rack of gear. He adjusted the radio's frequency; they'd be using a different channel today to keep their traffic off the main frequencies. Then he grabbed the bag holding forty pounds of climbing rope and set off for the rock face.

It was time to rescue poor Fred.

Again.

Lexi watched as Austin, Eric, and Chaska made their way up the rock face, moving smoothly up the vertical surface of the rock. Austin was in the lead, picking out the route they'd take to reach Fred, placing protection in the rock at short intervals. His fingers were white with chalk, his gaze turned upward. How he was able to hold on with just the tips of his toes and fingertips, she didn't know.

She'd watched him ski in high school, attending competitions to cheer him on. Yes, it had thrilled her to see him win, and, yes, it had turned her on, too. But she'd never really thought about how much strength or skill was involved.

But watching him climb was different. She couldn't *not* notice his skill, his motions strong and confident, even graceful, like an artist who worked with air and stone. Lexi couldn't take her gaze off him.

"Breathe, girl," Megs whispered.

Lexi hadn't even realized she was holding her breath. "How do they hold on?"

"Join me at the rock gym one of these days, and I'll show you."

Lexi stared at Megs. "Me? Climb?"

"Why not? Women are a force in rock climbing. Imagine the surprise on Austin's face if he saw you doing this."

The very idea made Lexi laugh. "There's no way I could ever climb *that*."

Could she?

Megs laughed. "Okay, just the rock wall, then. You ought to at least learn to belay. Then you can join him when he climbs. Everyone loves a belay slave."

"What's a belay slave?"

"Rock!" Austin's shout made Lexi jump.

A piece of rock fell through the air, just missing Eric's shoulder and crashing onto the ground twenty feet away.

Okay, so Lexi understood the helmets now.

"A belay slave is someone who stays on the ground and takes care of the slack in the rope so that the climber can't fall far. In the rock climbing world, a woman who does this for her man gets the nickname 'Belay Betty.'"

That didn't sound very flattering.

Austin reached Fred, treating him as if he were human. He checked for a pulse, then called via radio to let them know the victim was still alive and needed medical help.

Nearby, Ahearn was organizing other Team members for the vertical evacuation. While Lexi had been distracted watching Austin, they'd brought in rescue gear—a litter, an inflatable body cast, first aid gear, more rope.

A *lot* more rope.

Sasha led the Evac Team. If Austin was an artist, Sasha was a goddess, moving up the ropes Austin had set as if she were floating.

"Wow. She's good."

Megs nodded. "One of the best in the world."

What followed next was a long hour during which Austin and Eric got Fred off his rope and into the body cast and the litter, while the Evac Team, together with Chaska, worked out what Megs called "the anchor problem."

"They have to find a way to secure the ropes so that they're capable of supporting Fred, the litter, and three rescuers with their gear."

"That must be…" Lexi tried to guesstimate the math.

"We round it up to about fifteen-hundred pounds, just to be safe."

Wow. Okay.

Above, Chaska and Sasha climbed around like spiders, apparently looking for a way to create the needed anchor. They had to be at least three hundred feet off the ground, so it was impossible to see exactly what they were doing.

Lexi's cell phone buzzed. She glanced down at the screen.

Drat.

It was Kendra.

Not wanting to disturb the training, she walked back among the trees. "Hey, Kendra. How are—"

"Look, Lexi, I think it's best if you just stay out of this. Also, I don't appreciate being lied to—or manipulated—by anyone."

Lexi had known that's how Kendra would take it. "You and I haven't spoken since the day we had lunch. I didn't lie to anyone."

"You told Rose your father had hired Rain, but *you* were the one who did that."

Well, Kendra had her there.

"You know my dad. Do you think he would have let me hire Rain if he were dead-set against it? He would have fired her and sent her packing. He's just being stubborn because he hates to lose an argument. He loves you, Kendra, and he wants you back. That's why he let me do what I did."

"I don't believe you."

"Please have lunch with me again. You can vent. Maybe I'll vent, too. After all, I've been living with him for most of a week now."

That made Kendra laugh. "Okay, kid. Lunch Monday at that new Mexican place. Your treat."

"I can't make it Monday." She was doing her ride-along with Austin that day. "But I'm free on Tuesday."

"Okay, Tuesday. Just don't try to tell me your dad wants me back. Quit letting him use you. If he wants me, he needs to prove it and tell me himself."

"He's not using me. He doesn't even want me—"

But Kendra had ended the call.

"Well, hell." Lexi slipped her cell phone back into her pocket, wondering whether she was wasting her time.

By the time she had rejoined Megs, Austin and Eric had poor Fred in the litter. Then everyone but the two of them, along with Sasha and Chaska, climbed down again. Chaska stayed high above the others.

"Is he staying up there in case something goes wrong?"

Megs shook her head. "He's our brakeman. He's going to control how fast the litter and the other climbers come down."

Lexi found herself holding her breath again as Sasha clipped onto the head of the litter and Eric the foot, Austin standing on the litter and straddling Fred as if he were still giving medical care. Down they came, slowly and steadily, Sasha and Eric using their feet and hands to keep the litter from swinging into the rock face and jarring the victim.

When they reached the ground, Chaska let out a whoop from high above.

Cheers went up from the other members.

"Congrats, Belcourt," Megs said into her hand mic. "Your pretty piece of metal worked. But we're not done here, people. Stay focused!"

It took another hour to get Chaska and the ropes down and to move Fred down the steep scree slope at the base of the wall.

"Why don't they just take the trail?"

"This is much faster," Megs said.

When they reached the creek, Lexi got to see firsthand how a Tyrolean traverse worked. She watched as the rescuers set up the ropes and evacuated the litter safely to the other side, setting poor Fred on the ground near an imaginary ambulance.

"Time?" Megs asked.

Ahearn glanced at his watch. "Two hours and forty-two minutes."

"Not bad."

The remaining Team members sent the rest of the gear across the creek before following it over, their feet dangling above whitewater.

"Your turn, Lexi," Eric called to her.

She shook her head, took a step back. "Oh, no. I can't. I don't have a harness."

She was not crazy like they were. This was *not* her idea of a good time.

But no one was listening to her, or maybe they couldn't hear her above the water.

Austin crossed the creek again, a spare harness strapped to his gear. "Come on. I'll get you over."

She took the harness, looked down at it. "I don't even know how to use this."

"You can do it!" Sasha shouted.

"Come on, Lexi!" That was Eric.

"Lexi! Lexi! Lexi!"

Austin tucked a finger under her chin. "Trust me."

"If I fall in—"

"You won't. Even if you did, you have the best rescue team in the country standing right here—and you have me." He helped her into the harness, clipped her to the rope, then fastened what he called a "lead " to her harness. "I'm going to cross and then pull you over. All you have to do is hang on to this safety strap and step off the edge."

She shook her head. "Oh, God! I don't think…"

But he was already gone, moving across the rope again. When his feet touched the ground, he looked back at her.

He shouted to her, lead rope in his hand. "Come on over!"

"Oh, God." She squeezed her eyes shut and, barely breathing, stepped off the edge. She gave a shriek as the ground disappeared, gravity pulling her downward toward the center of the rope.

Austin's shout reached her over the raging water. "Open your eyes!"

Holding on tightly to the safety strap, she did as he asked. He was watching her, a smile on his sweat-stained face as he pulled her across the creek.

This wasn't scary. It was … *fun.*

She laughed, glanced down at the rushing water, and was almost sorry when the ride was over and her feet touched the ground.

Cheers.

"Look at her face." That was Sasha. "She wants to do it again."

Laughter.

"Well done, everyone. Let's break it down and get back to town," Megs called out. "First round of drinks tonight is on the Team."

Chapter Eleven

Austin took another drink of beer, Lexi beside him, their burgers devoured. Over on the rock wall, Sasha and Nicole were coaching Winona, Belcourt's little sister, on a 5.10 route, while the rest of them listened to Herrera brag about his four-hour climb of the Nose on El Cap.

"I'd just clipped in under the Roof when some *cabrón* went screaming by me in total free fall. Fucking BASE jumpers. Gave me vertigo."

Everyone laughed, except Megs.

She shook her head. "Idiots."

BASE jumping was illegal in Yosemite National Park, and more than one amazing climber had lost his life defying that law.

Lexi looked adorably horrified. "Why would anyone willingly jump off a cliff? What if the parachute doesn't work? What if you hit the cliff wall on the way down?"

"It's adrenaline addiction." Austin resisted the urge to plant a kiss on her lips. He hoped they'd leave soon and go back to his place. Oh, how he'd love to follow up today's vertical action with a little horizontal action.

Moretti grinned. "It's a hell of a rush. That's how I discovered climbing."

"You discovered climbing by falling?" Herrera rolled his eyes. "I always knew you were loco, man."

More laughter.

"Stay the hell away from my daughter!"

It took Austin a moment to realize the words were directed at him.

Lexi's father stood behind him, unshaven and drunk.

Lexi whirled and jumped to her feet. "What are you doing, Dad?"

"I'm doing what you're doing—having a drink."

Austin could tell the old man had had far more than a single drink. He got to his feet, too. "Let's get him home."

Lexi took one arm, Austin the other.

"Get your hands off me!" Her father jerked away, stumbled backward, somehow managing not to fall on his ass. "Keep your hands off my girl, too. You're screwing her again, aren't you? She didn't come home last night and—"

"Watch your mouth." Austin lowered his voice and got in the old man's face. "You can say what you want about me, but you will *not* talk about Lexi like that, not when I'm around."

"Oh, well, listen to you. You're a knight in shining armor." Bob Jewell fixed his gaze on Lexi. "C'mon, Lexi girl. You shouldn't be hangin' with him. You shouldn't waste your time with any of these losers. They let your mother *die!*"

That last word was shouted.

Lexi's face went beet red, her eyes pleading. "That's not true, Dad."

Austin was about to remove her father from the premises just like he would any other disorderly drunk, when Rain stormed up to them.

She looked furious, snapping her fingers in the old man's face to get his attention. "That's it, Bob. It's time to go. You know you can't come in here and cause a scene. Do you want Joe to ban you from the pub?"

"They let my wife die." His voice sounded whiny now, sad and tired.

"Let's go home, Dad." Lexi dropped a twenty on the table and then met Austin's gaze. "I'm so sorry. I'm so, so sorry."

With Rain's help, they maneuvered her father through the pub toward the front door, the old man alternately mumbling and shouting about his wife.

Austin wanted to go with Lexi to make sure she made it back to the inn safely, to make sure she knew none of them blamed her for what her father had said.

Eric came up beside him. "I know what you're thinking, but let her go. You'll only make things harder for her. You can call later, when she's got her dad settled."

"Who the hell was that?" Herrera asked. "And who is this Lexi woman you're hanging with, man? She is *fine*."

Megs answered for him. "Stuff a sock in it, Herrera."

*L*exi unlocked the back door and stood back to let her father enter. "Way to make a fool of both of us tonight, Dad. I'm not sure I'll ever be able to forgive you. I've never felt more humiliated."

"Don't know why you spend time with them anyway." He shuffled through the door, walked to the cabinet where he'd kept most of his liquor, apparently forgetting it was empty. "Where's the rum? Did you dump it, too?"

"I'm doing pro-bono work for the Team, Dad, and until tonight at least, I thought I was making some real friends."

"You don't need him."

"Do *not* talk to me about Austin." Oh, God, poor Austin! He'd stood up to her father, tried to protect her, tried to help. What must he think of her now? "I can't believe what you said to him, what you said in front of everyone."

Her father turned and glared at her, a confused look on his face. "Is that overgrown rock jock after you again?"

My God. Had her father forgotten what he'd just done?

She would have thrown every stupid word he'd said back in his face, but what was the point? He wouldn't remember five minutes from now, much less in the morning. "You're drunk, Dad. Go to bed."

Instead, he sat at the table. "What's for supper?"

"I don't know. What are you making?" She got herself a glass of water, reached into the cabinet, and got an aspirin, her head beginning to throb. "I ate at the pub."

"Oh, that's sweet. What kind of daughter are you?"

She slammed the glass down on the counter. "Why did I even come here? What was I thinking?"

"Kendra says you lost your job. That's why you're here."

"What?" Rage and humiliation crashed over her. "I quit, Dad. I filed a sexual harassment suit against an asshole who tried to bully me into sleeping with him, and I got a settlement. Did Kendra tell you that, too?"

From the look on his face, she hadn't. Or he'd simply forgotten.

She needed to get away from him, away from here. "I'm leaving."

Grabbing her handbag, she walked out of the house, needing to put distance between herself and her father, her blood boiling, tears pricking her eyes. She blinked the tears away and headed up the highway, not caring where she went or noticing that the sun had already set.

Why had she come back to Scarlet anyway? Britta was right. This wasn't her problem. If her father wanted to destroy his life, that was his decision. She didn't have to let him drag her down, too. She needed to get back to Chicago. She could live with Vic until she got a new job. She could start over.

Austin.

The thought of leaving him so soon put an ache in her chest. She'd made him no promises, but the hours she'd spent with him were the happiest she'd known in a long time. If she had her way, they would see where this *friendship* of theirs took them.

And then there was the audit.

"Shit!" She'd almost forgotten about that.

Okay, so she was going nowhere. Not yet.

Then again, there was a chance her father had just destroyed her relationship with Megs and the others. Just when she'd thought she'd found a place where she felt at home, he'd had to show up drunk and shoot off his mouth. He'd accused them of letting her mother die, insulting them in public, saying things that weren't true.

How could she ever look Megs in the eyes again?

She stopped when she realized where her footsteps had brought her.

She opened the cemetery's iron gate and threaded her way through the tombstones toward her mother's grave. She hadn't been here in years, but she knew where it was—there in the shade of the aspens.

Lexi ran her fingers over the engraved words.

Emily Ann O'Hara Jewell

June 5, 1960 – April 21, 1990

Beloved wife, mother, friend

"Mama." Lexi knelt on the ground. For a time, she could do nothing but cry, grief rising from some hidden place inside her. "We messed it all up. We're no good without you. Dad, well, he's a jerk who drinks all the time. Britta is on her own in San Diego. My life fell apart. I don't even know where I belong anymore."

She told her mother what had gone wrong in Chicago, told her why she'd come back to Scarlet, told her about Austin and what had happened earlier this evening at Knockers. She didn't know if her mother could hear her, but it felt good to talk to someone. And if she felt her mother's gentle presence—well, it was probably just her imagination. Only when she realized it was completely dark did she get back to her feet.

It wasn't safe to walk along the highway in the dark alone.

"Goodbye, Mama. I love you."

Wiping the tears from her face, she hurried back toward the gate.

Austin sat in his Tahoe on the shoulder of the highway, watching as Lexi left her mother's graveside and walked back through the cemetery. He'd been on his way to the inn to check on her and her father when he'd spotted her all but running up the road. Figuring she needed space, he'd parked across the road to keep an eye on her.

Dusk was the time of day when mountain lions came out to hunt, and more than one unsuspecting hiker had been attacked in these mountains. And then there were predators of the human variety, including the man who'd taken a shot at him.

Austin had watched when she'd stopped in front of the cemetery, had felt a hard lump in his throat when she'd knelt in front of her mother's grave, her grief piercing his chest. Why hadn't he understood how badly losing her mother had hurt her? It ought to have been obvious. She'd been four years old, for God's sake. That would crush a child.

Hawke's words had come back to him.

Kendra had no idea what she was doing and had never planned to be a mother, so the girls were basically left to deal with the loss of their mom by themselves.

And it had hit him that Lexi had, in truth, lost *both* of her parents.

Austin had never lost anyone close to him. His parents were alive and healthy, his grandparents, too. He'd been on rescues where people had died. It had shaken him up, but the loss hadn't been personal. The most grief he'd experienced had been when his first dog, Quinn, had died—and when he'd lost Lexi.

He was lucky.

Lexi passed through the iron gate and started down the highway toward town, apparently not noticing him.

He called to her. "Want a ride?"

Startled, she whirled around, eyes wide. "Austin?"

He climbed out of the vehicle. "I followed you."

"Oh." She didn't cross the road, but stood where she was, her arms crossed as if she were cold. "I'm surprised you even want to talk to me after that."

Unwilling to have this conversation by shouting back and forth, he waited for a Jeep to pass, then crossed the highway. "It wasn't your fault. I don't blame you. Neither does Rain or Megs or anyone else on the Team."

"Really?"

"Come here."

In a heartbeat, she was in his arms. "Oh, Austin, I'm so sorry. My father—"

"He's responsible for his own actions." Austin kissed her hair. "I have an idea. Why don't you go get your stuff and stay at my house for the next few days? You can take a break from the problems with your dad, and I can get my T-shirt and jeans back. You can take a hot bath or watch TV—just unwind."

He hadn't planned this, and the moment the invitation was out of his mouth, some part of him wondered if he was getting in over his head. They were just friends, after all.

"You don't know how much I would love to take you up on that, but I need to make sure my dad is okay. By the time we got home, he didn't even remember what he'd said. If anything were to happen to him…"

"You don't have to explain. Let's get you home."

"Thanks." She stood on tiptoe, kissed his lips. "And thanks for following me. It's creepy out here after dark."

They crossed the highway, climbed into his vehicle, and headed toward town.

Lexi found her father passed out on the sofa. She turned off the television, draped a blanket over him, then took a long, hot shower. She dropped her clothes—and the clothes she'd borrowed from Austin—in the laundry, smiling to herself at his last words to her.

Hey, don't feel like you have to wash the jeans.

She made her way back to her room, the annoying rattle of her father's snores following her down the hall. She closed the door, slipped into the T-shirt she used as pajamas, and called Britta, catching her up on everything that had happened with Kendra and their father since the last time they'd spoken. She reached the part where her father shouted at Austin in Knockers before Brit cut her off.

"Can't say I blame Dad for that. You're sleeping with that bastard again?"

Lexi couldn't help but smile. "Yes, and I'm enjoying every moment of it."

No man on earth was better in bed than Austin Taylor. It was a simple fact.

"You're not getting hooked on him, are you?"

"No! No, of course not. We're just friends—you know, with benefits."

"I thought you couldn't stand each other."

"That's what I thought, too." Lexi told her how they'd agreed to let the past go and had ended up in bed together. She skipped the intimate details—or most of them anyway. "It's not like either of us planned this."

"He broke your heart, Lex. I listened to you cry yourself to sleep every night for a month. Or have you forgotten?"

Lexi hadn't forgotten. "That was twelve years ago. We were both stupid teenagers. I hurt him, too, you know."

When her sister said nothing, Lexi went on. "This morning, he woke me up by getting me all hot and bothered. Then I went with him to one of the Team's trainings and watched him climb. God, if you could see—"

"Listen to yourself. You are falling for him again."

"Falling for him?" Lexi's pulse spiked. "No, I'm not! I just really love having sex with him. I'm leaving in a couple of weeks anyway. It's not like he and I can be together in the long term."

"Exactly. Remember that."

"He was there for me tonight." Lexi told her sister how he'd stood up for her and tried to help. "After I got Dad home, I went to visit Mom's grave. Austin followed me. I didn't even know he was there."

"Creepy."

"No, not creepy. It was getting dark. He watched over me, then offered me a ride home." It had touched Lexi more than she could say.

"So the man's not always an ass. How nice." Britta moved on. "You said Dad insulted the search and rescue team, too?"

Lexi filled her in on the rest—what her father had shouted to Megs and the others, what he'd said to her when they'd gotten home.

"Kendra let Dad believe you'd lost your job? What a bitch!"

"I guess I don't know that for certain." She didn't want to condemn Kendra unfairly. "Dad was so drunk, he might have forgotten the rest of the details."

"Oh, you *know* that's what she did. It was probably her way of getting back at you for letting her believe Dad had hired Rain."

Lexi hadn't thought about it like that. "You're probably right. I guess all's fair in love and war."

"Which one is this—love or war?"

Lexi suddenly felt weary. "I'm not sure."

For a moment, neither of them spoke.

Britta broke the silence. "Dad has a serious drinking problem."

"Yeah." It was time Lexi faced this fact. "God, Britta, what am I going to do?"

"Are you truly asking? If you are, you know you'll get an answer." Her sister was sometimes painfully direct.

"Of course, I'm asking."

"You can't fix him. Pack up and drive to California. You can stay with me for a while. We can hang on Mission Beach after work. You'll love it. We'll do a harbor tour and look at the sea lions. I'll show you the city. We can go to the clubs on Coronado Island, maybe meet some Navy SEALs. What do you think?"

Oh, it *was* tempting. She and Britta hadn't spent any real time together since the Christmas before last. "I would love that, but I have to finish the audit first."

"How long is that going to take?"

"A few weeks at least." Rather than trying to figure out why she'd just lied to her sister—she'd be done in ten days tops—she gave Britta an overview of what was involved in a forensic audit. "I'm probably going to have to meet with the district attorney to go over all of it. I might even be asked to testify."

"I'm proud of you for helping the Team. Really I am." The tone of Britta's voice implied she had reservations about this.

"But… There's a 'but' in there somewhere."

"I'm afraid you're going to get your heart broken again and find yourself stuck in that damned town if you don't leave soon."

Stuck in Scarlet?

"Trust me," Lexi reassured her. "That is *not* going to happen."

She wouldn't let it happen.

Chapter Twelve

Sunday was Austin's early shift. He'd planned to head back up to Russey Ranch, which was still closed to the public, but Sutherland had left him an email asking him to meet Tamiko Mori, the county's lead biologist, at Moose Lake to help set up motion-activated infrared cameras for a wildlife study. Sutherland had claimed Mori was behind schedule and needed his help, but Austin knew it was Sutherland's way of keeping him on light duty. This was the sort of job they saved for female rangers who were pregnant or staff who'd been injured.

Tamiko met him at the trailhead, a friendly smile on her face. "It's not what you're used to doing, is it?"

"You could say that."

The job was interesting at least and gave him an excuse to climb trees. He spent the next ten hours putting cameras together and positioning them where they had a clear view of the trail but where hikers were unlikely to tamper with them. The goal of the study was to determine how often mountain lions crossed the park's most heavily used trails. The more biologists knew, the better their chances of preventing conflicts between humans and animals.

After work, he drove home, took Mack for a quick walk, then stripped off his dirty uniform and stepped into the shower, washing a day's worth of tree sap, dust, and sweat off his skin, his thoughts turning to Lexi. She'd texted him earlier, thanking him again for giving her a ride home. He'd texted back.

No problem. Dinner?

Sure!

I'll pick you up at 6.

God, he wanted to see her.

Only two things about this bothered him.

First, Sunday evenings were set aside for family dinner. His mother always made a big meal, and the entire family gathered together. He'd brought Lexi to many of those family meals years ago, but if he showed up with her at his side now…

His parents would be gracious, but his sister might not be able to keep her mouth shut. Chey might be six years younger, but that didn't stop her from trying to protect him. She had a sharp tongue.

Second, he shouldn't *want* to see Lexi—not like this. They were only friends. He shouldn't spend his free time thinking about her, wanting her, wanting to be with her. He couldn't let her become a fever in his blood like she'd been before. He needed to step back, keep his distance, play it cool.

Nothing says 'playing it cool' like bringing her to dinner with the family.

Still, he couldn't seem to stop himself.

He called his mother. "Hey, would you mind if I brought someone tonight?"

"Lexi Jewell."

"How—"

"The word all over town is that the two of you are sleeping together. Who else would it be? I heard what her father said to you. Honestly, Austin, are there no other women in the state of Colorado who interest you?"

Shit.

"Lexi and I are just friends, Mom." Austin winced at his own words.

His mother wasn't going to buy that.

"You're a grown man. How you choose to mess up your life is your business. I just don't want to see you hurt again. Neither does Cheyenne. I have no idea how she'll take this."

"I'll deal with Chey."

Having spoken her piece, his mother relented. "Sure. Bring Lexi. God knows that poor girl could use some time with a functional family."

"We're a functional family?" Austin teased.

In truth, they had their differences, but at the end of the day, they were there for one another.

His mother laughed. "See you at six."

Now all he had to do was ignore the voice in his head warning him that this was a catastrophically bad idea—and explain to Lexi that they'd be eating with his family.

But first, he sent a text to his sister.

Bringing Lexi to dinner tonight. Behave.

Chey replied right away.

That bitch? WTF????

"Jesus."

*L*exi took Austin's hand as they headed up the stone walkway to the front door of the Taylor house, butterflies dancing in her stomach. She couldn't believe she'd agreed to have dinner with his family. Then again, anything was better than spending the evening with her father. "Chey hates my guts. Do you know she called me a bitch?"

"That was a long time ago."

"Tell her that." She glanced down at the silver sandals she'd chosen, their short heels clicking on the flagstone. She liked the way they went with the silver lace on her Rory Beca tank top, but maybe they were too dressy to wear with jeans.

"It's going to be okay. Quit worrying." Austin opened the door, held it for her.

Lexi took a breath to steady herself, then stepped inside, the savory scent of roasted chicken making her mouth water.

"There they are." Roxanne Taylor, Austin's mother, appeared from behind a partition that separated the dining room from the living room, a warm smile on her face. She took Lexi's hand, held it between hers. "So good to see you, Lexi."

"Good to see you, too, Roxanne." Warmth rushed through Lexi at the sight of the kind and familiar face. "You look amazing."

The past twelve years had left Roxanne almost unchanged. There were a few streaks of gray in her blond hair now and some smile lines on her face, but she could easily have passed for a woman in her forties.

Roxanne laughed. "Don't sound so surprised. It hasn't been *that* long."

She led them to the dining room, where Michael, her husband, was setting a bottle of Riesling on the already set table. His hair had gone to salt and pepper, his face as tanned as she remembered. He looked up as they entered, his smile so like Austin's. He reached out his hand, gave Lexi's a squeeze. "Glad you could join us."

A voice came from the kitchen behind them.

"If Austin is here, *he* should mash the potatoes. He's the one with the muscles." Cheyenne stood at the counter wearing shorts, a T-shirt, and an apron, an old-fashioned potato masher in her hand, her dark blond hair pulled back in a ponytail.

Austin turned toward his sister. "What happened to Ms. Liberated Doesn't-Need-A-Man-In-Her-Life?"

"You're not a man. You're my brother."

He chuckled. "I'm glad we got that cleared up. I guess I'd better help."

Roxanne followed her son into the kitchen. "The chicken is ready to come out."

Lexi glanced around her, tried to relax. She'd spent many Sunday evenings here with Austin and had fond memories of both the place and the people. It had once been her home away from home, a place she'd come to escape Kendra and her father. She had felt comfortable here, safe, wanted.

Most of the furniture was different. The walls no longer had wallpaper. Wood flooring had replaced the old shag carpet. Where school photos of Austin and Cheyenne had once hung, there were now paintings.

Michael interrupted her thoughts. "Can I pour you a glass of wine?"

"Yes, please." God, she needed a drink.

A few busy minutes later, they were seated around the table, Lexi to Austin's right. While they ate, Roxanne asked Lexi questions about her life in Chicago, probably trying to make her feel at ease. Was it truly windy there? How much snow did they get in the winter? Did she feel safe walking on the streets? What were some of her favorite places in the city?

Cheyenne cut in with the next question. "When are you going back?"

Lexi felt Austin tense, but she didn't take offense. "I need to finish the work I'm doing for the Team first."

Cheyenne looked mystified. "Why do they need *you?* You don't climb."

Okay, so Austin had been wrong. Cheyenne still hated her.

"She's helping us fix the mess Breece made." Austin's tone had a warning edge to it. "He embezzled thousands from us and hid his tracks."

Cheyenne looked unimpressed. "How long is that going to take?"

Lexi took a sip of her wine. "A few weeks at least."

"After that, you *are* going back, right?"

Michael leveled his gaze at his daughter. "That's rude, Cheyenne."

Cheyenne glared at her father. "You remember what happened the last time she sank her claws into him. He was a wreck. She's been back for less than a week, and she's already reeled him in again."

"Chey—" Austin tried to cut her off, but she kept going.

She looked to her parents for support. "You heard what her dad said to him at Knockers last night."

"That wasn't Lexi's fault." Austin's raised voice silenced his sister at last.

"For the record, I was wrecked by our breakup, too." Lexi took a sip of wine, fought to keep emotion out of her voice. "My sister feels the same way about your brother that you feel about me. I am *very* sorry about what my father said. He was drunk and completely out of line."

"How is he doing?" Roxanne asked, deftly changing the subject.

"He needs help." Lexi had spent the morning arguing with him, urging him to get alcohol counseling. "It's been very hard for him with Kendra gone."

The rest of the meal passed with a false sort of cheerfulness, Cheyenne's presence bringing tension to what would otherwise have been a fun meal. Afterward, Lexi helped clear the table, but she got shooed out of the kitchen by Roxanne when she tried to load the dishwasher. She and Austin sat with Michael on the back deck enjoying the cool evening air, Roxanne eventually joining them.

When enough time had passed that her departure wouldn't seem abrupt or rude, Lexi got to her feet. "I suppose I should get home. Thanks so much for the delicious meal. It was great to see all of you again."

Austin stood. "I'll drive you."

They'd just reached his SUV when he drew her into his arms. "I am so sorry, Lexi. Cheyenne is … well, she's just trying to watch out for me."

"I know she is." She rested her head against his chest. Even after all these years, it felt so natural. "I guess I had it coming, given what my father said to you."

"Bullshit." He kissed her hair. "Why don't we go to my place? I have a few ideas about how we could spend the time."

That made her smile. "I just bet you do."

Austin watched Lexi's sweet face as he thrust into her once more with agonizing slowness and then withdrew. Her brow furrowed. Her lips parted on a moan. Her neck arched, baring her throat to his kisses.

She opened her eyes, looked pleadingly into his. "*Don't ... stop.*"

Oh, he wasn't planning on stopping. "I could fuck you like this all night long."

Her pupils dilated, her eyes drifting shut again as he slowly thrust once more.

He kept the pace steady and slow, unable to take his gaze off her—the bliss on her flushed face, her pebbled nipples, the crimson fan of her hair.

"Ooh, this is *torture.*"

"Want me to go faster...?" He gave a few quick hard thrusts that had her crying out, then slowed down again, the transition earning him a deep moan. "Or do you want me to keep it slow like this?"

"*Yes!*"

He chuckled, shifting his tactics, keeping it slow for a while, then driving into her hard and fast, until she was frantic beneath him, her breathing ragged. "I love how you moan and smile at the same time."

She smiled—and moaned again.

Damn.

Okay, so maybe he couldn't last *all* night.

Forty-five minutes. He could last forty-five minutes, couldn't he? Okay, so a half hour. Ten minutes? Maybe he ought to have worn a condom after all. She felt too ... damned ... *good.*

He willed himself to relax and focus only on her response, not the way it felt to be inside her—her tightness, her slick heat. He could tell she was getting close. Her breasts seemed to swell, her chest flushing pink. There were no smiles now, only the moans and whimpers of a woman lost in sexual bliss.

Fast and hard—one, two, three, four, five—and then deep and *slow*.

It made his blood burn hot to know that he could do this to her—fuck her until pleasure made her come undone, her composure and control gone, her body desperate for what he could give her. And, God, he was just as desperate for her, his chest slick with sweat, his heart pounding from sheer lust.

What was it about Lexi that got to him like this? How did she make him want her so badly that he could never get enough? She was an addiction, an obsession, a disease.

One, two, three, four, five—and *slow*.

Without his permission, his mouth started talking, whispering nonsensical words against her fevered skin. "God, Lexi, you are so beautiful, so beautiful to me. I want you... I need..."

One, two, three, four, five—*slow*.

Her breath caught and held for a moment, then she came with a cry, her nails biting into his skin, her inner muscles clenching around him. He captured her cry with a kiss, staying with her until the tremors inside her had passed and she lay limp and still beneath him, her eyes closed. Then he let himself go, pounding into her until his world exploded into ecstasy. And for a time, he just breathed her in.

A slender finger trailed up his spine, her heartbeat slowing beneath his. He rolled off her, drew her into his arms. As they lay there in the dark together, her head pillowed on his chest, he did his best not to think about the fact that she'd soon be leaving.

"Can I tell you a secret?" she said.

He'd thought she was almost asleep. "Sure."

She seemed to hesitate. "After I left for college, I hated myself for what I'd said that night. If only I'd kept my mouth shut... All it took was a little distance from this place for me to realize that I *would* have come back here just to be with you. I didn't figure that out in time. I guess I was young and stupid."

He kissed her hair, now wide awake, his mind racing to take all of this in. "We were both young and stupid."

"It's too late now, but I wanted you to know."

Austin lay awake long after she'd fallen asleep thinking about this.

Lexi woke in Austin's arms early the next morning feeling languid and just a little sore. She closed her eyes, snuggled against him, savoring the feeling of lying beside him.

Beep! Beep! Beep!

His alarm went off, making her jump and waking him.

He reached over, smacked it off, then wrapped his arms around her, spooning her. "Morning can fuck off."

Lexi couldn't help but smile at the sleepiness in his voice. He must have worn himself out last night. He'd certainly exhausted her, driving her into some crazy sexual frenzy, making her feel like she was the only woman in his world. When it came to stamina, Austin was in a league of his own.

He stirred behind her. "Shit."

She rolled over, kissed him. "I don't think morning is going anywhere. When do you have to be at work?"

He brushed a strand of hair from her cheek, kissed her forehead. "You mean when do *we* have to be at work. You're doing a ride-along today, remember?"

"Oh, God." Lexi sat bolt upright. "I forgot."

While he dressed, took care of Mack, and made breakfast, she took a quick shower. She'd tucked a small makeup kit in her handbag, pretty certain she'd end up spending the night, and quickly applied mascara and lip gloss. Then she threw on the clothes Austin had peeled off her body last night and hurried down the stairs.

He was just setting plates on the counter, the puppy eating its own breakfast nearby. He took one look at her and shook his head. "The jeans are okay, but that top and those sandals—no. We're going to need to run by your place."

After Mack had gotten a quick walk and done his business, they left in Austin's SUV, swinging by the inn so that Lexi could change. She was in and out in a flash, switching into a T-shirt and a pair of running shoes, careful not to wake her father. Then they set off down the canyon toward the Forest County Parks and Open Space office.

After Austin had punched his time card, he handed Lexi a clipboard and a pen. "It's a standard release form. By signing it, you agree not to sue the county if something happens to you on this ride-along."

Ten minutes later, they were sitting in Austin's service vehicle on their way out of the parking lot, windows down to let in the cool morning air. For Lexi, it felt like a grand adventure.

"Fifty-six-twenty, show me in service."

"Fifty-six-twenty, good morning."

"Fifty-six-twenty, Moose Lake."

The dispatcher came back with the time. "Zero-eight-ten."

Lexi felt mildly cool now that she could understand some of the radio chatter—or traffic, as they called it. "We're going to Moose Lake?"

"It gets a lot of visitors on weekends, and this is Memorial Day—one of the biggest weekends of the year. I always head there on Monday mornings to check the trash and to make sure there's toilet paper in the bathrooms." He flashed her a grin. "I was on my way there last Monday when your call came in."

"I can't believe it's only been one week since we reconnected."

A lot had happened in those seven days.

He looked over at her, his eyes hidden behind his mirrored sunglasses, a smile on his lips. "Tell me about it."

"Are there any moose at Moose Lake?"

"Quite a few, actually. If you're lucky, maybe we'll see one."

"Oh, I hope we do."

Soon they were turning into the Moose Lake parking lot. She watched while he checked the restrooms and the trash bins. Then he checked in with dispatch and told them he was going on a foot patrol.

He lifted his pack onto his back. "You up for this, city girl?"

"Just try to keep up." She headed off down the trail, the warm sound of his chuckle following her. "Let me know if I'm going too fast for you."

The trail he chose encircled the lake itself, blue sky and white clouds reflected on the water's surface, cattails hugging the shoreline. Parts of the trail were rocky and exposed to the sunshine. Others were shaded by aspens, fragile blue columbine blooming in clumps amid the white trunks.

Lexi saw a side of Austin she'd never seen before. He knew the fancy Latin name of every flower, every tree, every little creature. He was even able to identify many of the birds by their songs. She could see on his face that *this* was his place. *This* was where he felt most at home. No wonder he'd never thought about leaving.

She watched from a distance while he nudged a fat bull snake off the trail with the tip of his expandable baton. "Come on, little guy. Go sun yourself somewhere safer."

She felt a tug in her chest, touched by his gentleness with a creature many people would find repugnant. "You know, for a tough guy with a uniform and a gun, you're basically a bunny-loving tree-hugger."

He looked over at her, his lips curving in a smile. "You've discovered my secret."

"Don't worry. Your secret is safe with—"

Lexi gave a startled gasp.

Bear.

He stood there, among the pines, something wrapped in a blanket in his arms. He'd come up behind them so quietly that neither she nor Austin had heard him.

"Ranger Taylor." His gaze moved to Lexi, a frown coming over his face. "I saw your truck. I thought you'd be alone."

"Lexi's doing a ride-along with me today. Are you okay?"

Whatever was in the blanket wiggled, and Lexi saw.

A tiny fawn.

Chapter Thirteen

Austin watched Lexi's eyes go wide as the little fawn poked its face out of the blanket. In a heartbeat, she was at Bear's side, the delight on her face sending warmth through his chest. But Austin was on the clock, and this was now official business. "Where did you find it?"

"Beneath the Pinnacles. It was about ten days ago. She was walking around her mama's severed head, crying her little heart out."

"Sounds like poachers." Austin loathed them. "Was it inside the wildlife closure?"

Bear nodded, looking a bit sheepish. He'd just admitted to violating the law, but Austin let that go for now.

"This girl is too little to survive on her own. I was gonna raise her up myself, but I need you to take her. These are bad times, dark times. The End Times."

It was unusual for Bear to surrender an animal. He had rehabilitated more than a few orphaned and wounded critters through the years, from a golden eagle to baby skunks. It wasn't strictly legal. Still, Bear knew what he was doing, so overworked wildlife officials had let him get away with it.

Austin considered both this and Bear's strange words—not that strange words from Bear were all that unusual. "What's going on, buddy? Is everything okay?"

Bear's gaze flitted to Lexi, then back to Austin. "A righteous man has regard for the life of his animal, but even the compassion of the wicked is cruel."

Ask a straight question, get a verse from Proverbs.

That was Bear in a nutshell.

"We'll take her." Austin reached for his hand mic and asked dispatch to tone out someone from the state Department of Parks and Wildlife. Before he could finish his call, Bear placed the bundled fawn in Lexi's arms and disappeared into the trees.

Lexi looked up at him, an expression of wonder on her face as the little fawn, who didn't seem to fear people, rested its head against her chest. "It's so cute."

"Be careful." Austin reached out, stroked the fawn's silky brown head. "If its legs get free, and it starts kicking, its hooves will cut you up."

"Can I help care for her?"

"That's for the wildlife folks to decide. Let's get her back to the truck."

Lexi crooned to the fawn, doing her best to reassure it as they made their way back down the trail. When they reached his truck, Austin took the baby animal from her and settled it in a large dog carrier, overriding Lexi's objections.

"I can't risk her getting loose in the vehicle and getting hurt or hurting one of us and causing an accident," he explained.

Then they headed toward town, Austin waiting for a call from dispatch that would tell him where to go with the orphaned animal.

But the fawn wasn't happy about being in the carrier or the moving vehicle, its little cries upsetting Lexi until Austin wasn't certain which one of them was most distressed. He couldn't help but laugh. "It's going to be okay."

"It's breaking my heart." Lexi turned in her seat and stuck a finger through the bars of the pet carrier, trying to comfort the little animal.

It latched onto her finger and began to suckle.

"I think it's hungry."

"We'll get it something to eat soon."

They were almost in Scarlet when dispatch let him know that state wildlife folks had no room and no one to send for the fawn.

"What does that mean? Are they just going to have you dump her?"

"God, no." Austin explained that standard procedure now was to call private animal shelters along the Front Range to see if any had room. "The only one in Scarlet is Aspen Wildlife Sanctuary. It's run by Chaska Belcourt's little sister, Winona. You met her at Knockers the other night, remember? She's a wildlife vet."

Lexi nodded. "She was the one climbing with Sasha and Nicole."

"The sanctuary is overflowing with baby animals right now. They got a trio of bobcat kittens last week." Austin was going to have fun with this. "If she takes in this fawn, she's probably going to need help with feedings, maybe with the kittens, too."

"Bobcat kittens?" Lexi sounded as if he'd just mentioned her favorite thing *ever*.

"Yeah, two females and a male. Fuzzy. Blue eyes. I just don't know anyone who has the time—"

"Hey, I have the time! I'll do it. I'll make the time. I'll help her."

Austin looked over at Lexi, fighting to keep the smile off his face. "You?"

Her eyes narrowed. "You knew I'd say that. You teaser!"

He couldn't help but laugh.

They arrived at the Aspen Wildlife Sanctuary ten minutes later. Winona met them in the parking lot and led them inside to an exam room, where Austin placed the dog carrier on the floor.

Winona knelt down, looked inside, cooing to the fawn in what must have been Lakota. "We've got five other fawns now. Most of them are bigger than this little girl, but it will work out."

"What do you mean?" Lexi asked.

"We like to raise fawns in groups so that they imprint on one another and not on people. I think they'll welcome her."

Austin's hand came to rest in the small of Lexi's back. "I need to get rolling, but Lexi would like to stay and help if she can."

Winona stood, her eyes narrowing as she met Austin's gaze. "Volunteers have to go through a screening process and then complete a six-session training course. But for special friends of Austin's, I guess we can work something out."

There was a resigned tone to her voice, and Lexi knew she was only doing this for Austin's sake. Then Lexi noticed the sign on the wall asking for donations and outlining the shelter's expenses.

She tore open her handbag, pulled out her checkbook, and quickly wrote a check for two thousand dollars. "I'd like to make a donation, too—you know, to help with what you do. I love animals."

"I can verify that." Austin's lips curved into a grin.

Winona took the check, looked down at it, her dark eyebrows shooting upward in surprise. She met Lexi's gaze. "For special friends of Austin's who make a significant donation, we can start today."

"Really?" Lexi fought to control her excitement, not wanting to seem too eager. "That's great. Thank you."

"Perfect." Austin ducked down, kissed Lexi. "I'll call you when I get off work. Leave tonight open for me."

The look in his eyes told her he'd make her glad if she did.

Lexi took his hand, squeezed it. "Thanks for a terrific morning."

"Okay, okay, you two. Not in front of the animals," Winona joked.

"Thanks, Win." Austin turned toward the door and was gone.

Winona handed Lexi a pair of nitrile gloves. "We need to examine her. Our first priority is hydration. If she gets badly dehydrated, she'll die."

"How do you do that?"

"I'll show you." Winona removed the fawn from the carrier, unwrapping the blanket and letting it stand on its four spindly legs. "I pinch together a section of its skin between its shoulder blades and pull it up like this. Then, I let it go. See how the skin went down right away? That means she's hydrated. If it had stayed up or returned to normal slowly, it would mean she needs fluids. Let's have a look at the rest of her."

The fawn endured the examination with patience, its tiny tail flicking back and forth, innocent dark eyes looking at Lexi, its little cries almost breaking her heart.

Winona looked beneath its tail, checked its ears, ran her gloved hands over its belly and legs. "I'm looking for injuries or parasites—maggots, lice, ticks."

"I think she's hungry," Lexi said.

"Fawns are always hungry. They'll eat until they make themselves sick." Winona got to her feet, retrieved something from a drawer, then shut off the lights and knelt down again. "This is a Wood's lamp. I'm checking her for ringworm now. If she has it, anyone who has held her probably has it, too."

"Really?" Lexi's skin itched.

Or maybe that was her imagination.

"It's relatively easy to get rid of, so don't worry." Winona turned on the device, which emitted a purple glow. She moved systematically over the fawn, looking through a built-in magnifying glass at the animal's coat. "She seems healthy to me. Bear took good care of you, didn't he, *tacicala*?"

"What does that mean?"

"It's Lakota for 'fawn.'" Winona got to her feet, put the light away.

Lexi tried to repeat what she'd heard. "Dachee…"

Winona repeated the word. "Dah-CHEE-chah-lah."

"Dah-CHEE-chah-lah."

"Not bad." Winona tossed her gloves into the trash, then washed her hands. "Would you like to give her a bottle of goat's milk?"

Lexi tried not to act too excited, but—*ohmygod!*—feed a fawn? "I'd love to."

*A*ustin headed back up the highway, his gaze resting for a moment on the empty seat beside him.

Knock it off, idiot.

If he missed her now when he'd just spent a night and morning with her, what was he going to do when she packed up her little car and drove back to Illinois?

God, he was screwed.

He put his mind back on the job, calling dispatch to let everyone know he was en route to the Pinnacles wildlife closure area at Russey Ranch, where he believed poachers had been taking deer.

In a moment, dispatch came back at him. "Fifty-six-twenty, we've toned out sheriff's deputy to meet you at the trailhead. Thirteen-oh-five."

A sheriff's deputy?

His mobile phone rang.

It was Sutherland. "You can't head up there with Ms. Jewell."

"I left her at Aspen Wildlife Sanctuary with the fawn."

"Oh. Good. We got word back from CSI on that backpack the shooter dropped. They found several prints. Turns out the guy who shot at you is John Charles Ready. He's wanted for armed bank robberies in Santa Fe, Moab, and Colorado Springs. The feds have been on his trail for months."

So that's why they'd toned out a deputy.

"Are the feds involved?"

"The FBI and Marshals Service have been there since this morning."

"Why didn't I know about this?"

"We're keeping it off the radio. We don't want to alert the bastard or bring the media down on our heads."

Okay, those were two good reasons.

Sutherland went on. "The feds think he might be hiding in a cave or maybe a mine shaft."

"If that's true, they've got their work cut out for them."

There were hundreds of mine shafts in these hills. Some were pits that were only a few feet deep. Some went deep.

"The feds have a hard-on for this guy. Try not to get in their way or piss them off. And, hey, Taylor, wear your Kevlar. I noticed you weren't wearing it last week. I don't give a damn how hot and heavy it is."

"Will do." Austin ended the call.

He arrived in the Russey Ranch parking area to find Deputy Julia Marcs waiting for him, her service vehicle parked in the only shade. She was talking to someone—a guy from the Marshals Service judging from the star on his baseball cap. Austin parked, retrieved his backpack, and walked over to them.

"Hey, Taylor." Julia shook his hand. "They sent me in to babysit you."

Austin laughed. "Are you sure you can handle this? You might break a nail or something."

The man in the baseball cap seemed to take this ribbing in stride, a slight grin on his face. He was well over six feet, his eyes concealed behind mirrored shades. He held out his hand, gave a firm shake. "Chief Deputy US Marshal Zach McBride."

"Austin Taylor. I'm a ranger with Forest County Parks and Open Space." Austin quickly filled them in on what Bear had seen and his reason for coming up to Russey Ranch. "The area is closed to the public through the end of June to protect wildlife. If we've got poachers up there, we need to act."

"Mind if I tag along?" McBride asked.

"The more, the merrier."

They hiked in silence up the trail, then left the trail and headed west near the place where Austin had almost been shot, contouring across the steep terrain before heading down into the valley. Soon the Pinnacles, a wall of jagged rocks spires, loomed into view. The spires served as prime nesting sites for raptors this time of year, while the valley, with its riparian habitat, offered elk and moose a quiet place to calve.

Austin stopped to get the lay of the land, trying to figure out what Bear might have been doing and thinking of the places mule deer liked to gather. He headed toward an area known as The Meadows. "This way."

"What are we looking for—a mule deer head?" Julia asked.

"At this point, there won't be much left—perhaps just the skull."

Nature wasted nothing. Even the bone would eventually be eaten, gnawed away by rodents, who used it as a source of calcium.

The afternoon waned on, the sun beating down hard from a cloudless sky. Austin was beginning to think he was wasting everyone's time, when Julia stepped on something that broke with a distinct *crack*.

Austin bent down to find the mandible of a mule deer, picked almost clean. Julia's boot had snapped it cleanly in half. Austin took a few photos with his cell phone, slipped on some gloves and examined it. "Let's see if we can find the rest of it."

After a few minutes, they'd found the key piece—the severed spine. The animal's head had been hacked off, probably with a saw.

"Poachers for sure." Julia held up a broken vertebra, her hands in nitrile gloves.

"Maybe not." McBride pointed to something up the mountainside.

Austin spotted it just below timberline, almost hidden by trees.

An abandoned mine shaft.

Lexi placed the third bobcat kitten on the scale, watching as Winona noted its weight. It mewed—a tiny sound that tugged at her heart—and tried to walk away, wobbling unsteadily on stubby legs.

Winona picked it up, checked its teeth, then handed it to Lexi. "Look at that round belly. They're thriving."

Lexi placed it gently back inside the crate near the barn cat who'd been recruited, along with her litter of four kittens, to care for the baby bobcats. "How did you know she would accept the kittens?"

"Cats have a strong maternal instinct in the few days after they give birth. I've seen them adopt puppies, baby squirrels, even ducklings. We were just lucky to have her nearby, and I thought we'd give it a try."

So far, Lexi had fed the fawn, cleaned poop out of a half dozen raccoon cages, given fresh water to an injured fox, watched Winona feed a sick bald eagle, and patted an enormous gray wolf named Shota on its head. Shota was the unofficial sanctuary mascot and Winona's pet—if anything that looked that untamed could possibly be called a pet. He lived in a large outdoor pen behind a tall fence, with a large dog house for shelter.

In the span of a few hours, Lexi had come to admire Winona for her skill with the animals and for what she'd accomplished. Truth be told, she was even a little envious. Lexi didn't know her whole story, but she'd gleaned from conversation that Winona had followed Chaska to Colorado, gone to college to become a vet, and had established this sanctuary last year—with the help of Scarlet Springs residents and some grants.

"I think you're doing a wonderful thing here—saving animals' lives. It must give you so much satisfaction."

Winona peeled off her gloves, and knelt beside Lexi, watching as the seven kittens —three spotted-and-striped bobcat kittens and four black-and-white barn kittens—crawled over one another, mewing, in search of milk. "I was raised to believe that the lives of animals are sacred, too."

Lexi waited for her to say more, but she didn't.

Instead, she got to her feet. "It's almost time to close up for the day. Thanks for your help. And thanks for the donation. Things are tight this time of year."

"I'd love to come back and help out again, but I don't want the fact that I'm Austin's friend or that I gave a donation to the clinic make you feel—"

Winona's smile cut her off. "I'd love the help. You're good with the animals, and I can see how much you care. You can add yourself to the volunteer schedule that's posted in the break room."

Lexi floated home, hardly able to believe that she'd held and fed a fawn, held baby bobcats in her hands, and patted a big wolf on the head. She couldn't wait to tell Austin about it. She was in such a good mood she didn't mind when her father demanded to know where she'd been all day.

"I did a ride-along with Austin in the morning. Bear brought him an orphaned fawn, and I've spent the afternoon helping take care of it. I got to hold bobcat kittens, too, and I met Winona's pet wolf, Shota. Have you ever seen him? He's huge."

Her father nodded. "I saw him when she first moved to town. He was just a pup then, skittish and wild. A lot of folks are nervous about pet wolves and wolf-hybrids, but that girl seems to know what she's doing when it comes to animals."

Austin hadn't called, so Lexi cooked a quick supper—spaghetti with meat sauce, garlic bread, and a salad—telling her father about her afternoon in detail. To her surprise, he listened, even asking questions. It was the first time since she'd been home that they'd had a friendly conversation.

"I wonder what that mama cat's going to do when those bobcat kittens grow to be bigger than she is," her dad mused.

"Winona said she hopes the cat will teach them how to hunt. She said—" Lexi's cell phone buzzed. She drew it out of her jeans pocket, expecting it to be Austin.

It was Vic. "Hey, Lex. I haven't heard from you for a while. I wanted to check and see how you're doing."

Lexi excused herself and stepped outside. "Things are going well. You'll never believe what I got to do today."

She quickly filled Vic in on her afternoon at the wildlife sanctuary, forgetting that she'd meant to keep the time she was spending with Austin secret.

"Wait. You went on a ride-along with *him?*" Her voice took on a note of suspicion. "Tell me you're not sleeping with him."

Lexi's hesitation gave her away.

"You are, aren't you?"

"We're just friends," Lexi said, adding, "with benefits."

"Well here's something that will help you forget him and remember where you belong. I bought us tickets to see Adele at the United Center on July tenth."

"Wow!"

"Tickets are sold out, but some guy at work had a couple of extras. We can do Taste of Chicago that weekend and finish it with the concert."

"That's fabulous."

"You don't sound excited."

"I am!" She was—sort of.

If she'd gotten this news a week ago, she'd have been jumping up and down. She loved Adele's music, and she loved Taste of Chicago. She looked forward to it all year—the food, the music, the art. But now...

She was enjoying herself here. She wasn't ready to think about leaving.

"You're getting caught up in that place, aren't you?" Vic let out an exasperated sigh. "I guess I'm going to have to fly out there."

Chapter Fourteen

It was after eight when Austin finally pulled into his driveway. It had been a long day, but a rewarding one. McBride and his team were going to find John Charles Ready, and Austin was happy to have helped in a small way. But for now, all he wanted was a shower, some food in his stomach, and Lexi.

The moment he stepped out of his vehicle, he called her. "Hey."

"Hey."

"Have you eaten?"

"Yeah. I would have waited but—"

"I'm glad you didn't. It's late. We had one hell of a day."

"I'd love to hear about it. Want company?"

Hell, yeah, he did. "Give me ten minutes to take a shower."

"I'll see you soon."

The soft feminine tone of her voice was like caffeine.

Reenergized, he went inside, let Mack out to do his business, then filled the puppy's bowls with kibble and fresh water. When Mack was settled, Austin took a shower, cool water sluicing over his skin, washing away the day's sweat, dirt, and sunscreen. He had just stepped out of the shower when he smelled something cooking, the delicious scent making his stomach growl.

What the... ?

He dried off, slipped into a pair of jeans, and headed down the stairs, hair uncombed and damp, to find Lexi pulling something from the oven. She'd changed from jeans and a T-shirt to one of those sexy sundresses, her hair tied up in a messy bun.

She set the baking sheet on top of the stove. "Spaghetti is easy to reheat in the microwave, but not garlic bread."

He stood there, stared. "You brought me dinner."

"I'm as surprised as you are." She gave a little shrug, looking embarrassed to be caught doing something domestic. "But we had leftovers, so…"

"I'll never tell anyone," Austin promised.

She put two pieces of garlic bread on plates piled high with salad and spaghetti and set it on the table, then grabbed silverware, a napkin, and two beers from the refrigerator. "Bon appétit."

"Thanks." Austin took his first bite, the sauce thick and tangy. "How did it go at the shelter?"

While he ate, Lexi told him how she'd fed the fawn, helped weigh the bobcat kittens, and done other things around the place. Her face glowed with happiness, her eyes bright with excitement. He found himself wondering what it would be like to come home to Lexi every day, to share meals with her, to talk about each day's ups and downs with her, to go to bed each night with her. A sense of rightness slid through him—followed by a longing so intense he lost track of what she was saying.

Do you like torturing yourself, dumb shit?

What the fuck was wrong with him? She was leaving for Chicago soon. He couldn't get stupid and forget that.

"Oh! I met Shota. He let me pet him. I was nervous at first, but he walked right up to me like we were old friends."

Austin put his emotions on lockdown, willed himself to focus on the moment. "He's not usually like that with strangers."

"Really?" She smiled. "He's beautiful."

"Animals are good judges of character."

Lexi took a drink of her beer, her eyes going wide. "I haven't let you get a word in, and you had such a long day."

Austin wiped his lips on the napkin. "I found the remains of the fawn's mother. Deputy Julia Marcs and I met with a deputy US marshal and searched near the Pinnacles till we found it."

"Poachers?"

He shook his head. "It looks like the guy who fired at me might have been living up there. We found a mine shaft that showed signs of habitation. There were scorched animal bones, wrappers from energy bars, water bottles, all with his prints."

"So they've identified him."

"His name is John Charles Ready. He's wanted for armed bank robbery."

Lexi's face went pale. "He's a fugitive?"

Austin took Lexi's cell phone and called up Ready's mug shot online. "Agents are distributing these posters around town in case he comes in for supplies."

Lexi picked it up. "What a creep."

The man had dark hair, brown eyes, a bad complexion, and a moon-shaped scar on his left cheek that would be easy to recognize.

"He could have killed you. Do you think he's still up there?"

"There's no way of knowing. There are so many caves and mine shafts in that area." Austin set his fork aside, took a drink of his beer. "Damn, that was good. You can bring me dinner every night."

Her eyes narrowed, a smile tugging at her lips. "Don't you just wish."

While Austin loaded the dishwasher, Lexi slipped upstairs and walked into his closet, an idea half-formed in her mind. She searched through his clothes and his ranger gear. But what she was really looking for was a distraction.

Her conversation with Vic this evening had left her feeling down. Until that phone call, she'd felt free to stay in Scarlet as long as she wanted. Now there was a hard and fast date for her return to Chicago. The thought of going back so soon had left her feeling just like she had as a teenager when summer vacation was almost over.

You're being ridiculous.

July was a little more than a month away. It's not like she was leaving tomorrow. She had lots of time left.

She found one of Austin's uniform shirts and pulled it off the hanger. Quickly, she undressed until she was naked, then she slipped on his shirt, leaving it unbuttoned.

Austin called up the stairs to her. "Hey, Lexi, I'm taking Mack out for a walk."

"Okay." That gave her more time.

A few minutes later, she stood just inside the back door, waiting for him, her belly full of butterflies, her pulse tripping. Apart from his uniform shirt and duty belt, she was naked, a pair of handcuffs in her right hand.

God, she must be crazy. She'd never done anything like this before. If it backfired, she would fire her ovaries.

She heard Mack's excited bark, heard Austin's voice calling him. Then the handle turned on the door, and Mack rushed in, Austin behind him.

Lexi fought not to squirm and stood her ground—though she did have to push the puppy's inquisitive nose away more than once.

Austin saw her, stopped dead in his tracks. He said nothing, his pupils going dark, his gaze sliding over her and coming to rest on the handcuffs.

Somehow, Lexi managed to speak without laughing. "You're coming with me."

His eyes narrowed. He leaned against the counter, arms crossed over his chest. "And if I refuse?"

A trill of excitement passed through her. He was playing along.

She hooked the cuffs onto the belt, drew out the baton, and slapped it against her palm. *Ouch.* "Resistance could prove … *painful.*"

A single eyebrow arched, an amused twinkle in his eyes. But when he spoke, he was all seriousness. "All right, then."

She pointed toward the stairs with the baton. "Go."

He walked ahead of her to his bedroom. "What are you going to do to me?"

"Nothing you don't deserve." She had to bite back a giggle. What part of her was coming up with this stuff?

When they reached his bedroom, she gave him his next order. "Undress."

He did as she demanded, taking his sweet time, turning it into a masculine strip tease, the sight of his cock making her squirm.

"Now, lie down on the bed, hands over your head."

He complied, the muscles of his bare torso shifting, his shoulders broad against the mattress. "I'll make you pay for this."

A shiver of anticipation ran down her spine.

"You wish."

She straddled him, let her breasts hang above his face as she closed one cuff around his left wrist and passed the other behind one of the brass bars of his headboard.

He could easily have overpowered her, but he let her have her way, his gaze moving over her. She snapped the other cuff around his right wrist, and fastened it, a series of metallic clicks signaling his total surrender.

She looked into his eyes. "You are my prisoner."

What a rush it was to have all this man and muscle under her control. He was hers to do with as she pleased. She indulged herself, running her fingers through the crisp curls on his chest, thumbing his flat nipples, exploring the firmness of his pecs, shoulders, and biceps. Soft skin, hard muscle.

"You're enjoying this." He was still in character, his voice hard.

"You bet I am." She was already wet, her body aching for him.

She bent down and kissed him long and hard. But there didn't seem to be a passive bone in his body. His mouth answered hers, his head lifting off the pillow as he tried to take control of the kiss from her.

She tore her lips from his, kissing and caressing her way down his throat, over his chest, and across his abdomen, lavishing attention on those sexy obliques before taking his erect cock into her mouth.

He sucked in a quick breath, the muscles of his abdomen tensing. "I'm nothing but a toy to you."

"Play time." She tasted him, teased him, stroked him with her hand and tongue, getting more turned on by the minute. She looked up, found his eyes squeezed shut, every muscle in his body tense, his hands clenched around the brass bar that held him fast. But she couldn't let him come—not yet.

She wanted him inside her now.

Austin moaned in sexual frustration as Lexi quit going down on him, his hips instinctively thrusting upward. "What the hell is it with you and fellatio interruptus?"

She smiled, her lips wet and swollen. "I'm not done playing."

He hadn't realized Lexi had this side to her. He'd gone along with this just to see what she'd do. And, *damn*, it had been worth it. Although being cuffed to the bed didn't really do anything for him—he was used to being the one in control—it made him horny as hell to watch her getting so turned on.

She straddled his hips, took hold of his cock, and lowered herself onto him, taking all of him inside her.

Ooooh-kay, so he could go for this.

She was slippery-wet and hot.

"You really *are* enjoying this."

But she was beyond answering.

She rested her palms against his chest for balance, then began to move her hips, grinding her clit against him, his cock held deep inside her. They'd done it like this a lot as teenagers when she'd been learning how to climax with him, so he knew from experience that it wouldn't make him come. But it was perfect for her.

Her breasts swayed as she moved, those sweet puckered tips taunting him. He wanted to touch them, wanted to caress them, wanted to suck them into his mouth, but he couldn't move. The triangle of dark red hair peeking out at him from beneath his duty belt made him want to taste her there, too, but he couldn't do that either. All he could do was lie there and let his body be her sexual playground.

Boy, do you have it rough.

She was getting close now. Her eyes were squeezed shut, her lips parted, every exhale a little moan. She came with a cry, her head falling back, her inner muscles clenching around him.

He felt a hitch in his chest. He'd never seen anything more beautiful than the bliss on her pretty face, nothing more beautiful than Lexi.

She collapsed against him, her heart pounding so hard he could feel it against his chest, her body still apart from her breathing.

He waited for her to recover, wanting to hold her, wanting to kiss her. When she hadn't budged a few minutes later, he gave a little thrust of his hips. "Hello? I'm the guy whose stiff cock is still inside you. Remember me?"

She laughed, a soft sleepy sound. "Oh, don't worry. This isn't over."

She sat up, adjusted her hips, and spread her legs wider. "Ride me from below."

She didn't have to ask him twice.

He started slow, thrusting upward, her pussy clenching him like a fist. But he was too turned on to hold back for long. Faster, harder. Soon, he was almost beyond control bucking into her with everything he had and on the brink of coming, his fists closed around brass.

But Lexi was right there with him, her breathing ragged, her thighs drawing tight against his hips. She reached down to touch herself, her fingers stroking her clit, and it took every shred of his self-restraint not to lose it right then.

"Austin!" She cried out his name, the two of them reaching that bright, sweet crest one after the other.

They lay there together, drifting, Lexi still on top of him, his wrists still cuffed, her fingers caressing his shoulder.

"Are you going to unlock me?" he asked when he could speak again.

She sat up, looked around. "God, where did I put the key?"

"Lexi."

She laughed and pulled it out of his shirt pocket. "It's right here."

She had removed it from his county key ring.

"What a sneaky thing you are."

She reached up to unlock the cuffs, but the key slipped from her fingers and fell behind the headboard. "Oops. Sorry."

Austin did his best to be patient as she climbed off him and disappeared from view beneath his bed.

"Why, hello, dust bunnies. You have a village down here, Austin."

He heard the *clink* of metal on metal.

"Oh, shit." After a moment, her head popped up to his right, her eyes wide. "It fell into your heating vent."

She *had* to be teasing him.

"You've had your fun. Now unlock me."

"I'm not joking. I tried to get it, but my fingers bumped it right in."

Austin didn't know whether to laugh—or get irritated. But with Lexi sitting there, almost naked, her tousled hair spilling over her shoulders, her skin still flushed from fucking his brains out, he couldn't feel angry.

There were men who'd pay to be in his position.

"There's a bolt cutter…" No, that was in his service vehicle.

"I could try to break the chain with a hammer."

Austin shook his head. "That won't work. These are made to restrain professional bad guys, remember? You're going to have to remove the vent.

You can pry it up with a screwdriver from the toolbox in the hall closet downstairs."

"I already thought of that. The center support for the headboard is sitting right on the vent. I'd have to move the entire bed first."

There was no way she could do that alone—especially with him in it. "Damn it."

"I have an idea." She turned and ran out of his room, still wearing only his uniform shirt and duty belt.

Austin relaxed into the pillow.

This ought to be good.

Lexi dialed the non-emergency number for the Scarlet Springs Fire Department. "May I please speak with Eric Hawke?"

A man moved the phone away, shouted, "Hey, chief, it's for you!"

"This is Hawke."

"Hi, Eric. It's Lexi. I have a little problem, and I need your help. But please don't send a truck with sirens or anything. Um… It's kind of a delicate situation, so I would appreciate your discretion."

"Are you all right?" He sounded worried.

"I'm fine. It's Austin." How could she explain this? "Just come to his place by yourself and bring whatever you would use to, oh, say, break chains or something."

"Chains?"

Oh, God, she might as well come right out and tell him.

"Austin is handcuffed to his bed, and I dropped the key down the heating vent."

"You … what? No, don't repeat that. Are they his duty cuffs?"

"Yes."

He coughed, a sound suspiciously like a strangled laugh. "Got it."

"Please don't tell anyone. I don't want to embarrass him. You're his best friend. He'd trust you."

"I won't tell a soul. See you in a few minutes."

That weight off her shoulders, Lexi hurried up the stairs. She needed to get dressed before Eric got here and—God!—she needed to get Austin back into his jeans.

"Who were you talking to?" he asked when she walked into the bedroom.

"I called Eric, and—"

Austin's head came up, a horrified look on his face. "What? You called *Hawke*?"

"What else was I supposed to do?" She searched the room for her dress and panties and put them on. "I told him to come by himself and not to use sirens or anything. He promised not to tell anyone."

"Jesus, Lexi!" Austin started to laugh and kept laughing as if she'd just said the funniest thing he'd ever heard.

She grabbed his jeans off the floor. "What's so hilarious?

"You called the fire department and told the fire chief that I am handcuffed to the bed?" He laughed even harder.

She nodded. "I had to do something."

He dissolved into laughter again. "The FD ... will have to generate ... a report ... for that call."

"Wh-what?" Some of the blood rushed out of her head. "I didn't mean—"

"I know you didn't. Put my jeans on me before he gets here."

It wasn't as easy as she'd thought it would be, but between his pushing and wriggling and her tugging, they managed to get them up his legs and over his bare ass.

She started to pull up the zipper.

"Whoa! Stop! You need to adjust the goods, honey, or you're going to catch my dick in the zipper."

"Oh." She took his now soft penis in her hand, but she wasn't really sure what to do with it. "Up, down, left, right. What do I do?"

Austin dissolved into laughter again.

Before she could finish zipping him, there came a hard knock at the door.

"Lexi?" Eric called for her.

She tossed the sheet over Austin's still exposed junk. "Be back in a minute."

She hurried barefoot down the stairs and opened the back door.

Eric stood there in his turnout pants and a dark blue Scarlet FD T-shirt, a box of tools in his right hand. He grinned. "Your dress is inside out."

"Shit." Why hadn't she noticed? "He's upstairs."

Mack whined from his crate, recognizing Eric.

Eric bent down, said hello to the puppy, then grinned at Lexi. "Let's not keep your prisoner waiting."

Lexi followed Eric up the stairs, wondering if she'd ever be able to look him in the eyes again after tonight.

When they reached the bedroom, Austin was no longer laughing. He met Eric's gaze. "Hawke."

"Taylor." Eric's gaze traveled over the room from the baton on the bed to the duty belt that sat beside it and Austin's uniform shirt on the floor.

Lexi cringed, certain that Eric was able to tell exactly what they'd done.

"Not a word," Austin warned him.

Eric nodded. "Hey, I'm a professional."

He set the box down, opened it, and took out a small tool, an awkward tension stretching between the two men as he bent over Austin and went to work. A moment later, Austin was free.

He sat up. "Thanks."

Eric bit his lower lip, clearly trying not to laugh. "Don't mention it."

"I won't." Austin reached beneath the covers and zipped his fly, then got out of bed. "And you'd better damned well never mention it either."

"I'll report it as a prank call—or something." Eric put the tool away and closed his toolbox. "I just want to know one thing. Whose idea was it?"

Heat rushed into Lexi's face. "Mine."

Eric winced as if in pain. "*Damn.* You are one lucky sonofabitch, Taylor."

"You've done your duty, so please *get the hell out of my bedroom!*"

Lexi could hear Eric laughing all the way down the stairs and out the door.

She turned to face Austin. "I'm so sorry. You're angry with me, aren't you?"

"No." He drew her into his arms. "Hawke is right. I'm a lucky guy."

She let out a relieved breath.

"That doesn't mean you're off the hook." He tucked a finger under her chin, forced her to look into his eyes, his lips curving in an evil-sexy smile. "You are going to pay for that. Oh, baby, you are going to pay."

Chapter Fifteen

Austin awoke with Lexi in his arms, sunshine streaming into his bedroom. There was no alarm today. It was the start of his weekend. But there was a hungry puppy who needed to go outside.

Reluctantly, he slipped out of bed, threw on a pair of shorts and a T-shirt, then went downstairs to let Mack out. When he and Mack came back inside, he found Lexi making coffee. She'd put on one of his T-shirts and a pair of boxer briefs, the sight of her delicious round ass in his underwear giving him a jolt of testosterone.

She slipped into his arms. "Morning."

He kissed the top of her head. "Morning, beautiful."

They made breakfast together and carried it out to the table on his deck, talking and sipping coffee, Mack sniffing around the back yard. The summits of the Indian Peaks rose white against a blue sky to their west, the forest alive with the calls of Steller's jays, woodpeckers, and mountain bluebirds. It was as close to a perfect morning as anyone could hope for—unhurried, peaceful, warm. But it wasn't their surroundings that made it perfect for Austin. It was the company.

Morning sunshine filtered through the trees, making Lexi's tousled hair glow like copper. In this light, her skin seemed almost translucent, her eyes impossibly green. Her face lit up as she spoke, her hands wrapped around her coffee mug.

Austin was struck again by that sense of rightness—and a knife-sharp longing.

You're in love with her.

The realization hit him in the solar plexus, adrenaline shooting through him.

No. No fucking way.

He refused to be in love with her.

"What do you usually do on your day off?"

It took a moment for her question to sink in, his pulse still tripping. The answer came out on its own, his mouth on auto-pilot. "Laundry."

She laughed. "That sounds exciting."

He tried to snap out of it. "Hawke and I both have the day off, which doesn't happen very often. We're talking about meeting Moretti in Rocky Mountain National Park to do some crack climbing."

That's what he needed—sun, sweat, and severe pain. That would straighten his head out fast. Because he could *not* be in love with her.

"I have no idea what that means. Climbing in cracks? Climbing on crack? Because, honestly, I think you must have to be high on something to think that hanging five hundred feet in the air is fun."

"You're welcome to come along if you want." What the hell had he just said? Jesus! His mouth was always making things worse.

She got to her feet, stretched. "I can't. I've got a busy day. I put myself on the schedule to help at the shelter for a couple of hours this morning. Then I'm having lunch with Kendra. After that, I'll be heading to The Cave."

While they loaded the dishwasher, she told him about her most recent conversation with Kendra and explained why her stepmother was angry with her. He did his best to listen but was too caught up in his own thoughts.

How had he let this happen? What the hell was wrong with him? Had he forgotten somewhere along the way that this was just a temporary thing?

No, he hadn't forgotten. He'd walked into this with his eyes open. What a fucking idiot he was! In a few weeks, she'd drive away, and he would have to forget her. Again.

No big deal, right? It was so easy the first time around.

A hand touched his forearm.

"Are you okay?"

He nodded. "Yeah. Why wouldn't I be?"

"You look angry. Are you sure you're not upset with me about last night?"

"I'm sure." He reined in his emotions, drew her into his arms, willing himself to savor the moment. "Besides, I'll get my revenge."

She looked up at him from beneath her lashes. "What are you going to do to me?"

He couldn't help but laugh at the expression on her face—part seduction, part nervousness. "Don't play innocent with me. After last night? I don't know what I'll do, but you can bet I'll come up with something—and not even Scarlet's fire chief will be able to save you."

Lexi squeezed her eyes shut. "How am I going to face Eric again?"

Austin wasn't much looking forward to that either. "He's seen stranger things. He told me a story once about a call involving two guys, peanut butter, and a foot-long fluorescent light bulb—"

Lexi pressed her fingers to his lips. "I don't think I want to know."

She turned and hurried upstairs, reappearing a few minutes later wearing her own clothes, her hair tied up. "Will I see you again tonight?"

Austin knew he ought to make up an excuse—buddy night, county staff meeting, important appointment in Timbuktu—anything to put some distance between them so he could have time to breathe and straighten out his head. But he couldn't do it.

"Unless I get called out with the Team, I'm free."

"Be careful climbing today, okay?"

"Me? Always." He kissed her, soft and slow.

Then he watched her go.

Lexi was five minutes late getting to the restaurant. Kendra was already seated and sipping a margarita. "Sorry I'm late. I'm volunteering at the wildlife shelter and lost track of time."

"Aren't you the do-gooder? First, you help out the Team. Now the wildlife shelter. Whatever will they all do when you go home?"

Lexi was used to Kendra being snarky, but this was harsh even for her, those last words heavy with sarcasm. Determined not to let Kendra provoke her, she picked up the menu. "I'm starving. What's good here?"

"No idea. The place opened a month ago, and your dad didn't feel like bringing me. He thought we ought to save money and stay home. He's such a skinflint."

A server in a white peasant shirt and black skirt approached the table, bringing Lexi a glass of ice water. "Are you ready to order?"

"Well, I've been sitting here for ten minutes, so I'm ready," Kendra answered.

"Go ahead. I'll make up my mind." Lexi scanned the menu, settling on the fajita salad and a glass of iced tea.

The server left with their orders, an awkward silence filling the space.

Lexi decided to plunge ahead. "I'm sorry you felt misled by what I told Rose."

"You're sorry I *felt* misled? I *was* misled."

Okay, that had been a lame apology.

"I didn't mean any harm. Rain *is* working at the inn, doing housekeeping Friday through Tuesday. Do you think my father would have let me hire her if he didn't want her there? Do you think he'd sign her paycheck?"

Kendra looked away, frowned. "He said he had nothing to do with it."

"It's true that I did the foot work, but he could have stopped me." Okay, so Lexi had told him he had no choice, but he was the sole owner of the business. He could have thrown her out and fired Rain. "You know him, Kendra. If he admits that he's okay with Rain working there, it's like admitting he was wrong."

"Yeah. He doesn't much like that."

The server brought Lexi's tea, interrupting the conversation. Lexi squeezed lemons into the beverage, stirred it, sipped.

Kendra's eyes narrowed. "You were standing right beside him when he called last night. I know you were."

"He called you?" This was news to Lexi.

"Oh, come on! Don't lie to me. You told him what to say."

"I wasn't home. Dad and I had a nice supper—we actually talked, no arguing—and then I went out for the night."

"Off to sleep with Austin the beefcake boy, huh? Hey, I don't blame you. Get it while you can, girl. You won't stay young and pretty forever."

Lexi had to bite her tongue and count to five. "What did my dad say?"

"He said he missed me and wanted this to end. I figured you'd written something down for him to say."

"You figured wrong. Don't believe me? Call my dad and ask him."

"Let him squirm for a while." Kendra licked salt off the rim of her glass, then took a sip of her margarita. "I'm surprised you're still defending him after what he did at Knockers. Oh, yeah, I heard all about it."

Lexi had figured as much. "I'll be the first person to admit my dad can be a jerk, but he loves you as much as he is capable of loving anyone."

Kendra shook her head. "Not true. He loved your mother more. She was his entire world. I don't hold a candle to her—and neither do you or your sister."

Okay, *that* hurt.

"Don't bring my mother into this." Lexi hated when Kendra spoke of her.

"Your dear, sainted mother." Kendra gave a laugh, then took another drink. "I've lived my entire life in her shadow."

"You can't seriously be jealous of a woman who's been dead for twenty-six years."

Kendra's face screwed up with rage, her voice taking on an edge. "Don't tell me what I can and can't feel. I spent my best years raising *her* children and trying to help *her* husband move on with his life."

Now they were treading on dangerous ground.

Lexi had listened to Kendra complain about not wanting to be a mother for as long as she could remember, and she was sick of it. "If you didn't want to deal with children, you never should have married a widower with two tiny kids."

Kendra shrugged. "Hindsight is twenty-twenty."

This wasn't going the way Lexi had intended. She drew a breath, tried to let go of her anger. "I'm sorry you feel you've had to compete with my mother's memory. We can't help the fact that we miss her."

Kendra gave a little laugh. "Miss her? You barely even knew her."

Those words hit Lexi right in the heart.

She found herself on her feet. "Maybe I should stop trying to help my father win you back. Maybe he's better off without you. He's a jerk. He drinks too much and says hurtful things. But you? You're deliberately mean. You're bitter and mean."

The server stood a few feet away, their plates in her hands, her eyes wide.

"I'd like that to go, please. I'll pay up front." Lexi looked down at Kendra, who sat there gaping up at her. "You can pay for your own lunch."

Austin tossed his rack of climbing gear and his pack into the back of Hawke's truck then got into the passenger seat. "I meant it. Not a word."

Hawke gave a snort. "Shouldn't you be in a great mood after last night? If I were in your shoes—"

"You're not."

"Ooo-kay." Hawke studied him for a second. "Did you and Lexi have a fight?"

"No. Nothing like that." Austin felt like an ass. "Sorry. I have a lot on my mind."

"Yeah? Like what?" Hawke knew him too well.

Shit.

"I'm in love with her again." Austin waited for Hawke to say "I told you so" or call him an idiot, because, God knew, he deserved it.

He'd done this to himself.

Instead, Hawke nodded. "You never stopped loving her."

That couldn't be true, because… "Well, fuck."

They drove up the highway toward Rocky Mountain National Park, windows down, classic rock playing on the radio, silence helping Austin's tension to ebb.

"Moretti wants to hit Crack of Fear and practice his offwidth," Hawke said.

So that's why Hawke was wearing a long-sleeved shirt.

A 5.10d climb, Crack of Fear was the toughest offwidth crack in the state. The crack was too wide for fingers or hands and too narrow to fit one's entire body. Climbers had to get creative, stacking hands and fists, using bent arms, feet, knees, and any other body part they could shove into the rock like cams. It was exhausting, painful, brutal, dangerous. No one climbed offwidths without donating a little skin and blood, not to mention the occasional limb.

It was exactly what Austin needed. "Sounds good."

Moretti was waiting for them at the trailhead, a big smile on his face. "You two ready to get beat up?"

They grabbed their gear and headed up the trail, shooting the shit along the way. The hike helped Austin get his mind off Lexi and on the climb. About a half hour later, they reached a rock spire called the Rat's Tooth. It would take them up to the base of Crack of Fear. They broke out the gear—harness, climbing shoes, chalk, Moretti's rack full of Big Bros and #4 and #5 Camalots—and then it was time to tape up.

Hawke took out his tape roll, looking up at the three hundred feet of offwidth stretching above them. "Why the fuck are we doing this?"

Moretti grinned. "Sack up, buddy."

Austin taped his wrists, hands, and each finger, hoping to keep some skin. "Bring on the pain."

They let Moretti lead. He was newer to climbing and needed the experience. Besides, he loved the bragging rights that came with this shit.

They set a good pace through the Rat's Tooth. Then they hit a thirty-foot stretch of offwidth, and the punishment began. Hand stacks, fist stacks, heel-toe cams. Austin forgot about Lexi, his mind focused only on the climb as they grunted and growled their way up the crack toward the ledge that marked the end of the first pitch.

One by one they caught their breath on that ledge, taking turns being on belay. Then they hit the second pitch, a mean ten-inch crack that stretched upward for seventy feet. They paid for every inch of that distance, then transitioned to a tricky undercling, moving to the left. The third pitch was easier, but Austin's muscles were so pumped by now that it didn't feel easier.

Moretti let out a whoop when he reached the summit, then he switched to a belay stance, enabling Austin and Hawke to finish. They took a few minutes to savor the view and the endorphin high, then rappelled down and hiked back to the parking lot.

"Man, you're a mess." Hawke tossed his pack into the back of his truck. "You should've worn long sleeves."

"I'm no worse off than the two of you." Sure, Austin was bleeding from his right elbow and knuckles on both hands, but they'd been nicked up, too. "Shit, look at Moretti's knee."

"That's nothing. Check out your face, bro," Moretti pointed to the driver's side mirror on his Jeep.

Austin looked at his reflection. "Shit."

Somehow, he had managed to scrape his cheek and forehead. "That's what happens when you pick a fight with a rock."

"Meet you two at Knockers for a beer?" Moretti asked.

"Hell, yeah," Hawke said. "I'm up for that."

Austin pointed to his battered face. "This climb was your idea, Moretti, so you're buying the first round."

"You're on."

Lexi took her lunch home. It was Rain's day off, so her father was busy cleaning rooms upstairs. She ate in the kitchen alone, her conscience at war with her own rage. She'd lost her temper with Kendra—and it had felt wonderful.

But had she made things harder for her father?

She'd been surprised to hear he'd called Kendra, though she doubted it had done him any good. Kendra saw everything through a lens of bitterness. She'd said she wanted him to call her and say something nice, and then when he'd done just that, she'd rejected him. Was she punishing him?

Maybe her father truly was better off without her.

Except that he wasn't. He was miserable.

Britta was right. Lexi should never have gotten involved in this. If her father and Kendra couldn't fix their lives, what could she possibly do to help them?

She grabbed her files, shoved them in her handbag, and walked to The Cave, doing her best to shake off her bad mood, willing herself to think of the good things that had happened today. She'd had breakfast with Austin—after an amazing night. She'd gotten to feed the fawn again this morning. And she'd be seeing Austin again tonight.

Don't pretend you don't have feelings for him.

Well, of course, she did. They were old friends, special friends. But his life was here in Scarlet, while hers was in Chicago. That's just how it was.

And if some part of her wished it were different?

She shoved that thought aside.

She arrived at The Cave to find Megs and Ahearn doing an inventory of first-aid kits, which were spread out across the conference table, the radio quiet for now.

Megs looked up from her clipboard. "Are we in your way?"

"I can work at the ops desk." Lexi took her files out of the handbag that was serving as a briefcase and spread them out, moving the mic to make room.

Now that she knew what to look for, she moved faster, working through the remaining four months of the previous fiscal year in a couple of hours. She organized what she'd found to make it easy for Megs and the other Team members to understand and explain to law enforcement. So far, she'd found proof that Breece had embezzled almost sixty grand from the Team.

What a jerk!

She must have said this aloud, because Megs came to stand beside her.

"How bad is it?"

Lexi swiveled in her chair. "Do you want the good news or bad news first?"

"There's good news?"

"The good news is that you're not going to have any trouble prosecuting Breece once the police catch up with him."

Megs didn't seem cheered by this. "And the bad news?"

"Between this year and last year, he stole almost sixty grand."

"That scum-sucking bastard." Megs leaned against the desk, a look of disbelief on her face. "I have no idea how we're going to make up for that. How can we possibly explain this to our donors? Jesus!"

"I have some ideas about that. We can talk about it when I've finished the audit."

Megs rested a hand on Lexi's shoulder. "I'm so grateful to you for your help. I wish we could do something to repay you, but all you're getting is a lousy Team T-shirt."

Lexi laughed. "It will be my favorite T-shirt, truly. It will be the one I'm proudest to wear. But, you know, there is one thing you could…"

Men's voices came from the other side of the door.

Austin.

He and Eric were back from climbing.

Oh, God. Eric.

She would just pretend nothing unusual had—

The door opened, and the two of them walked in, followed by Jesse Moretti.

"Oh, my God! What happened?" Lexi got to her feet and hurried over to Austin.

He had abrasions on his forehead and cheek. His right elbow was badly skinned, and his knuckles were split and bloody. Eric and Jesse weren't much better off.

She looked from Austin to the other two. "Did you fall?"

Jesse laughed. "We got the shit beat out of us."

Austin and Eric were laughing, too.

"You got into a *fight?*" Lexi gaped at them.

Megs rolled her eyes. "God save me from climbers' egos."

Mitch got to his feet, a big smile on his face. "How was Crack of Fear?"

"Brutal and amazing," said Eric. "But, hey, don't sign me up for that shit again anytime soon."

It took a moment for all of this to sink in.

Lexi glared at Austin. "This is all from *climbing?*"

"Offwidth climbing," the three men said together.

Whatever that meant.

"We're heading to Knockers for a brew and some grind and wanted to see if anyone wanted to join us," Jesse said.

Eric chuckled. "What Moretti really wants is an audience so he can brag about what a badass lead offwidth climber he is."

"Fuck you, Hawke."

"Not today, buddy."

Megs sat at the table, picked up a pen. "Ahearn and I need to finish this inventory of the first-aid kits, but we'll be over shortly."

Austin caught Lexi, drew her close. "You coming?"

"I need to wrap up what I was doing first."

He kissed her. "We'll see you in a bit then."

"Come on, man. I'm starving." Eric caught Lexi's gaze, smiled. "Hey, Lexi."

Lexi felt herself blush to the roots of her hair. She went back to the desk, hoping that no one had seen. But Megs was watching her.

"Before those three smelly brutes walked in, you were saying…"

Lexi had to think. "Oh. Yeah. There is something you can do for me, if you want. I mean, you don't have to. Don't feel obligated to—"

"Just come out with it."

"Teach me to climb? I mean, I know I can't become an expert like you are. Just teach me what you can. I just want to surprise Austin."

Megs smiled. "You got it."

Chapter Sixteen

Austin took the last swig of his jalapeño stout, listening while Lexi and Winona talked about Lexi's new favorite subject: wildlife rehabilitation. As much fun as she seemed to be having, he could tell something was bothering her, worry lurking behind those green eyes and hiding behind her smile. He hadn't had a chance to ask her yet, not with all of his friends crowded around them.

Not that he wasn't preoccupied himself. He'd spent the past hour or so doing his best to come to grips with his feelings. He loved her, and there wasn't a damned thing he could do about it. Oh, sure, he could quit seeing her or quit sleeping with her, but he wasn't that smart. He would have the rest of his life to miss her. He might as well enjoy what they had—whatever it was—for as long as it lasted.

Or maybe that was the beer talking.

They'd long since demolished their dinner, Team members scattered across the pub from the dance floor to the pool tables to the climbing wall. Up on stage, Davey Jane, an all-female Denver newgrass band, was laying down a beat that was equal parts bluegrass, Cajun, and rock.

"Does leave their fawns for hours at a time, so most of the time when people come to me with a fawn, it isn't truly orphaned," Winona was saying. "But Bear knows what he's doing. He's lived up there with the animals all his life."

"Hey, speaking of Bear, has anyone seen him?" Rain came up behind Austin and set another iced tea on the table in front of Lexi.

Winona shook her head. "He usually preaches at the roundabout not far from the sanctuary, but I haven't seen him there for a few days."

"We saw him near Moose Lake a couple of days ago," Lexi said.

Austin wasn't worried. "If I had a dollar for every time Bear disappeared and the entire town decided he must be dead, I'd be able to pay the Team's bar tab. You never know with Bear."

Rain laughed. "I guess he'll come around when he gets lonely—or hungry."

Sasha leaned across the table, shouting so Winona could hear her. "Hey, Win, can you be my belay slave for a little while? Nicole isn't here, and I want to show those two smelly rock jocks how to climb like a girl."

Over on the wall, Herrera failed to stick a dyno and fell. Moretti, on belay, caught him and let him hang.

"Sure." Winona got to her feet. "Thanks for your help today, Lexi."

"Move over, boys!" Sasha called out in challenge.

For the first time since this morning, Austin and Lexi were more or less alone. "How did it go with Kendra?"

Her face crumpled into an expression of misery. "I blew up at her."

So that's what was bothering her.

Austin took her hand in his. "Knowing Kendra, she probably deserved it."

"Oh, she definitely deserved it." Lexi gave him the short version of the story. "I got up and walked out with my meal. I made her pay for herself, even though I'd agreed it would be my treat."

"You shouldn't feel guilty for standing up for yourself."

"I don't. It's just…" She took a sip of tea, looked down at the table. "What if I just ruined any chance my father had with her?"

"The two of them made a big mess of things before you got involved."

"Yeah. I guess so." She lifted her gaze to his. "Dance with me?"

"You want to dance with a sweaty, scraped-up climber?"

"You bet." She smiled, got to her feet, held out her hand.

If she had asked him to go with her straight into hellfire, he'd have done it.

He stood, took her hand, led her onto the dance floor. "Do you remember your two-step and country swing, or has city life ruined you?"

She laughed, rested her hand on his hip. "Just try me."

Austin led her around the dance floor, mixing two-step with country swing. Lexi didn't miss a thing. She was easy to lead, responding to his every cue, the body connection between them every bit as powerful on the dance floor as it was in bed. Austin wasn't even conscious of leading her. He lost himself in the moment—the rhythm of the music, the smile on her face, the excited flush in her cheeks. He ended the song with a dip, her head arched back, his lips almost touching her pulse.

The next song was slow and romantic, giving Austin an excuse to hold her close. She rested her head against his chest, the scent of her shampoo teasing him, the feel of her sweet in his arms. He ran his hand slowly down her spine, her touch burning him through his T-shirt. He found himself wishing the two of them were alone.

She stopped moving, whispered. "Let's go home."

"Honey, you read my mind."

It was a ten-minute drive from Knockers to Austin's place, but it felt like an eternity to Lexi. "I can't wait. Can't we just park?"

"Aren't you the impatient one?" He reached over to take her hand, heat arcing between them at that simple touch. "You think having to call Hawke was embarrassing, try being interrupted by cops."

Lexi knew most of Scarlet's police force. "Yeah, no. Let's not do that."

"Besides, I really need a shower. Ball sweat just isn't sexy."

Okay, so he had a point. Still, there was an upside to this. "Good. I'll help."

He laughed again. "You shouldn't distract me while I'm driving."

"I used to distract you. Do you remember?" She'd spent a lot of time sitting right next to him on the bench seat of his old pick up, doing naughty things to him that just weren't possible in modern vehicles with center consoles.

"Mmm, hell, yes." He gave her hand a squeeze. "It's a wonder we're still alive."

When they got to his house, Austin let Mack out and fed him, while Lexi brushed her teeth, got the freshly laundered sheets out of the dryer, and made the bed. By the time she was naked, Austin was on his way up the stairs, Mack following behind him.

"Sit, Mack. Stay. Good boy." Austin stopped at the foot of the bed, took off his T-shirt, his gaze on her.

Lexi was halfway to him, ready to kiss his brains out. "Oh, God!"

She stopped, stared.

He laughed. "That bad?"

He had a deep abrasion on his right shoulder and dark bruise on his inner arm next to his bicep. With his scratched hands, bloody knuckles, his right elbow, and his face, he really did look like he'd gotten into a fight—or been in a wreck.

She held out her hand. "Come."

She got a clean washcloth, then started the shower, tested the water, and stepped under the spray, moving aside to make room for him.

He finished undressing and followed her into the shower, breath hissing from beneath clenched teeth when warm water hit his skin. "*Shit.* That stings."

"I bet it does." She soaped up the washcloth and washed his abrasions one by one, careful not to hurt him, water rinsing away soap, blood, and dirt. "You know, rather than climbing, you could just jump in front of a car or pick a fight with a bear or something."

He chuckled. "Less effort and same results—is that what you're saying?"

His arm went around her waist, and he drew her against him, silencing whatever she'd been about to say with a kiss, his cock hard against her belly.

"Stop. You're hurt."

He didn't stop, but yanked the washcloth from her hands and backed her against the wall, tiles cold against her skin, his body shielding her from the spray. "Those are just scratches."

"Deep scratches." She slid her hands over the muscles of his arms, savoring the hard feel of him.

"Mmm… You said 'deep.'" He cupped one of her breasts, tugged at the wet nipple with callused fingers, his lips doing wicked things to hers.

Heat flared to life in her belly.

But it only got better.

The hand that had teased her breast slid down the wet skin of her belly to cup her, fingers that had the strength to hold his body weight gentle as they explored her.

"*Austin.*" Lexi wrapped one leg around his waist, making room for him.

He made the most of it, stroking her, caressing her, penetrating her until she was ready to scream. Then he took hold of himself and guided his cock inside her.

Oh, sweet Jesus!

She opened her eyes, found herself looking into his, the tenderness she saw there putting an ache in her chest.

How was she ever going to live without him?

"Lexi, I…" He brushed his thumb over her cheek but didn't finish, instead kissing her deep and slow, his hips beginning to move.

There was nothing in the world like the sweet sensation of his cock thrusting into her, each stroke golden. Wet skin on skin. Steam and pheromone. The sound of her own moans. The heat inside her exploded, bliss raining down on her as he, too, fell over that sweet edge and joined her in paradise.

A moment or so later, she noticed a rhythmic thumping sound that wasn't her heartbeat or their bodies rocking against the tiles.

Mack.

The puppy sat outside the shower, tail wagging against the floor.

Austin looked over his shoulder. "What part of 'stay' do you not understand?"

Austin indulged Lexi afterward, allowing her to go crazy with the adhesive bandages and antibiotic ointment. Truth be told, he was touched. She cared about him. He knew she did. He'd seen it in her eyes in the shower—a longing as deep as his own.

"Are you finished, Ms. Nightingale?"

Still naked, she fussed with the large bandage on his elbow, trying to make it stick. "Do you want an Advil or something?"

He shut the first-aid kit, caught her around the waist, kissed a bare breast. "Quit worrying about me. I'm *fine*. Come to bed."

They hadn't been asleep for long when Austin's pager went off.

THREE STRANDED CLIMBERS, FIRST FLATIRON

They had to be kidding. At midnight?

Shit.

He got out of bed, peeled off a few bandages that weren't sticking well, then slipped into a clean pair of climbing pants and a long-sleeve Team shirt.

Lexi sat up. "What's wrong?"

He bent down, kissed her. "The Team just got toned out to rescue some stranded climbers. Go back to sleep. I'll be home in a few hours."

Team members were still talking about their middle-of-the-night rescue when Lexi arrived at The Cave the next afternoon. She'd already heard the story from Austin over breakfast, but it was just as funny when Creed retold it.

"They were sitting on top, drunk off their asses, with this pony keg dangling down the rock face, attached to the lead climber's harness with a daisy chain of quick draws. I couldn't believe it, man."

Lexi couldn't believe it either. "Who is stupid enough to get drunk while rock climbing? Isn't that suicide?"

Megs shrugged. "In Yosemite in the sixties, there were climbers dropping acid while climbing El Capitan."

Good grief!

"Could you make people pay for a rescue when it's their fault? Maybe it would serve as a disincentive for people to do these kinds of things." It seemed fair to Lexi—and perhaps a way to recoup some of their stolen money.

"Nah, man, that's not our style," Creed said.

Megs shook her head. "Most accidents are someone's fault. A climber who gets in over his head. Someone getting drunk or doing drugs on a climb. A hiker who stays out too late and gets benighted. Skiers who go beyond the ropes and set off an avalanche. If we made people pay for rescues, they'd wait to call in until their situation was desperate, and more people would die."

Lexi supposed that made sense. "Colorado is lucky to have you."

Creed laughed and headed off toward the kitchen. "That's what we think."

Lexi got down to work, finishing her audit of the Team's records from the year before last. When she finished this, she'd be more or less done with the audit, and then...

She'd have kept her promise to the Team, and, since she'd given up trying to help her father and Kendra, she'd be free to go back to Chicago and start her new life. She should feel excited about that.

Instead, the thought seemed to suck the light out of the room.

Austin.

This whole friends-with-benefits plan wasn't working out the way she'd thought it would. How could she have known that spending time with him would reawaken her feelings for him? She'd thought what they'd had was over.

Liar, liar.

"You look like someone just canceled Christmas." Megs interrupted her train of thought. "Are you okay?"

Snap out of it. You still have a month here.

Lexi smiled. "I'm fine."

"I talked with everyone on the Team except for Taylor, of course, and we've got a lot of volunteers willing to give you some climbing lessons. We just need to find out from you when you'd like to start and what times you've got available."

Lexi took out her cell phone and opened the calendar app. "I'd like to do it while Austin is at work, so there's no chance of running into him by accident."

She came up with a list of dates and times over the next two weeks, which Megs wrote down on a notepad. Then she got back to work. But her mind wasn't really on the audit, her thoughts drifting to the one thing she didn't want to think about—leaving Austin and Scarlet.

Two hours later, she'd made it through only three months' worth of records. She was closing up her files when Austin and Eric walked in. Austin had Mack on a leash.

"Hey, boy!" Lexi got to her feet and knelt down to scratch him behind his ears.

"I think she's more excited to see the dog than you, Taylor," Eric said.

Austin's gaze met Lexi's, a grin on his face. "Looks like it. I'm going to get him some water."

The moment he'd disappeared into the kitchen, Eric turned to Lexi. "I've got some time later this week if you want to hit the rock gym."

Lexi took out her cell phone to look up the times she'd given Megs, and they bent over it together, settling on an hour Friday afternoon and another on Sunday.

"Just an hour?" Lexi asked.

Eric laughed. "Honey, if you can handle more than that, we'll keep going."

The kitchen door opened, and Austin stepped out, a bottle of water in his hands and a thirsty puppy on his heels.

Eric stepped away, said something to Megs, while Lexi closed her calendar app and slid her phone beneath the stack of files.

She smiled at Austin. "Did you catch up on your sleep?"

There had to be an explanation for what Austin had just seen—Lexi and Hawke huddled together, smiling and whispering over her cell phone like they were arranging a hook-up. They'd moved apart the moment he'd come out of the kitchen, as if they hadn't wanted him to see them. But he *had* seen.

"Come on, boy. Let's leave Lexi in peace." He led Mack from the room and went to work inspecting the ropes that had been used in last night's rescue, pulling the length of rope through his hand and letting it coil up in its bag.

"Give me one of those." Eric grabbed another rope.

Austin knew Eric was attracted to Lexi. He always had been. In high school, he'd been more than a little jealous of Austin's relationship with her. Still, Austin didn't believe for a second that his best friend and girlfriend would fool around behind his back. Hawke knew how Austin felt about her. Then again, was Lexi actually his girlfriend?

No, they were just friends. They'd made no commitments.

Son of a bitch.

Austin hated himself for doubting them, hated the way it made him feel even to imagine the two of them together. He decided to be an adult about it and ask. "So, hey, what were you and Lexi talking about in there?"

Hawke frowned. "In where?"

"In the ops room just now. I walked out from the kitchen, and you were bent over her cell phone talking together."

Hawke didn't look up from the rope in his hands. "Oh, that. Nothing much. She wanted to know when you and I have another day off together. I think she's planning some kind of surprise. I don't know."

"Huh." A surprise.

"Do I need to rearrange what's left of your face?"

Austin looked up to find Hawke glaring at him.

"I would never mess around with another man's woman—especially not when that man is like a brother to me."

And immediately Austin felt like an idiot. "Sorry, man."

"Yeah, you'd better be." Eric went back to work. "She would never do that. I don't care what kind of arrangement you have. She's not that kind of woman. Besides, she cares about you. I'm not sure why she prefers you to me. I'm better looking, and my cock is at least three inches longer than yours."

"Okay, *that* is bullshit." Austin couldn't help but grin.

"Are you two really comparing dick sizes?" Sasha walked in through the open bay doors. Her gaze dropped to Hawke's groin. "Hey, if you need an impartial judge, let me know."

She headed off toward the ops room, a smile on her face.

Hawke's gaze followed her. "Did she just check out my bulge?"

"What bulge?" A rough patch of rope scraped across Austin's palm. He held up that bit of rope, saw that a few of the fibers were frayed. Worse, the rope was flat as if it had been pinched. "Another one bites the dust."

He wound the rope around his arm and carried it over to the recycling bin.

"How many does that make so far this year?" Hawke asked. "Five?"

"Yep. Megs is going to be thrilled."

"Did you hear Breece stole at least sixty grand from us?"

"Yeah." Lexi had told him. The news had made him want to crush Breece.

"We could've bought a lot of ropes with sixty grand."

Speaking of ropes…

Austin walked back to the recycling bin and took the rope back out, stashing it near the door. He still had to get his revenge on Lexi, and he had a pretty good idea of what he was going to do. He could use some rope that he wouldn't mind cutting to size.

Hawke watched him. "What the hell are you going to do with that?"

Austin grinned. "Wouldn't you like to know."

Hawke rolled his eyes. "Jesus."

Chapter Seventeen

Lexi stopped by the inn after work and packed a few things in her carry-on bag to take with her to Austin's. She'd been spending every night at his place, so it made sense to bring her toiletries and a few changes of clothes with her. She was on her way out to her car when she saw her father sitting on the bench in the backyard.

He looked shabby, his hair uncombed, his face unshaven.

She didn't want to feel sorry for him, but she did. He'd done what Kendra had said she wanted him to do, only to have Kendra throw it in his face. Lexi couldn't imagine how he must feel.

She left her bag just inside the back door and walked over to him. "Hey."

"Hey." He moved over to make room for her.

She sat beside him. "How are things going with Rain?"

"She does a good job. I only have to show her once."

"That's good. I'm glad it's working out."

"Yeah. Thanks, by the way. You hired the right person."

Lexi had known her father all her life. She ought to know what to say to comfort him. But she didn't. "I saw Kendra yesterday. She told me you called her."

He nodded. "She thought you put me up to it."

"I'm sorry. I told her I wasn't even here, and I think she believed me."

"It's hard to tell with Kendra. The woman loves to hold a grudge."

That was the truth.

Lexi decided to tell him all of it, because he'd find out anyway. "She said some pretty awful things. I got angry and walked out on her."

"You did?"

Lexi shared the gist of the conversation. "I was so angry I left and made her pay for her own lunch."

"Served her right."

Wait. What? She and her father had just agreed on something.

Lexi was tempted to note the date in her calendar. "You're not angry with me?"

He shook his head. "But she's not wrong, you know."

Had her father just told her that Kendra was right, that he didn't really care about them? She supposed that wasn't a surprise. But still...

Blinking back unexpected tears, she shot to her feet. "I'll talk to you later."

"You're going to *his* house again, huh?"

She clamped down on her emotions and turned to face her dad once more.

"I'm only going to be here a couple more weeks." Had she truly felt sad about leaving this afternoon? Ha! If it hadn't been for Austin, she'd have jumped in her car and left Colorado tonight. "I want to spend as much time with him as I can before I go."

"You'd rather spend time with him than your old man. That's okay. Can't say I blame you for that."

Was that hurt in his eyes? Good grief!

Why should she care how he felt when he didn't seem to give a damn about her feelings? She would go to Austin's house. She would turn and go right now. She would walk away. But she couldn't, something holding her to the spot.

Damn it!

A sense of resignation washed over her. "How about we order pizza and play some checkers?"

God, she must be an idiot! Choosing time with her dad over Austin? Besides, she hated checkers.

The surprise on her father's face was real. He nodded, some light returning to his eyes. "I think I've got a coupon for Mr. Fatty's somewhere."

Angry as hell at herself for caving like this, she pulled out her cell phone. "Hey. It's me. I'm going to have dinner with my dad tonight and spend the evening with him. I'll be over later, say, nine?"

Austin sounded surprised. "Is everything okay?"

She couldn't explain, not with her father sitting there. "Yeah. See you later."

Her dad got to his feet. "You still like pepperoni and black olives?"

She wanted to say that what Mr. Fatty's served didn't deserve to be called pizza, but she bit her tongue. "Love it."

She turned and followed her father back inside.

Austin watched Lexi park and walk around to the back door. He put Mack in his crate with a chew toy. "Sorry, but I've learned I can't trust you, buddy."

He'd spent the evening setting everything up, the thought of what he was going to do to her making him incredibly horny. He'd never gone so deeply into his own fantasies with any woman before, and he was a little worried about how Lexi would take it.

Would it turn her on, or would she decide it was too kinky?

He waited until she knocked, then opened the door and killed the lights.

"Austin?" She stepped inside.

He moved up behind her, clamped a hand over her mouth, turning her surprised cry into a squeak. "Not a word. Do you understand?"

Her body stiffened, but she nodded.

He bent one arm behind her back, using it to guide her. "Upstairs. Now."

She allowed herself to be marched up the stairs. "What are you doing?"

There was a hint of laughter in her voice.

He jerked her back against him, using just enough force to set the tone, the pulse at her wrist tripping beneath his fingers. "I said not a word."

When she turned toward his bedroom, he stopped her.

"No, not that way. I have something else planned for you tonight, honey." He pushed her down the hallway toward one of the empty bedrooms—not so empty now—and opened the door.

She sucked in a breath, her gaze moving over the room.

Dozens of candles illuminated the little scenario he'd created for her. Handcuffs dangling from the ceiling. The rest of the homemade sex swing tied up out of the way for now, its homemade ankle restraints visible. The digital camera he'd set up in front of the swing. The flatscreen TV he'd placed right where she'd be able to see it.

He nudged her deeper into the room and slammed the door, locking it behind them. *Click.* "No one will be able to hear you, so scream all you like."

"This is your revenge." Her voice was breathless, equal parts excitement and nervousness.

She was playing along.

Hot damn.

"I told you I'd make you pay."

She put up a brief and half-hearted struggle, offering just enough resistance to make him use his strength.

"Fight if you want, but you don't stand a chance." With very little effort, he brought her to the center of the room, stretched one arm at a time over her head, and cuffed her to the ceiling. "You're mine until I decide to let you go."

She glared up at him. "When will that be?"

He ducked down, kissed her roughly. "I'm going to fuck you so long and hard you'll have trouble remembering a time when my cock wasn't inside you."

The look of arousal on her pretty face was unmistakable.

She hid it behind a mask of fear. "Don't hurt me."

"I won't unless you force me to."

Then he realized he was faced with a problem he hadn't considered. Her arms were cuffed over her head, and she was still fully dressed. There were only two ways to get her naked—uncuff her or make use of the folding army knife in his pocket.

Smooth move, idiot.

Not wanting to look like a total bondage newbie—which he was—he would much rather go with the knife.

"You won't need clothes anymore." He drew the knife out of his pocket, opened it, let her see the blade, giving her a moment to realize what he was about to do.

She sucked in another breath, but didn't object.

His gaze locked with hers as the knife sliced through the fabric of her dress and then her bra. He saw her pupils dilate, heard her quick little intake of breath when the fabric fell away from her skin, her need heightening his own.

He stepped back, the breath leaving his lungs as he took in the sight of her—hands chained above her head, eyes wide, puckered nipples peeking through strands of red hair, candlelight dancing over her pale skin, her feet still in heels.

Damn.

She was every fantasy he'd ever had come to life, and he was so hard now that it hurt to be inside his jeans.

"Hurry up and get it over with." She was good at this make-believe thing, her voice laced with fear.

"What fun would that be?" Besides, he hadn't spent three hours figuring all this shit out only to have it be over in five minutes—which was a very real danger, considering how turned on he was. "I'm going to take my sweet time and enjoy your body the way it was meant to be enjoyed."

Now for the final touch.

He turned on the camera and then the television, an image of beautiful, naked Lexi filling the screen.

Her gaze shifted from him to the image of herself, her eyes going wider.

He stripped off his shirt, then moved in on her.

Lexi's pulse raced as Austin strode shirtless toward her, one hand unzipping his jeans, his erection springing free. She forgot about the image of herself on the TV screen, almost moaning at the sight of his cock, her body already wet and aching for him.

He took her chin in his hand, forced her to look at the television. "Look at you—helpless, vulnerable, no one to save you."

Seeing herself like this was so stunningly erotic that it didn't occur to her to feel self-conscious or even to wonder whether he was actually taping this.

He stood to the side out of the camera's way. "Don't take those pretty green eyes off the screen."

She watched as he pushed her hair over her shoulders to expose her breasts, then palmed her, his thumbs teasing her nipples to points, the sensation seeming to travel straight to her belly. She whimpered, the ache inside her overwhelming. "*Please.*"

"Please what?" He lowered his head to nip the skin beneath her ear, his hand moving from her breasts to cup her, one finger sliding inside her. "You're wet. Your body is giving you away. You like what I'm doing to you."

Oh, God. Did she *ever*.

But if she'd thought he was going to put her out of her misery, she'd been wrong.

He withdrew his hand, raised his middle finger to his mouth, and tasted her, his eyes drifting shut. Then, without warning, he nudged a knee between her thighs, forcing her legs apart. "Wider."

Then he knelt down and took her with his mouth.

Lexi's hands grabbed onto the strap that held the handcuffs, her knees almost buckling at the hot shock of his tongue against her as he tasted her, teased her, tormented her. She must have been wiggling too much because one of his big hands moved to cup her ass, holding her in place for him, angling her pelvis.

Two thick fingers slid inside her.

Oh, sweet heaven!

Then she remembered the TV screen. She opened her eyes to see herself chained from the ceiling, Austin's head between her legs, the muscles of his back shifting while he devoured her.

It was too much—his tongue stroking her, his lips tugging on her clit, his fingers fucking her deep and slow. Bliss gathered into a tight ball low in her belly, sensation carrying her upward until…

Austin stopped, got to his feet, and stood there, a satisfied grin on his face, while she hovered on the edge of a climax she couldn't quite claim.

She gaped at him. "You can't stop."

He stepped away from her. "I can't?"

"Safe word!" She blurted the term.

His brow furrowed in confusion. "Safe word?"

Oh, God, they were both such beginners.

She told him what she'd heard. "When someone can't take what the other person is doing they have a safe word."

He leaned in, her scent all over him, an amused grin on his face. "Don't tell me you're undone by *one* round of cunnilingus interruptus. Remember what you did to me? Three's a charm. Besides, Lexi, honey, you don't have a safe word."

"Oh, you *bastard!*" Torn between sexual frustration and laughter, she tried to squeeze her thighs together, anything to ease that ache, but he stopped her, kicking her feet apart again, his forcefulness only heightening her lust.

He shook his head. "Bad girl. What am I going to do with you?"

He disappeared behind her, her gaze snapping to the television screen for some sign of what he meant to do next. He reached around with one hand to torment her more, the sight of his busy fingers between her thighs bringing her frustration to a peak.

Then he caught her around the waist with one arm and thrust himself into her.

Lexi's cry mingled with his moan, the feel of his cock inside her like deliverance. "God, yes, fuck me."

He plunged into her, and she could see it all—his fingers digging into her hips, the expression of sexual anguish on his face, her breasts bobbing, his cock disappearing into her up to his balls.

She came hard and fast, his thrusts driving her orgasm home.

But he didn't let himself come. When her climax had passed, he withdrew from her, walked to the side, and reached up.

"Time to get serious."

She had no idea what he was talking about until a homemade sex swing fell from the ceiling above her.

Oh. My. God.

It took a few minutes to fasten her into the thing. Then with some tugs on a few different ropes, he had her off her feet, her knees drawn back, her ankles bound by straps, her legs spread wide.

It was all there on the TV screen, every inch of her bared to the camera, to Austin. She was exposed, completely vulnerable.

"That's more like it." He stood there for a moment, his gaze moving over her, a muscle clenching in his jaw, the heat in his eyes scorching her, taking her breath away.

Then he stepped in front of the camera, grabbed hold of her waist, and slowly buried himself inside her.

He pounded into her, every thrust making her cry out, the sheer pleasure of it staggering. But he felt it, too. "You *feel* ... *so* ... *good.*"

She came again, the pleasure searing through her like molten gold. She thought he would join her, but the moment her climax subsided, he stopped and held himself still inside her, drawing deep, even breaths, his muscles slowly relaxing. He was trying to make it last, putting all his strength and stamina into making good on his threat.

I'm going to fuck you so long and hard you'll have trouble remembering a time when my cock wasn't inside you.

Oh, she could only be so lucky.

Again and again he went as long as he could without coming, until his chest was slick with sweat and Lexi hovered on the brink of an unbelievable third orgasm, her heart thudding, her toes curled in her shoes.

He looked into her eyes, his chest rising and falling with each slow, steady breath. "You are the most beautiful thing in my world."

Her heart melted. "Austin."

Then he began to move again, cutting off anything else she might have said, the feel of him inside her perfect. But this time, he didn't stop, driving relentlessly into her, bringing her to a third shattering climax, her gaze locking with his as he finally let himself go inside her.

Austin let himself catch his breath, holding onto the straps of the swing for balance, certain the earth had just shifted beneath his feet, his cock still inside her, the aftermath of orgasm sliding through him like warm honey.

Holy hell.

That was all his brain could manage at this point.

Lexi's eyes were closed, her body limp, her lips parted.

He felt a hitch in his chest, overwhelmed by the need to hold her. He took off her fancy heels, untied her ankles, then unfastened the climbing harness and unlocked the handcuffs, catching her in his arms as she slumped, boneless, against him. Then he carried her to his bed and wrapped his arms around her, kissing her cheeks, her closed eyelids, her lips.

She opened her eyes, ran her hand up his sweat-slick chest, her gaze soft. "You're the most amazing man I know."

It wasn't "I love you," but it was better than nothing.

Afraid he'd say something dangerous or stupid if he said anything at all, he bent down to kiss her.

She turned her head away, her lips curving in a naughty smile. "Of course, you'll pay for that. I don't know when or how, but I'll get my revenge."

He chuckled. "Sorry about the dress and the bra. I'll have to take you shopping."

"The sacrifice was worth it."

For a time, they lay together in silence, Austin drifting toward sleep.

Then Lexi spoke. "I told my dad what happened with Kendra."

Austin opened his eyes. "Yeah?"

"He wasn't angry, but he said she wasn't wrong, that he doesn't care about her or about Britta and me as much as he cared about my mom."

Ouch.

"He told you that?"

"Not in those words, but isn't that what he meant? I was so angry I wanted to throw my stuff in the car and drive back to Chicago tonight. If it hadn't been for you—and the audit—I probably would have."

She'd wanted to leave because of her father, but she'd stayed because of Austin.

Austin liked that.

He held her closer. "Kendra said a lot of things. I guess you can't know for certain what he meant if he didn't spell it out for you."

"I suppose that's true." She gave a little laugh. "He acted hurt that I've been spending all my time with you."

"So you stayed with him."

"I even played checkers with him. I hate that game."

They certainly had a strange family dynamic, but Austin wondered whether Lexi could see it the way he did. "Your father probably wouldn't give a damn what you did with your time if he didn't care about you. If your leaving bothered him, it's a good sign he actually *does* love you."

She raised her head off his chest, looked up at him. "You think so?"

"Yeah, I do. The fact that you stayed and played checkers with him even though you hate the game proves that you love him, too."

She rested her cheek against his chest again. "He makes me so angry."

He kissed the top of her head. "The people we care most about are the ones with the power to hurt us."

As they drifted off to sleep, Austin found himself wondering whether Lexi's dislike for Scarlet Springs had anything to do with the town itself or whether she'd been running from her father this entire time.

Chapter Eighteen

Lexi pushed her cart through Food Mart, grabbing a few things for lunch with her dad and other things to take to Austin's for dinner tonight. She needed something that would be quick and easy for supper because Austin would be exhausted from a long work day and she would be tired from her first climbing lesson.

Good God! Was she really going to do this?

Yes, she was. There was no backing out now, not now that everyone on the Team—apart from Austin, of course—knew about it. She'd feel like a coward.

"Hey, Lexi. Good to see you."

It took a moment for Lexi to recognize her high school English teacher, her once-dark hair now completely gray. "Hey, Mrs. Beech. I was so sorry to hear about the loss of your husband. How are you?"

She'd already run into Rose, Conrad, and the guy with the bushy beard who ran the marijuana shop across the street from the inn, whatever his name was.

"Oh, I'm getting along all right. I hear you and Austin Taylor are back together."

Did everyone know about that?

Of course, they did. This was Scarlet.

Mrs. Beech smiled. "I always liked him. He was such a good kid—and not hard on the eyes. You should stop by the house sometime before you head back to Chicago. I love catching up with my students—at least the ones who've done well. And you've certainly done well, haven't you?

"Thanks." Lexi was touched by the invitation. "I'll try to make it by."

She moved on to the produce aisle, where she picked up some organic romaine lettuce, scallions, tomatoes, and a cucumber for a quick dinner salad to go with the marinated chicken breasts she planned to make for dinner. She heard someone speaking French and looked to see Sandrine and her husband fussing over a display of table grapes, neither of them looking impressed with the fruit.

Sandrine smiled and waved when she saw Lexi.

Lexi waved back, then pushed her cart over to the busy deli counter, thinking of picking up some sliced turkey breast for sandwiches.

"You again."

Lexi turned to find Cheyenne standing behind her in a sports bra and yoga pants, a basket on her arm, her blond hair tied up in a messy bun. "I can't leave until I finish the work I'm doing for the Team."

Cheyenne stepped closer, lowered her voice. "Austin is in love with you, you know. No, he didn't tell me that. He doesn't have to. Your coming back here was the worst thing for him."

Lexi's pulse spiked, a rush of adrenaline drowning out that last part.

Austin wasn't in love with her. Was he?

Cheyenne was still talking. "Do you know how long it took him to get over you the first time? I don't even want to think about how he's going to feel when you run away to Chicago again."

Lexi fought back a surge of guilt. They hadn't made each other any promises. They were just friends—very special friends. But she couldn't explain that to his sister. "We are *not* having this conversation in the middle of Food Mart."

The anger faded from Cheyenne's face, worry taking its place. "Look, I know I probably come across as a bitch. It doesn't matter. Austin is my brother, and I don't want to see him hurting. You—well, you're like his personal brand of kryptonite. It was selfish of you to get involved with him again."

"I don't want to do anything to hurt him. I never—"

Cheyenne turned and walked away, leaving Lexi to stare after her.

Austin spent a couple of hours of his Friday morning in a department meeting with the feds. Chief Deputy US Marshal Zach McBride, whom Austin had already met Monday, was there, along with a handful of suits from the FBI, the two agencies bringing Austin and the other rangers up to date on their manhunt for that bastard Ready. They hadn't found him, and they disagreed on where he might be.

McBride believed he was probably still somewhere in Colorado, living off the land, while the FBI seemed to think he'd moved on.

"Why steal a hundred grand and then go live like a caveman?" Sutherland asked.

McBride explained. "The dye pack in the money bag detonated as he was fleeing the scene. The money—if it wasn't incinerated—is dyed bright red. Those dye packs reach about four hundred degrees to prevent thieves from pulling them out, so there's a good chance most of the bills were burned."

Austin had always wondered how those things worked. "So he steals the money and ends up with nothing but red hands."

"That gives new meaning to the phrase 'caught red-handed.'" Sutherland laughed at his own humor.

Austin could tell from the weary look on McBride's face that he'd *never* heard that lame-ass joke before.

McBride went on as if he hadn't heard. "I think it might be a good idea for your rangers to work in pairs over the next couple of weeks, especially if they're hiking off trail or working in the backcountry. It's your decision, of course."

Austin ended up riding shotgun in Hatfield's truck, the two of them making a circuit of picnic areas to check restrooms and haul away trash before heading up to Haley Preserve, one of the county's newer acquisitions that hadn't yet been opened to the public. The property abutted Russey Ranch to the west. If Ready had kept moving westward after he'd fired at Austin, he would have had to cross Haley.

They parked at the only trailhead in the park, then backtracked to a gully that separated Haley from Russey, more or less following the property line. Careful to stay clear of old mine shafts, they hiked uphill along that gully, looking for signs of human encroachment. Neither of them spoke, the sun beating down on them, Austin's body armor stifling and heavy.

A red-tailed hawk circled overhead, hunting for a meal, its trademark cry unmistakable. A pissed-off Abert's squirrel scolded them from a nearby tree. Then on the hillside across from them, something moved.

A bear cub. No, make that two... no, *three* bear cubs.

They played together near a thicket of chokecherry bushes, one up a tree, the other two rolling on the ground together.

Austin and Hatfield shared a glance, only one question on their minds.

Where was Mama Bear?

Austin would bet she was napping in that thicket. He wasn't worried that she would attack. Bears rarely attacked people, and he and Hatfield were far enough away to make that unlikely. Still, he hated to disturb her.

They watched for a few minutes, both grinning.

This was why Austin loved his job. Where else could he get paid to hike and watch wildlife?

They moved westward, away from the bears, stopping when they'd gained the sandstone ridge above. To their east was Russey Ranch and the Pinnacles and to the west, the snowcapped mountains of the Indian Peaks Wilderness.

Austin and Hatfield scanned the surrounding countryside through binoculars, trying to take advantage of the high ground.

"Holy shit! Is that Bear?" Hatfield pointed to the southwest.

For a moment, Austin thought Hatfield was talking about the four-legged kind. Then he saw a small cabin that sat in a clearing roughly midway between South Scarlet Creek and the Peak-to-Peak Highway. A man was hard at work splitting firewood.

"Yep, that's Bear." Austin lowered the binoculars. "Shit."

He'd known Bear had a cabin up here somewhere. What he hadn't realized was that Bear was homesteading on public land.

"Think he's got a permit to cut wood up here?" Hatfield asked.

"Yeah, right."

The answer, of course, was no. Haley Preserve was just that—a preserve. No hunting, no harvesting firewood, and certainly no homesteading allowed. Austin had no choice but to report it, and once he did, the county would take action.

Shit.

Leaving Bear homeless was not on his wish list. But maybe if he spoke with the county attorney first, he'd be able to help Bear through this.

"Mind if I handle this myself?" he asked.

Hatfield shook his head. "Be my guest."

"Let's keep this between us for now."

"You got it."

The two took a different route back to the vehicle, trying to cover as much of the Haley property as they could. But again they found nothing. Hot and sweaty, they checked in with dispatch, then climbed back into the sweltering vehicle and drank deeply from their canteens.

"So what are you up to tonight?" Hatfield turned on the vehicle, started up the AC. "Want to come to my place to catch some MMA?"

Austin shook his head. "Not tonight. I've got plans."

"Oh, yeah. Lexi. Can't say that I blame you for choosing to spend time with her over me. How do you two know each other?"

Austin gave Hatfield, who'd come to Scarlet Springs from Denver, the short version of the story—how he, Lexi, and Hawke had grown up here and gone to high school together and how he and Lexi had dated during their senior year.

"That explains why she knows Hawke so well, too." Hatfield said. "I ran into her and Hawke at …"

He caught himself, fell silent, his flushed face getting redder.

"Lexi and Hawke were … what?"

He shook his head, looked away. "You didn't hear anything from me. I didn't say a word. Lexi will kill me. Hell, Hawke will kill me. The entire Team will kill me."

So Lexi and Hawke *were* conspiring about something, and everyone on the Team seemed to know about it but Austin.

"What are you talking about?"

"Nothing, man. Forget it. It was nothing." Then he threw the vehicle into gear and started down the road.

Austin didn't push Hatfield, but he was sure about one thing. Whatever Hatfield had been about to tell him, it sure as hell hadn't been nothing.

*L*exi drove to the rock gym, willing herself to quit obsessing over what Cheyenne had said to her at Food Mart and get her mind on the afternoon's adventure. She was really going through with this. She was really going to try rock climbing.

Eric and Sasha met her in the parking lot, and they walked inside together, Eric using one of his guest passes to cover her admission fee.

The gym's rock wall was easily twice as high as the wall at Knockers, climbers moving up and down it like spiders, ropes trailing after them like webs.

What the hell was Lexi doing here?

Sasha dug in her backpack and held something out—climbing shoes and a climbing harness. "Do you know how to put all this on?"

Lexi felt herself blush at the sight of the harness, her mind flashing back to Austin's homemade sex swing. "I imagine it's pretty self-explanatory."

She stepped into the harness, letting Sasha adjust it to fit her wider hips and waist. Then she slipped her feet into the strange shoes. The mirror across from her gave her a glimpse of herself. She wasn't all lean muscle like Sasha, but she couldn't tell by looking at herself that she'd never set foot in a rock gym.

"The first thing we're going to do is teach you to belay," Eric said.

"Okay."

Eric led her toward the rock wall, the floor beneath their feet turning to soft padding that made her feel like she was walking on marshmallows. People called out to him and Sasha, and it was clear that they knew almost everyone there.

When they reached the wall, he took hold of one of the free ropes and gave it a quick tug. "The routes here are top-roped. The ropes are anchored to the top of the climbing wall. When you do top-rope climbing, the person on belay stays on the floor and manages the slack, making sure the climber has enough rope to keep going but not enough to hit the ground should he or she fall."

"Okay." That made sense.

He held up an oblong metal device. "This is a grigri. You clip it onto your harness with a carabiner here." He reached down, grabbed a loop on her harness, gave it a little tug, then handed the grigri to Sasha.

Sasha slipped the carabiner through the loop on her own harness, then showed Lexi first how to lock the carabiner and then how to pass the climbing rope through the grigri. "Am I overwhelming you yet?"

"Not at all." Lexi shook her head. "Okay, just a little."

Sasha smiled, went over it again. "Okay? Then let's belay."

Eric tied into the other end of the rope, while Sasha showed Lexi how to take up the slack by pulling the rope through the grigri with her right hand and how to let it out again by releasing the brake.

"Is belay on?" Eric asked.

"On belay," Sasha replied.

"Climbing," Eric said.

"Climb on."

Sasha belayed while Eric climbed, showing Lexi how to take up the slack as Eric climbed higher.

"What if he falls? Won't the rope just slide back through?"

Sasha grinned. "Hey, Hawke, could you fall for me, please?"

Twenty feet above them, Eric simply let go. Rather than hurtling toward the ground, he hung in mid-air, sitting in his harness as if it were a swing.

Sasha smiled. "See? He can't go anywhere. Are you ready to try?"

"Sure." Butterflies danced in Lexi's stomach.

Sasha shouted up to Eric. "I'm going to dirt you."

"Okay."

Sasha released the brake, holding onto the rope as it slid slowly through the grigri, lowering Eric to the floor.

It was then Lexi noticed that everyone was watching them—okay, maybe not everyone, but almost everyone. Then she remembered that Sasha was a celebrity, one of the most famous female climbers in the world.

"Man, that chick is lucky," said a woman standing off to their right. "I'd pay cold, hard cash to have private lessons with Sasha Dillon."

"Forget Sasha Dillon," said another. "Who's that man she's climbing with? He is freaking *hot*."

"That's Eric Hawke, our fire chief. He's on the Team, too."

"Hot, a badass climber, and a firefighter. I think my panties just melted."

Neither Sasha nor Eric seemed to hear them.

Sasha handed Lexi the grigri. "Do you remember what to do?"

Lexi nodded. "Please don't let me kill anyone."

Sasha laughed. "Don't worry. That's *not* going to happen."

Austin arrived home to find Lexi's car parked on the side of his house. He'd given her a key, figuring it would be easier for her if she didn't have to come and go on his schedule. His job meant early mornings, and volunteering for the Team meant he could get toned out at any time. It was the first time he'd ever given a woman the key to his house, and he had to say that he liked arriving to find someone else already home—as long as that someone was Lexi.

He found his back door unlocked, the house silent, the kitchen empty. Lexi didn't come to greet him, and neither did Mack. The puppy wasn't in his crate, either. "Lexi?"

He was about to pull out his cell phone to call her when he spotted strands of red hair spilling over the end of his sofa. "Lexi?"

He found her sound asleep, the puppy curled up at her feet. He felt that familiar hitch in his chest. He couldn't blame her for being exhausted. Their sex life had been keeping them both up late.

Mack opened his eyes, gave a few lazy wags of his tail in greeting.

Austin tousled the puppy's ears and was about to tiptoe upstairs to take a shower, when Lexi stirred, and her eyes opened.

She smiled, reached out her hand. "Austin."

"Hey." He bent down, kissed her, aware that he was sweaty and dirty. "I was about to take a shower. Keep sleeping."

When he came back downstairs, he found her in the kitchen, dinner already in the oven. Whatever it was, it smelled delicious. "You made dinner."

"I know, right?" She walked over to him, a teasing smile on her face. "Don't get used to it. I'm not much of a domestic goddess."

He started to say that he wouldn't have a chance to get used to it because she'd be leaving soon. But the words died on his tongue, the thought turning to lead in his chest. Then he noticed the large bandage on her shin. "What happened to you?"

"Oh, I wasn't watching where I was going and hit my shin against the side of one of those metal litters. Lucky for me everyone at The Cave knows first aid. Eric bandaged it. He says he thinks I bruised the bone."

Austin knelt down to examine it. "I think he's right. You're getting a hematoma. You should elevate and ice it."

He scooped her into his arms and carried her back to the sofa, moving the coffee table close so she'd have a place to rest her foot.

"What about dinner?"

"I'll finish it." He walked back into the kitchen to get an ice pack. "Who the hell left a litter where someone could trip over it? I bet Megs blew a gasket. She's got zero tolerance for workplace accidents."

"It was my fault. I'm a klutz."

This from the woman who danced like a dream. "You are *not* a klutz."

He sat down on the coffee table, placed the ice bag gently on her shin. Then he saw a fresh bruise on her inner arm. "Did I do this?"

He hadn't exactly been gentle in bed lately.

"No! No, I just … I fell. I guess I'm a little more banged up than I thought." She winced as she settled onto the sofa. "I'm a little sore."

"You know what you're doing after dinner?"

"Dishes?"

He laughed. "Wrong. You're going to take off your clothes, lie down on my bed, and let me give you a massage with cannabis oil."

She stared at him like he'd lost his mind. "Will it make me high? I don't want to be stoned."

"It's great for relaxing stiff muscles. Hey, trust me."

Lexi lay face down on Austin's bed, moaning as his hands moved over her back, taking the stiffness out of muscles she hadn't known she had. Rock climbing, as it turned out, was a lot of hard work. She'd hit the steep part of the learning curve today.

Though she'd made it to the top of the rock wall once, it hadn't been graceful. She'd fallen at least a dozen times, banging herself up and finally striking her shin hard against a large foothold called a jug.

Eric had ended her lesson there and then, bandaging and putting ice on her shin. "Live to climb another day."

She hated lying to Austin about it, but if she were to tell him the truth, her surprise would be ruined. Now she needed to make sure the Team was in on her fib.

"Hey, relax." Austin's voice was deep and soothing.

Lexi drew a deep breath and let her worries go. She'd done something today that she'd never done before, and she was proud of that.

She lost track of time, Austin's hands working wonders on her neck, her shoulders, her quads, her back, and her aching arms.

"Man, the muscles of your forearms are tight. You must have reached out to stop your fall or something."

"Mmm," she said. "Where did you learn to do this? Was it part of your paramedic training or something?"

He laughed. "No. I learned it from a friend."

It was the tone of his voice that roused her suspicions.

"Was that friend by any chance a woman?"

"Jealous?"

"Yes." She *was* jealous. She didn't want to think about the other women Austin had been with over the past twelve years.

Warm lips kissed her temple. "Don't be. There's not a woman in the world who matters to me the way you do."

"Really?" Maybe Cheyenne was right. Maybe he *was* in love with her.

"Really." He kissed her again.

"Watch out, or you'll get high from kissing me."

"That happens all the time anyway." His words hit her right in the heart, unleashed a strange ache behind her breastbone.

Confused by her own emotions, she tried to think it through, but couldn't, her thoughts unraveling before they could form, chased away by the magic of Austin's hands. But this was no therapeutic massage he was giving her now, his touch becoming decidedly sensual, callused fingers tracing the ticklish skin of her sides, a big hand cupping her ass, a knee nudging her thighs wider. Her body responded, desire for him flooding her.

"I want to be inside you." His breath was hot against her cheek.

"*Yes.*" She started to roll over, but he stopped her.

"You don't have to move a muscle."

Oh, she liked that idea, given that most of her muscles were sore.

She heard his fly unzip and felt a shiver of anticipation, his hands coming down on either side of her shoulders, his hips pressing against her buttocks, the head of his cock nudging against her until it found its way home.

He buried himself with one slow thrust, then rocked into her until she was panting against the pillow. He filled her so perfectly, filled her as if he'd been made for her. She came, her aches and pains carried away in a wave of bliss.

Chapter Nineteen

Lexi rushed around her bedroom trying to find her sports bra, cell phone in one hand, Vic on the line. "I can't talk long. Eric will be here any minute to pick me up to take me to the rock gym."

"The rock gym?" Vic sounded horrified.

"I've been taking climbing lessons for two and a half weeks now." Had she left her bra at Austin's house? No, she'd never worn it there.

"Why in God's name would you do that?"

"I thought it would be a fun way to surprise Austin."

Today was the day.

It was Saturday, so he would be getting off work soon. Megs had asked him to stop by The Cave to discuss something urgent. When he got there, she would drive him to the rock gym, where Lexi, Eric, and most of the rest of the Team would be waiting for him. Then, with Eric or Sasha on belay, Lexi would climb the 5.9 route she'd climbed two days ago—hopefully without falling.

"You're still sleeping with him."

It wasn't a question.

"Yes." She tossed dirty clothes around, looked beneath the covers of her unmade bed, glanced inside the closet.

Where the hell was her damned sports bra?

"Austin is the guy who broke your teenage heart into little pieces, remember?"

Lexi wasn't surprised by Vic's reaction. She'd had an almost identical conversation with Britta yesterday when she'd been doing laundry.

Laundry! Her bra was in the dryer. She'd thrown it in the dryer yesterday while talking with her sister.

She rushed down the hallway. "That's how it started anyway, but I really like it. My muscles are sore all the time now, and I banged my shin up pretty badly the first day. It left a huge bruise that still hasn't gone away."

"What's not to like about that?" Vic's voice dripped with sarcasm.

Lexi bent down and dug through the dryer—towels, socks, panties. "It's exciting to do something I've never done before."

It was even more exciting to discover that she didn't suck at it. She'd never thought of herself as athletic, and no sport had ever held her interest. But climbing, with its complicated movement problems, was a lot like dancing—figuring out which moves went next so she could climb smoothly up the rock.

She couldn't say why, exactly, but something about climbing made her feel more confident. When she'd finished that 5.9 route two days ago, she'd stood there at the top of the wall with her fist in the air, feeling like a hero.

"Apart from beating yourself up to impress a guy, how are things?"

Lexi found her sports bra—thank God!—and hurried back to her bedroom. "I'm doing well. My dad and I have been getting along pretty well the past couple of weeks."

"That's new. How about the audit?"

"I'm almost done." She could have finished more than a week ago, but she kept finding little ways to help Megs, each of them nothing more than an excuse to spend the afternoon at The Cave.

"I bet you'll be glad to have that out of your hair."

From outside, came the honk of Eric's horn.

Shit.

"Actually, I'm really going to miss working there. Hang on just a sec." Lexi put the phone down, stripped off her T-shirt and bra, then wriggled into her sports bra and pulled on her yellow Team T-shirt. She picked up the phone again. "I've discovered that I really love doing pro bono work."

"I hear it's not very lucrative."

"Very funny." Lexi tried to explain. "My work at Price and Crane involved doing tax preparation for wealthy clients. Whom did that help?"

"Wealthy clients who paid your very nice salary."

"But I'm really making a difference here. I'm helping the Team to do its job, and they save lives. They show me a lot more respect than my Chicago clients did."

That was true about Winona and the volunteers at the wildlife sanctuary, too.

When it came down to it, Lexi was having a great time here.

Whoa. That was a strange thought.

She grabbed her handbag and headed for the back door, waving to her dad as she breezed through the kitchen.

Vic changed the subject. "I know you're in a hurry. I just called to let you know I bought my plane tickets."

"Plane tickets?" Lexi hurried toward Eric's Silverado. "You're really coming?"

She'd thought Vic had been joking.

"I took Friday and Monday off, so I'll be there next Friday. I'm not sure how I'll survive without lattes for four days, but someone has to be there to watch out for you. I'm afraid Scarlet Springs has sunk its claws into you. I know how much you hate that place. I don't want to see you unhappy."

Lexi didn't know what to say.

"Don't sound so excited."

"Oh, I am!" But she wasn't, not the way she should be. Vic's arrival would mean spending less time with Austin, and she had only *two weeks* left here.

"I'll send my itinerary so you can pick me up at the airport."

"Great. See you Friday." Lexi ended the call, sadness stealing over her.

Her precious time here was coming to an end.

She opened the passenger door and climbed into the front seat of Eric's truck. "Sorry. I couldn't find my bra."

Eric grinned. "I'm sure none of us would mind if you climbed braless."

She glared at him. "Right."

Austin parked at The Cave, sweaty, tired, and ready for a shower. Megs had said she needed to see him right away, so she was just going to have to deal with him the way he was. He was late getting off work because he'd gone to visit the county attorney about Bear, looking for a way to let the old man stay in his cabin. If it had been up to Austin, he'd have let Bear stay where he was. But it wasn't up to Austin.

He walked in through the bay doors to find the place all but deserted, Rescue One and Rescue Two parked and plugged in.

Megs sat at the ops desk, keys in her hand. She glanced at her watch when he walked in. "It's about time. Come on."

"Where are we going?" He followed her toward her car.

She smiled. "Please shut up, and get in the vehicle—and *don't* ask any questions."

"Okay." What the hell?

She started up her Subaru and headed toward the highway. "Some of us were talking about having a surprise going-away party for Lexi. She's leaving two weeks from today, which doesn't give us a lot of time to plan."

Megs went on about dates and cakes, but Austin barely heard her, his stomach knotted. He'd been trying not to think about it, trying not to count the days, trying not to let what was going to happen down the road ruin the time he had with her now. But the closer he got to saying goodbye, the harder it became.

"Are you listening to anything I've said?"

"Sorry. Long day." It was then he realized where they were. "The rock gym? What the hell are we doing here?"

"I said no questions."

They finished the drive in silence, as Megs turned into the enormous lot and parked her Subaru.

She fired off a text message to someone, then looked over at Austin. "Inside."

He climbed out and walked toward the entrance, wracking his brain to figure out what planning a surprise party for Lexi had to do with the rock gym. He came up with precisely nothing. Then he noticed Hawke's truck. Harrison's and Moretti's vehicles were here, too. And Ahearn's. And Herrera's. "What the—"

"Shut your trap." Megs opened the door for him, then followed him inside.

Nicole was standing by the front desk, talking with Sasha. She glanced over her shoulder as they walked in, and both women smiled. "Hey, Megs. Hey, Taylor."

Sasha, who was wearing a climbing harness, hurried onto the climbing floor.

"Is anyone going to tell me what's going on?"

Nicole just smiled and followed Sasha.

"This way." Megs walked after them.

Austin followed. And then he saw her.

Lexi stood together with most of the Team members, wearing a climbing harness, climbing shoes, and her yellow Team T-shirt. She smiled when she saw him, her eyes holding both excitement and nervousness. She didn't walk over to him. Instead, she turned to Sasha. "Shall we?"

Sasha smiled. "We sure as hell shall."

And it clicked.

Conspiring with Hawke. Bruises. Her battered shin. Sore muscles and fatigue.

He gaped at her. "You've been learning to climb?"

She flashed him that lethal smile, the one that made his heart constrict and turned his brain to mush. "Surprise!"

Around them, Team members laughed.

Lexi walked over to the wall, Hawke and Sasha standing close to her, offering her advice as if they were her coaches. She nodded, took a few deep breaths, and shook out her hands, her brow furrowed in concentration.

"Nervous?" Herrera asked Austin.

"Nah," he lied. "Why would I be? I know she's in good hands."

He could just make out what Lexi was saying.

"What if I mess up? My stomach is full of butterflies."

Hawke rested his hand in the center of her back, leaned down. "Hey, don't psych yourself out. You can do this. Really, you can."

He was a good friend to her. Austin liked that.

"Tell those butterflies to fuck off," Sasha said. "You are going to crush this."

Lexi nodded, took another deep breath.

Then Hawke and Sasha stepped back, and Sasha took up the slack.

"On belay," she called out.

"Climbing," Lexi replied.

"Climb on, girlfriend!"

Megs looked over at Austin. "Hang on to your nuts."

Austin could see the colored strips of tape that marked the various routes. He expected her to climb the rainbow—ignoring the colors and using any foothold or handhold she could to get to the top—so when her first handhold was marked with red tape, he didn't think much of it. But her next handhold was a red, too, and that little peanut hold she caught with her left toe—that was also a red.

What was she climbing—a 5.8? No, a 5.9. Okay. Wow.

She kept her weight over her feet, her hips pushed in toward the rock face, her movements graceful.

Holy shit.

Lexi wasn't just *trying* to climb. She *was* climbing.

*L*exi had worried that she'd be too nervous to climb with Austin and the entire Team watching her, but after the first few moves, the only person she was aware of was Sasha, who shouted encouragement up to her.

"You got it. Crimper to your left."

Lexi found the crimper, caught it with the fingertips of her left hand, then stemmed to the right, reaching for a bigger handhold. She had climbed this route so many times in the past week that she almost had it memorized. She did her best to keep her weight on her legs, her pelvis "fucking the rock," as Sasha liked to say. But the muscles in her forearms were already pumped, her hands sweating.

She put her foot on a nice fat jug and took advantage of the stability to shake out her arms and chalk her hands one at a time, letting the muscles rest while her gaze traveled up the route, picking out her next move and the next.

She reached up again, caught a pocket with two fingers, then slapped her open palm against a sloper, sweat and chalk helping her to stick the move so that she could lunge up and catch another crimper. Her feet dangled, and for a moment she thought it was over. Then one of her toes caught. There it was—that little edge.

Her heart, which was already pounding, started to race, adrenaline shooting through her. She'd made it past the sloper. She'd stuck the crux move. She could do this.

From the ground below, a dozen voices cheered her on.

"Take it easy. Don't rush it." That was Sasha.

"You nailed it." That was Eric.

"You've got this, babe. Just shake it out." *That* was Austin.

She dug into an undercling, leaned back, and shook her hands out one at a time, as much to give the adrenaline time to pass as to rest her muscles. From there, she moved at a steady pace. When she reached the top of the wall a few minutes later, she raised both arms over her head, let out a whoop, a cheer rising from below. She looked down to see her friends smiling up at her, Austin most of all.

Heart still thrumming, she sat in the harness as Sasha lowered her to the mat.

The moment her feet touched the floor, Sasha gave her a high five and followed it with a hug. "Way to kick ass. I knew you could do it."

Then Austin was there, sweat stains on his uniform, a wide grin on his face. He reached out to untie the rope from her harness. "So this is what you've been up to. I'm betting you didn't trip over a litter after all."

"Sorry I lied to you." She hadn't liked that part of it.

"Oh, don't worry about that. I'll get even." He drew her against him, kissed her forehead. "My Lexi is a badass climber. That was … *amazing.*"

She shook off the praise. "I'm not such a badass. Finishing a five-nine route in a rock gym is nothing compared to what all of you do."

She knew the truth. She was still very much a beginner.

"He's not just blowing smoke up your ass," Eric said.

"He's not," Sasha agreed. "You've got natural talent."

Megs piped up. "You know I never say anything I don't mean. For someone who started two weeks ago, you've come a long way very quickly."

For Megs, that was high praise.

"Thanks." Lexi felt a rush of gratitude. "Thanks to all of you for taking the time to teach me over the past couple of weeks."

"Hey, thanks to you for stepping up to help the Team," Megs said. "Drinks at Knockers, and Lexi's first one is on me."

Austin sat at the table, beer in hand, watching as Lexi belayed Sasha, who was slaying a 5.12 route on the rock wall.

Two weeks. That's all he had with her.

Damn it.

The whole situation was fucked up—their arrangement, her plans to leave Scarlet, his obsession with her. He'd spent the past month pretending, lying to himself, telling himself that he'd be able to handle it when she left again. He'd carved out a world of hurt for himself, and it was staring him right in the face.

Hawke scooted down the bench to fill in Lexi's empty spot across from him. "You sure weren't expecting that today, were you?"

Austin shook his head. "I don't know why I didn't figure it out—all those bruises, her shin. I guess I never imagined she'd even want to try climbing."

"When Megs told us that she wanted us to teach her how to climb, I thought, 'Yeah, that won't last beyond the first hour.' I guess I underestimated her Colorado blood. She worked hard, and she did it for *you*, man."

Austin hadn't missed that part of it.

Hawke studied him for a minute. "You okay?"

"She's leaving for Chicago two weeks from today. She has her plane ticket."

"Have you told her how you feel? Have you asked her to stay?"

"What good would that do? It didn't make a damned bit of difference last time."

"Dude, you were eighteen—and so was she. She *had* to leave for school. It was a completely different stage of your lives, a different situation."

Austin watched her lower Sasha to the mat. "I don't want her to stay because of me. She would only end up resenting me later. She needs to stay because she wants to stay, because she wants to live *here*."

"Give her time. She loves you. She might come around."

What Hawke had just said reminded him of what Lexi told him that night after they'd had dinner at his parents' house.

All it took was a little distance from this place for me to realize that I would have come back here just to be with you.

"Maybe."

Lexi walked up to them, sat beside him, slipped her arm through his. "I was impressed with all of you before I knew anything about climbing. Now I'm in awe."

"You should be," Hawke joked.

Austin pressed a kiss to her forehead. "Ready to leave this place?"

She gave him a sexy look. "Is it bedtime?"

Hawke shook his head. "Lucky bastard."

They drove back to his place, Lexi chattering a million miles a minute, almost bouncing in her seat, still high on excitement and adrenaline. "On a scale of one to ten, how surprised were you?"

Austin considered this, trying to set his bad mood aside. She'd worked hard for tonight—to impress *him*. "I knew you and Hawke were up to something, but I never imagined it would be this. Eight."

"Were you really impressed with my climbing?"

"*That* was a full ten on the blow-me-away scale."

She seemed to bask in his praise, and he wondered how often her old man or Kendra had taken the time to say anything kind to her.

"I cannot wait to get you inside and rip off your clothes."

As it turned out, there were more practical things to see to first. Austin let Lexi have the first shower so he could feed Mack and take him for a short walk. While she blew her hair dry, he washed off the day's sweat and sunscreen, the hot spray doing nothing to clear his mind.

He should end the lie. He should tell her how he felt—all of it.

And if that meant she walked away, and he lost these last two weeks?

Towel around his hips, he stepped out of the bathroom to find her waiting for him in bed. She got up, crossed the room, removed his towel with a yank. Then she surprised him again, dropping to her knees and taking him into the heat of her mouth.

"Jesus." He was hard in an instant because—*damn!*—she was just that good.

He slid his fingers into her hair, gave himself over to her, let his mind go blank.

Lexi was here with him tonight, and that would have to be enough.

*L*exi lay in Austin's arms afterward, her body still singing, her fingers trailing through his chest hair. Sex had been somehow different tonight, more tender, more intense. She wondered about that for a time but soon started to drift. She was almost asleep when he spoke.

"I've been lying to you."

"What?" She opened her eyes.

"I've been lying to both of us. I thought I could do this, but I can't."

Oh, no.

She propped herself up on one elbow, looked down at him, cold fingers closing around her heart. "What do you mean?"

He reached up, brushed a strand of hair from her cheek. "I said I could do this 'friends with benefits' thing, but I can't."

God.

Austin was dumping her. He was dumping her again.

She sat, did her best to face it. "You want to end things."

"God, no." He sat up, the sheet falling to his hips.

Relief washed through her.

"Last time, I pushed you away. I was so upset over the fact that you were leaving that I used the first excuse I could find to end it. It wasn't a conscious thing. I think some part of me just wanted to get the loss behind me. Or maybe it was easier to let you go if I could find a reason to be angry. Who knows? I was an idiot."

He gave a little laugh. "I won't do that this time, but I want you to know that we are no longer *just* friends. We're lovers."

Her heart gave a hard kick. "Austin—"

He leaned over and silenced her with a kiss. "Not long ago, you told me you realized you'd have come back to Scarlet just to be with me. You said you didn't figure that out in time. Well, that was my fault, wasn't it? This time, I'm going to trust you. I'm going to trust in us. But I'm done pretending. You're not my fuck buddy, Lexi. You're the woman I love."

Her heart was thrumming now. She wanted to tell him that he couldn't possibly love her because, if he *did* love her, she would have to face the fact that she loved him, too, and that would turn her entire life upside down.

Was she in love with him, too?

Well, shit!

Chapter Twenty

Austin's alarm woke him. He tried to shut it off before it could wake Lexi, but when he sat up, she sat up too, her cheek coming to rest against his back, her arm sliding around his waist. He laced his fingers through hers. "Morning."

"Morning."

He got dressed while she made coffee and scrambled some eggs. When he came downstairs, she was just putting breakfast on the table—scrambled eggs, toast, sliced cantaloupe, OJ, and lots of coffee. The windows were wide open to let in the fresh morning air, a bank of storm clouds rising over the Indian Peaks to the west.

"Thanks. This is amazing. You didn't have to do this, you know." He didn't want her thinking that a change in their relationship meant that he expected her to take over in the kitchen. He wasn't a Neanderthal.

"I don't mind." She met his gaze for a moment, a new vulnerability in her eyes. "You have a long day ahead of you and need a good breakfast, and I have to eat, too."

Neither of them brought up last night's conversation. She hadn't said a word then, either. She'd just stared at him through wide eyes, reminding him of a cornered rabbit. When he'd held her as they'd fallen asleep, he'd been able to feel her heart pounding. It had made him smile to himself.

He had forced her to face her feelings for him—and she was terrified.

He took a sip of his coffee. "It's Father's Day—"

"Shit. Really?"

He laughed. "We'll be having a big family cookout tonight. You're welcome to come if you want. Chey will be there, of course."

Lexi shook her head. "I should make dinner for my dad. Besides, Cheyenne doesn't want me around. I ran into her in Food Mart. She told me I was your kryptonite."

"What?" *That* pissed him off. "I hope you didn't let that get to you."

He would have to talk with his sister tonight. She was loyal to a fault, but she needed to learn when to keep her opinions to herself.

Lexi shrugged. "I figured if you wanted me out of your life, you'd tell me. You didn't have trouble with that last time."

"Ouch." There was truth in that.

She smiled sweetly over the top of her coffee cup. "Besides, kryptonite makes Superman limp. I do *not* make you limp."

"Um ... no." He couldn't help but laugh. "Do you want a ride home?"

Lexi shook her head. "My car is here. I'll clean this up, take Mack for a walk, and then drive in."

He glanced at his watch, tossed back the last of his orange juice, then got to his feet, quickly making his lunch and tucking it into his pack. "Will I see you tonight?"

He'd meant it when he'd said he wouldn't push her. Given what he'd told her last night, it wouldn't surprise him if she needed some space.

She stood and wrapped her arms around him. "Just try to keep me away."

Her perfect answer melted tension he hadn't realized he was carrying. He tilted her face upward, kissed her. "I'll text when I leave my parents' place."

And then it was time for him to get to work.

He said a quick goodbye to Mack. "You're a lucky little shit. You get to spend the morning with my woman."

He scooped his pack onto his shoulder, gave Lexi a long, slow goodbye kiss and walked out to his Tahoe, his heart feeling lighter than it had in days.

Lexi stood in the greeting card aisle in Food Mart, looking through the Father's Day cards. Given that she and her father were actually getting along, she felt it would be right to honor the day. The only problem was the cards themselves.

The people who made them seemed to think that every father and daughter had a close relationship and a lifetime of happy memories. They didn't take into account the people who cared about their fathers, but rarely got along with them. She settled on a blank card with a wolf on the front and filled it out in the checkout lane.

Dear Dad,

I'm glad we've had this time together. Wishing you a very happy Father's Day.

Love,

Lexi

The house was silent when she got home, last night's dinner dishes still in the sink, the curtains closed despite the fact that it was almost noon.

She set the card and the groceries for tonight's supper on the table. "Dad?"

She found him sitting on the sofa in the living room, a bottle of rum in his hand.

Damn it!

He was drunk again—in the middle of the morning.

"Dad, I thought you'd given this up." She reached for the bottle.

He jerked it away. "Don't!"

The rough, hostile tone of his voice stopped her cold.

"What's wrong?"

"Kendra's divorcin' me." He pointed to papers sitting on the coffee table.

"What?" Lexi picked them up, glanced through them.

Holy shit. Kendra had done it. She'd filed for divorce. And she'd dropped the papers off on Father's Day. What a bitch!

"She wants half the inn." The words were slurred, but Lexi understood.

"I'm so sorry." Lexi sat down beside him.

He glared at her. "This is partly *your* fault. You think you can come here and get into everyone's business. You made it worse."

The words hit Lexi in the face. She fought to push her hurt aside. He'd just gotten devastating news, and he was drunk. There was no sense in getting upset over things he wouldn't remember saying once he was sober. "I can help you pay for an attorney. We can fight this. We can—"

He staggered to his feet. "Don't want your help. You've done enough. Go back to Chicago. I didn't ask for your help. Go live with your sister if you don't have a job."

"I'm not here because I'm broke and need a place to live, Dad."

Why even bother trying to set him straight? It was pointless.

She stood, reached out for him, afraid he was going to pitch onto his face. "You're going to fall if you're not careful. Let me help you get to bed."

He didn't seem to hear her but repeated himself. "Go back to Chicago. I didn't ask you to come here. Go live with your sister."

She reached for him again. "You need to lie down. I'll make some coffee."

He shouted at her, rage on his face. "Leave me 'lone!"

Lexi stepped back from him. "Okay. If that's what you want."

"She wants half the inn. Half of *my* goddamned inn."

Fighting tears, Lexi bolted for her room, slamming and locking the door behind her. She took out her cell phone and called Austin. He was at work and wouldn't get her voicemail for hours, but she knew he'd call her back.

She left a message, trying to keep her voice from shaking, then ended the call and started to pack. If her father didn't want her in his life, she wouldn't impose herself on him. She would move her things to Austin's house. She knew he wouldn't mind. She was practically living with him anyway.

It took a couple of trips to carry her suitcases to her car. She came back inside to check her room, the bathroom, and the laundry for anything she might have left behind. Then she walked back through the kitchen, saw the groceries and the card. She put the food away, then picked up the card.

Tears blurring her vision, she set it on the table, then turned and walked back out to her car. She sat in the driver's seat, setting her handbag down on the floor.

"Are you leaving, Lexi?"

Lexi almost jumped out of her skin. "Rose."

Her neighbor stood next to her open car door in a white gauze bowie blouse and jeans, red beads around her neck. "I heard shouting and came over to see if your father was okay. Oh, but you've been crying. Come here!"

It was a sign of how awful Lexi felt that she actually got out of the car and let herself be swept up in Rose's patchouli embrace.

"Come over to my place, sweetheart. You can tell me all about it."

And to think Lexi had *almost* made it through a visit to Scarlet without getting a Tarot reading.

*O*t was late afternoon before Austin finally got a lunch break. The Team had been toned out to help a kayaker who'd been separated from his kayak while practicing rolls in Middle Scarlet Creek. The RP had seen a kayak floating upside down in the creek and called 911, fearing the worst, and for a time, the swift-water rescue unit had thought they were searching for a body.

As it turned out, the kayaker had washed downstream but had managed to climb onto a pile of logs, branches, and other debris left over from the catastrophic 2013 floods. Beat up and stranded in the middle of the creek, he shouted and waved when he saw rescuers making their way slowly down the water in their own kayaks.

The whole affair had taken place on a stretch of the creek that transected county park land, so Austin had acted as incident commander during the rescue. He'd helped rig a Tyrolean traverse over the pile of debris so that the Team could bring the kayaker out that way. The victim was now en route to the hospital with a suspected head injury and some lacerations that needed stitching.

Whitewater could fuck a person up.

Starving, Austin sat in the shade of ponderosa pines at the Moose Lake picnic area, pulled his lunch out of his pack, and ate, a breeze from the west taking the edge off the heat, driving those storm clouds over the mountains.

They'd have a thunderstorm this afternoon.

His sandwich disappeared far too quickly, and he was glad he'd taken the time to pack some carrot sticks and an apple. While he munched, he dug out his cell phone and saw he had a call from Lexi. He listened to her voicemail.

Hey, Austin. I hate to bother you. My dad is drunk and shouting. Kendra filed for divorce. He says it's partly my fault. He told me to leave. He wants me to go back to Chicago. I can't stand being near him right now, so I'm packing up and heading to your place. I hope that's okay. I know you're at work, but I really wish I could hear your voice, even for a minute.

She'd been upset when she'd left the message, on the verge of tears, her voice shaking. *Damn it!* Austin wished he could drive to the inn, sit the old man down, and give him a piece of his mind. Bob had certainly earned it.

What kind of father blamed his daughter for his marital problems and then threw her out of her home? Bob had turned into an angry drunk. He'd alienated his wife, and he'd lashed out at Lexi—again.

Well, the old man's loss was Austin's gain.

She was moving in with him. That's all there was to it.

He had to admit it touched him that she'd turned to him, that she wanted to hear his voice. He glanced at the time on the message and saw that she'd called more than an hour ago. *Damn.* He wished he'd thought to give her the number for his work phone.

He dialed her number, but she didn't answer. He called his house next, but she didn't pick up there, either. He called her cell phone once more. Still no answer. This time, he left a message.

"Hey, Lexi. I'm so sorry the shit hit the fan with your dad today. He's wrong. None of this is your fault. Of course, you're welcome to stay at my place. You can stay for as long as you need. Make yourself at home, and let Mack cheer you up till I get there. See you later. If you need me, call my work cell phone."

He left her the number, then ended the call with, "I love you."

God, it felt good to say those words.

A tiny chipmunk—*Tamias minimus*—darted out from behind a tree, moving closer in staccato bursts while Austin packed up his garbage, careful to remove the crumbs and other micro-trash that could attract birds and small wildlife.

"Sorry, buddy. You're cute, but I won't feed you."

He looked down in time to see the chipmunk dart between his feet, grab a piece of apple he hadn't realized he'd dropped, then run full-speed for the trees.

"And *that* was chipmunk for, 'Fuck you, human.'"

Lexi reached for another tissue, wiped tears from her face. "Then he told me to get out and go back to Chicago. Can I have more sangria?"

She'd already told Rose everything else, the words spilling out of her—her ordeal at Price & Crane, how she and Austin had gotten back together, what had happened with Kendra and her father.

Rose had actually closed her shop for the afternoon and made her lunch, the whole time listening—really, truly listening—as if she understood exactly how Lexi felt.

"Of course, you can." Rose poured more of the delicious fruity drink from a glass pitcher. "So your dad is drunk again, and he told you to get out."

Lexi nodded. "Is there a lot of alcohol in this?"

"Don't worry about that now, sweetheart."

Lexi was pretty sure there was. Her face felt flushed, her blood warm, but then it was hot outside. "If I could, I'd get in my car and drive back to Chicago right now and never come back again."

"What's stopping you?"

Other than the fact that she was most likely over the legal limit?

"I need to say goodbye to the Team and Winona at the wildlife sanctuary." Her throat got tight, more tears spilling down her cheeks. "And I would have to leave Austin."

"You don't want to say goodbye to any of them, do you?"

Lexi shook her head. "For the first time, I feel like I'm doing something that matters. I feel like I'm a part of something. I feel needed."

"You *are* needed."

But it was more than that. "I love working with Megs and the Team, and I love the animals. It's been the most fun I've had in a long time."

As much as she loved her life in Chicago, it was the truth.

"And what about Austin?"

Lexi rolled her eyes. "Last night, he had to go and make everything worse by telling me he loves me. Can you believe that? Now I don't know what to do because I'm afraid I love him, too."

Rose nodded in understanding. "What you're experiencing, Lexi, my dear, is spiritual dissonance."

"What?" There was a name for feeling torn apart like this?

"Spiritual dissonance." Rose gave her a gentle smile. "It's when your ego wants one thing, but your heart wants another."

"Spiritual diss … disso…" Lexi tried to repeat the term but gave up.

Rose stood, reached for a leather-bound bundle on a nearby shelf. "Fortunately, that's something we can fix. I'm going to smudge you to purify you of all of that old energy. That's what's holding you back."

Lexi watched Rose open the bundle. It held an abalone shell, a braid of grass, and a large dark feather that could only have come from a bald eagle.

"I'm pretty sure that's illegal."

"That's just the paper law," Rose said. "It was given to me by a Lakota medicine man."

Lexi watched while Rose lit the grass braid, said a few words she didn't understand, then wafted the smoke over herself with the feather. Then she did the same to Lexi, walking behind her as if trying to get the smoke on her entire body.

Lexi coughed, took another drink. "Is that marijuana? I don't smoke—"

"No, dear. It's sweetgrass." Rose set the shell and grass braid aside, then carefully bundled up the feather and set it back on the shelf. "You are now in a sacred and safe space. You are free of the energetic entanglements of your past. You can imagine any future you want for yourself."

Whether it was the sangria, the soothing sound of Rose's voice, or something in the sweetgrass, Lexi felt herself relax. "I want to be with Austin. I want to open my own CPA firm. I want to do pro-bono work for the Team and other nonprofits. I want to help at the animal sanctuary. I want to go for walks along the beach, spend time with Vic at museums and concerts, but that's all in Chicago."

She had two worlds, and they were worlds apart.

So Rose helped her draw up a list of pros and cons to living in Scarlet Springs.

Whoa! Was Lexi even considering this?

The cons of staying in Scarlet were obvious: being near her dad and Kendra; missing Vic and Lake Michigan and good pizza; and missing out on all the culture that comes with living in a big city. There were an equal number of pros, but they were big things: being with Austin; doing work that mattered alongside people she admired; having friends again; feeling that she fit in; being able to afford to open her own business; and no damned lawn chairs in parking places when it snowed.

"Seriously?" Rose asked. "They do that?"

A heavy feeling settled in Lexi's chest as she realized where this conversation was leading her. "I feel like a failure. I spent my whole childhood wanting to get away from this place and now..."

"No, dear, I think you spent all your life wanting to get away from your father." Rose reached for her deck of Tarot cards. "Let's see what the cards have to say."

Chapter Twenty-One

By the time Lexi left Rose's, it was almost five in the evening, and the sun had disappeared behind a wall of thick, dark storm clouds, gusts of wind carrying the scent of rain. Austin would be getting off work soon. Had he gotten her message?

She stood in the driveway of the inn, feeling emotionally drained and uncertain what to do. She refused to go back inside the house so that her father could yell at her again, and she wasn't sure she was sober enough to drive to Austin's. Her mother had died because of a drunk driver, and she wouldn't get behind the wheel if there were any chance at all that she could be a danger to others.

What did Rose put in her sangria anyway?

She decided to walk to The Cave and see what was happening. She had an official appointment with Megs tomorrow morning to go over her final report, but that didn't mean she couldn't drop by to say hello.

Fat raindrops started to fall as she hurried along the sidewalk down First, thunder grumbling in the sky above. When she reached Third Street, she glanced over at the wildlife sanctuary, saw Winona's car in the parking lot, and decided to stop there first to get out of the storm. She hurried across the street, calling a quick greeting to Shota, who had taken shelter from the rain inside his dog house. She found the back door unlocked and stepped inside.

She could hear the chatter of raccoons coming from the back. Winona was probably cleaning enclosures or giving the animals their evening feed.

Lexi turned down the hallway—and froze.

Oh God!

Bear lay face down on the floor, unconscious. And Winona. She lay on her back just inside the first treatment room, also unconscious.

What had happened?

Adrenaline mixed with the alcohol in Lexi's bloodstream. She reached into her pocket for her cell phone, but it wasn't there. Had she left it at Rose's?

No, she'd left it in her car.

She hurried over to the wall phone, dialed 911. "I'm at the Aspen Wildlife Sanctuary in Scarlet Springs. We need an ambulance. Two people are hurt. I don't know why. I just found them lying unconscious on the floor and—"

"Hang up."

She whirled toward the man's voice.

John Charles Ready.

Her heart seemed to stop. Her mouth went dry. *"Oh, God."*

Where had *he* come from?

She recognized him from the wanted poster—dark hair, brown eyes, scar on his left cheek. He had a rifle slung over one shoulder, his blue T-shirt stained a strange color of red. His right hand was bandaged, but it was his left hand that held her gaze.

He was pointing a revolver at her, his finger on the trigger.

He reached out, snatched the receiver from her, and hung up.

As if from a distance, Lexi heard her own voice. "It's too late. They're on their way. If you shoot me ..."

"I'm not going to shoot you—not now anyway. Thanks to that fucking call you just made, I need you."

In the distance, she heard sirens.

"What? No! I—"

He shoved the revolver against her breastbone. "You'll do as I say. If you scream or try to get away, things will get bloody. Got it?"

She nodded.

He forced her out the back door, where Shota paced the fence of his enclosure, growling low in his throat. It was in Lexi's mind to loose Shota on him, but the wolf would probably end up getting shot. She couldn't let that happen.

He pressed car keys into Lexi's hand, pointed toward Winona's car. "Get behind the wheel."

Lexi stopped. "I can't drive. I've been drink—"

He shoved her. "Move!"

The sirens drew nearer.

Lexi opened the car, sat in the driver's seat, while he slid into the seat behind her. She started the car, saw that the gas gauge was on empty, but said nothing.

He wanted to abduct her? Fine. Let's see how far he would get on fumes.

Through the seat back she felt the barrel of the revolver nudging her.

"Drive."

Austin was on his way back to the county building, driving through a heavy thunderstorm, when dispatch toned out paramedics for two injured parties. A few minutes later, dispatch toned out the Scarlet Springs PD for an armed robbery and abduction. Concerned now, he listened for the location of the call.

Aspen Wildlife Sanctuary.

What the hell?

Lexi.

Lexi didn't volunteer on Sundays. She couldn't have been there. But Winona, Belcourt's little sister...

Jesus.

"The suspect's name it John Charles Ready. He is wanted for a string of bank robberies and for attempting to shoot a local park ranger."

Austin turned on his overheads, waited till traffic cleared, and flipped a U-Turn. The city of Scarlet wasn't within Austin's jurisdiction, but the people who worked there were his friends. If ready had harmed Winona or any of her volunteers ...

He hadn't gone a mile when his work cell phone rang.

It was Hawke.

Austin's stomach sank.

Shit. This couldn't be good news.

"Pull off the road if you're driving," Hawke said.

Dread closed in on Austin, his pulse picking up.

He kept driving, switched his phone to speaker. "Was Lexi there?"

"You've been following it on the radio?"

Austin felt his teeth grind. "Was Lexi there?"

"Yes. Now, listen to me."

Jesus, no.

Austin felt like he'd just slipped into a bad dream. He drew to the side of the road, put his vehicle in park. "I'm listening."

"We don't have all the details. Lexi found Winona and Bear unconscious here at the sanctuary and dialed 911. Ready was still in the building. He walked up on Lexi and forced her to hang up. Dispatch caught the whole exchange. About that time, Frank at the gas station saw her climb into Winona's car with an armed man fitting Ready's description. He called 911, told dispatch they were headed west up the highway. The sheriff thinks Ready forced his way into the sanctuary to steal drugs and shot up Winona and Bear because gunfire would attract attention. Then Lexi walked in on him and dialed 911, so he took her hostage in case he was pursued."

Lexi taken hostage.

Austin could barely think, but his mouth seemed to work. "Does McBride know?"

"Yeah, he knows. The US Marshal Service and the FBI just pulled up. The sheriff's department and PD are here."

"How about Bear and Winona?"

"They're going to be fine, thanks to Lexi. Winona was close to respiratory arrest when I arrived. Based on the vials I saw on the floor, it looks like Ready injected them with ketamine. They're at the ER."

Jesus.

Austin's mind raced, searching for a way out. "Are they sure Lexi was the RP?"

"I listened to the 911 call myself," Hawke answered. "It was Lexi."

Son of a bitch.

Hawke went on. "There's a BOLO on the car. They're going to hunt him down, and they're going get Lexi back safe and alive."

"Tell McBride I want in."

*L*exi stumbled uphill, wet to the skin and shivering, pine needles and mud slippery beneath her sandals. She wanted to wake up, to open her eyes and discover that this was just a nightmare, a weird dream brought on by too much of Rose's sangria. But the cold and the man with the gun were only too real.

He's going to kill you when he's done with you.

The thought left her feeling dizzy, almost sick, hopelessness seeping through her skin as the ugliness of her reality became apparent to her. He was using her as a hostage, a human shield in case police or federal agents came after him.

Did the police know she was the one who'd called 911? Did they realize she was missing? Did Austin know? What if no one came for her?

Don't think about it now.

Thunder crashed overhead, so near it sounded almost metallic, blue-white flashes of lightning all around her. The car had run out of gas on a forest access road about ten miles west of town. At first, Ready had thought Lexi was faking the empty gas tank and had been incensed. He'd held a gun to her head, threatening to kill her if she didn't get moving. When he'd realized that the tank truly was empty, he'd backed off.

Thank God for that at least.

He forced Lexi to hike straight up the mountainside. There was nothing up there but more forest, so where was he taking her?

She knew better than to ask. He'd made it clear more than once now that he'd kill her if she caused trouble. He'd already hurt two of her friends. He was also sick and in pain—and that was making him short-tempered and mean.

They'd been hiking up the mountainside for maybe ten minutes when Lexi had no choice but to stop and catch her breath. Fortunately, he was breathing hard, too.

A burst of thunder made her gasp. "It's not safe ... to be out ... in a thunderstorm."

"You think I'm afraid ... of lightning?" He sneered at her, breathing hard. "Get moving."

She trudged onward, the climb arduous, her feet slipping with each step. She was afraid he'd shoot her if she fell or didn't move fast enough. She glanced back over her shoulder, saw that he was struggling to keep up with her, his face flushed. With that hand as infected as it was, she wouldn't be surprised if he had a fever.

Could she exhaust him or make him collapse?

It was worth a try.

Bit by bit, she quickened her pace, her gaze on the mountainside above her.

Click.

"Stop!"

She turned to find him struggling for breath, the cocked revolver pointing right at her. She glared at him. "You tell me to go … and then you tell me to stop."

She waited while he caught up with her, rainwater running in rivulets down her legs, pooling in the little indentations her sandals left in the rocky soil. At least it was raining. On a dry day, she wouldn't have left footprints at all.

"I should have shot you up and brought the other girl," he said when he'd caught up with her. "She at least knew how to keep quiet."

The storm slowly passed to the east, leaving the forest soaked and silent. And then she heard it—the rotors of a helicopter.

He jabbed her in the back with the barrel of the revolver, pointed to what looked like the entrance to an abandoned mine shaft about twenty yards to their right, yellowish mine tailings heaped around it. "Over there. Now. Run!"

She did as he demanded, knowing he was right behind her, but when she got to the small, dark opening, she stopped. No way. "We can't go in there. It's a mine shaft. There could be deep holes or—"

"That's why you're going first. If you fall, I'll stop." When she didn't move, he fired a shot, striking the ground near her feet, making her scream. "Get inside."

The blast echoing in her ears, Lexi bent down and stepped into the pitch darkness, one thought rising above her adrenaline.

Rose sure hadn't seen this in her cards.

By the time Austin reached the wildlife sanctuary, the place was surrounded by reporters, police tape cordoning off the entire grounds. It looked like most of Scarlet was there, too, a crowd standing across the street. They weren't just there to gawk. Scarlet Springs was a small town, and when something bad happened to someone, it touched almost everyone one way or another.

He parked his service vehicle down the road, pushed his way through the news crews, then ducked under the police tape, fighting to control his emotions.

Do not lose your shit. Do not lose your shit. Do not fucking lose your shit.

If McBride or Sutherland thought he was too shaken up to do his job, they would sideline him. He'd have to sit on his ass at incident command rather than playing an active role in the search. He couldn't let that happen.

He found Hawke and his crew packing their first-aid gear into the red and white rescue truck and strode over to them. "Anything new?"

Hawke shook his head. "I'm just the fire chief, buddy. They're not keeping me in the loop. McBride asked me some questions. He seems to agree that Ready took Lexi hostage in case the cops went after him."

Austin could think of a lot of reasons a violent criminal like Ready would want to take a woman captive, and he didn't like a single one of them. "Where is McBride?"

"He's around back." Hawke stopped him with a palm in the center of his chest. "Man, you've got to pull yourself together. Get that look out of your eyes."

"What look?"

"The one that says your entire world is on the line here. The one that tells me you want to find Ready and rip him to pieces."

That's exactly what Austin wanted to do. "He's going to pay for this."

"Damn straight. But first, we focus on finding Lexi."

Austin took a deep breath, nodded. "If anything happens to her…"

"Lexi is tougher than she looks. She'll be okay."

"Yeah." Austin couldn't let himself imagine any other outcome, not if he wanted to help her. "Want to ride along?"

"You think they'll let you in?"

"I'm not giving them a choice."

"I'm coming, too." Belcourt walked up to the tape barricade, his brown eyes blazing. "That bastard almost killed my sister."

The two men walked with him to the rear entrance of the building, Hawke catching him up on other things along the way. "They've closed Knockers. Rain went to the hospital with Bear, said he ought to have someone be family for him. Megs has the Team on standby in case they're needed. Kenzie and Gizmo are also on standby. Everyone is doing all they can."

Until Lexi was safe, no one was doing enough.

They found McBride on the phone, a couple of FBI agents standing nearby, the sheriff's CSI unit still processing the crime scene.

McBride saw him, ended the call. "Taylor, I'm glad you're here. I just got confirmation that a state trooper found the stolen vehicle about ten miles west of here."

Thank God!

Do not lose your shit.

"That's good news."

McBride showed him the exact location on an electronic pad. "It's parked here on a forest access road that runs through county land. Are you familiar with the area?"

McBride didn't seem to know that Austin and Lexi were connected.

Austin nodded. "Yes. There's not much up there—just open space."

"I could use your help. You can follow us up."

Austin was on his way back to his service vehicle, Hawke beside him, when he heard Rose calling for him.

Shit.

The last thing he wanted was the latest gossip or a psychic prediction—unless, of course, she could tell him where to find Lexi.

She waited for him at the tape barricade, then shoved something in his hands—a piece of paper. "Lexi spent the afternoon at my place. She was pretty torn up about what happened with her dad. I tried to cheer her up. We talked for a few hours. I thought you should have this."

Austin looked at it—a list of pros and cons. It took him a moment to realize what they represented. Lexi was thinking about staying in Scarlet?

Rose patted his arm. "Whatever happens, you should know that Lexi loves you."

*C*old to the bone, Lexi crouched down in the pitch black, the air heavy with an unfamiliar stench, unseen somethings brushing against her damp skin and hair.

Cobwebs? Spiderwebs?

Something rustled overhead, a chorus of tiny squeaks coming from above them.

Bats.

Oh, God.

She tried not to think about that. The real problem wasn't the creatures that might be living here—which, by the way, probably included snakes. *Ew.* The problem was the monster behind her and the very real risk of having the ground vanish from beneath her feet. Some of these old mines went hundreds of feet down. Without light, she wouldn't be able to tell whether her next step would land her on terra firma or tumble her into a deep ventilation shaft.

"Don't you at least have a flashlight or a lighter or something?" Her voice echoed—proof that this mine went deep.

Icy fingers dug into her arm. "It's in my bag. Hang on. And don't you even think about trying to get away from me."

She could hear him digging through his junk, bats that had been disturbed in their sleep stirring above them.

Click.

Light flooded the space.

Lexi bit back a gasp, her pulse rocketing.

The passage they stood in was narrower than she'd imagined, a bat colony numbering in the thousands no more than a foot above their heads. Guano covered the rocky floor—that explained the stench—while slender roots tangled with spider webs all around her. Bending lower, Lexi moved forward.

She'd gone maybe twenty feet, when the ground ahead of her dropped away, a ventilation shaft shored up with rotting timbers opening at her feet.

Instinctively, she stepped backward. "That's as far as we go."

Ready sat on a stone not far from the shaft's edge and pointed to the place beside him. "Sit."

"I'm not sitting there."

He grinned. "Don't tell me you're afraid of heights."

"No, of course not. You have BO."

He gave a snort but said nothing.

She sat back against the rock wall on what looked like the remains of a railway tie, just beyond his reach and out of sight of the edge.

He didn't object. "Not a sound."

He turned off the flashlight, plunging them once again into darkness, the only light coming from the mine's small opening ten yards away.

From outside, Lexi could hear the drone of the helicopter's rotors. Had the pilot spotted Winona's car? Did she even want police to find it, given what might happen? She had no doubt this bastard would open fire on anyone who entered the mine after them. She didn't want innocent people to die trying to rescue her.

If she'd been brave, she would have picked up a rock and hurled it at Ready's head—or kicked him backward into the shaft. Now it was too dark to see him anyway.

She wrapped her arms around herself, still shivering.

The sound of the helicopter's rotors got fainter, then disappeared.

It was gone.

She didn't know whether to feel relief or despair.

Time passed, minutes creeping by like hours. She wanted to ask him what he'd done to Bear and Winona and why he'd shot at Austin, but he didn't seem like the kind of bad guy you saw in the movies who filled up gaps in the conversation by telling you why he'd done all the evil things he'd done in his life.

It was then she noticed that her left foot—the foot nearer to Ready—was sinking as if the earth had turned into quicksand or…

There came a knocking sound.

Clunk. Clunk. Clunk.

No!

She leaped up and ran toward the mine's entrance, but it was too late. There was nothing beneath her feet, nothing to grab onto, no way to pull herself to safety. She heard herself scream. Ready screamed, too, rock and rotted timbers groaning.

Darkness swirled around her as she fell.

Chapter Twenty-Two

Austin reached the abandoned vehicle ahead of the feds and parked right behind it, the state trooper who'd called it in waving as he drove up.

"That's my sister's car for sure," Belcourt said.

Hawke, who had crammed himself into the vehicle's narrow backseat, followed Austin out of the driver's side door, while Belcourt hopped out on the passenger side. The three of them hurried over to the car.

Austin introduced himself to the trooper who said his name was Stewart, then looked in through the open driver's side window.

"No blood." Hawke said what he was thinking. "No sign of violence."

"Yeah." Austin wanted this bastard.

"I was catching speeders down on the highway and using this road to loop back around after each stop when this car just showed up," said Stewart. "One minute it wasn't there. Twenty minutes later it was. I'd just heard the BOLO and realized it was the car everyone was looking for, so I called it in."

"Did you see where the occupants went?" Austin asked.

Stewart shook his head. "The car was empty when I found it."

Damn it.

McBride came up behind them. "Good work, trooper."

Stewart shook his hand. "I think you all should know, I heard a gunshot and a scream about ten minutes ago. The search chopper—"

Austin's heart hit his breastbone. "Gunshot?"

Son of a bitch. *Lexi.*

"Yeah." Stewart pointed up the mountainside. "Sounded like a handgun to me. I'd have gone to check it out, but I figured I'd better wait for backup."

Fuck.

"You did the right thing." McBride looked over at Austin. "Taylor, you and I need to talk."

Austin exchanged a glance with Hawke and Belcourt, then followed McBride to the other side of the road.

"Your boss tells me you and Ms. Jewell are involved."

"What does that have to do with anything?"

"Don't you think that's something you ought to have disclosed at the outset? I can't have you up here if there's any chance that your emotions are going to impede your judgment. You know that."

"Have you seen any sign that my judgment is impaired?"

"Other than your passing my vehicle going eighty miles an hour?"

Okay, McBride had him there.

"Sorry about that." He laid his cards on the table. "I love her. I can't let this bastard hurt her. Every second he's alone with her, there's a chance..."

He couldn't even say it.

McBride studied him for a moment, mirrored sunglasses concealing his eyes. "I know what it means to love a woman and to want to protect her. I'll let you be a part of this only so long as you hold it together. Pull another stupid stunt like that or put yourself or someone else at risk, and I'll have you forcibly removed. Got it?"

"Got it."

Forest County SWAT arrived, followed by Kenzie and Gizmo, the minutes seeming to drag on while McBride and the cops discussed options and made plans. Lexi was out there somewhere, perhaps shot, maybe even dying. A fucking eternity had gone by before everyone had geared up and was ready to move out.

Kenzie was carrying something in an evidence bag—Lexi's yellow Team T-shirt. She took it out, let Gizmo sniff it, then led the dog over to the car. He jumped inside, sniffed around, then hopped out and set off down the road, following the little gully, his paws splashing in the storm runoff.

They'd gone perhaps a quarter of a mile, when Kenzie stopped the dog. She looked back at them. "It's the rain."

"The rain?" McBride asked.

"Water holds scent well, but in this terrain the trail Gizmo is picking up might easily have come from somewhere else. We should make certain they didn't go off the road somewhere uphill from this drainage. Otherwise, we'll just be following the scent caught in the runoff and not our quarry."

Damn it.

Belcourt's shout came from behind them. "They went this way!"

Austin turned to find him standing on the mountainside above the vehicle.

"Who is he?" McBride asked.

"He tracks for the Rocky Mountain SAR," Austin lied.

Hawke shot him a sidelong glance, spoke in a whisper. "You do remember that he's a federal agent, right?"

Austin shrugged. "What the hell else was I supposed to say? 'He's an engineering geek who climbs rocks and volunteers for the Team, and, by the way, he says he cuts sign and Ready assaulted his sister'? That would get him a one-way ticket out of here. He deserves to be in on this as much as anyone."

"No argument there."

Austin followed Kenzie as she led Gizmo back up the road, climbing the embankment toward Belcourt, where two sets of footprints were visible in the mud.

And immediately Gizmo was off, Kenzie behind him. "Let's find her, boy."

Lexi held onto a twisted bit of rail with all her strength, two thoughts breaking through her pain and panic. She was still alive, and she was no longer falling.

Okay. That's good.

She had landed … on something hard and wooden. It was so dark that she couldn't see her own hands, much less what was around or beneath her. Afraid to move, she let go with her left hand and reached slowly out to feel around her.

To her right, there was rock. To her left and in front of her, nothing as far as she could reach. Below her, there were wooden support beams and then… nothing.

Oh, God.

Reflexively, she grabbed onto the iron rail again, her heart slamming so hard that it hurt, terror making her mind go blank. Her jerky motions made whatever was beneath her move, too, made it bob and bounce. And for a time, she sat there, pressed up against the rock, afraid to breathe, her hands clutching at cold iron.

Apart from whatever she'd landed on, she seemed to be sitting in midair.

Slowly, her terror began to recede, chased away in part by pain. Her right leg hurt horribly. She reached down with her left hand and felt a painful bulge in the middle of her shin. It really *was* broken.

And, no, she couldn't get dizzy and pass out thinking about that because she had no idea where she would end up if she fell off this little platform. Solid ground might be a few feet below her—or it might be hundreds of feet down.

Then it hit her: Where was Ready?

"Hey, jerk, are you there?" Her voice echoed through the pitch black.

Silence. Not even the squeaking of bats.

She was alone.

A surge of panic overtook her again, left her feeling sick.

No, she couldn't do this. She couldn't fall apart.

They would find her. They would find Winona's car, and that would lead them to search the area. They would see the tracks she and Ready had made. Or maybe they'd bring in search dogs. The dogs would follow their trail here. Even if they didn't know she'd been the one who'd called 911 or that Ready had abducted her, they'd come this way because the dogs would catch his scent.

All she had to do was stay alive until they got to her.

She could do that—if she didn't fall asleep and if whatever she had landed on didn't break free and if there wasn't another cave-in that buried her or sent her plummeting into the darkness below.

Don't think about it.

Right. Because there were so many other things to think about sitting here in total darkness over a chasm with a broken leg and bat poop in her hair and probably splinters in her butt.

Oh, Austin.

An image of his face filled her mind, put an ache in her chest, tears stinging her eyes. He'd bared his heart to her last night, and she hadn't said a thing. She'd been so freaked out that she hadn't told him how she felt about him. Now, she might never get that chance.

Did he know she was missing? He was probably in his parents' backyard now grilling steaks and enjoying Father's Day with his dad. But he would figure out something was wrong. When she didn't return his calls and didn't show up at his place, he would come looking for her.

Her father probably had no idea. He probably didn't…

Lexi felt herself start to slide. Her head jerked up. She reached up, her hands closing tightly around the iron rail.

When had she started to drift off?

She must be in shock or hypothermic or something, because she was shaking.

Stay awake. Stay awake. Stay awake.

She tried talking to herself, but she'd started to drift off again, the motion of the beams she was sitting on rousing her once more, cold sweat dripping down her forehead. Or was that water? Was it still raining? She was thirsty.

Snap out of it!

If she couldn't stay awake, she was dead.

She'd started to drift off again, when she noticed a glow. And there beside her was a small man. Dressed like a miner from the old days, he knelt there in the darkness, worry on his sweat-stained face, a candle stuck to his helmet.

She gaped at him, astonished. "Who…"

He grinned. "'allo, me purty. Ye don' 'aff to be afeard. This 'ere be Cousin Jack."

A ustin kept close to Belcourt, who truly knew how to track.

"She was moving faster than he was." Belcourt pointed to faint footprints. "She stopped here, turned back to look at him. Then they headed off that way at a run."

Gizmo sniffed at a particularly deep footprint.

"The water pooled up here," Kenzie explained.

Then Gizmo, too, veered off in the direction Belcourt had pointed, moving faster up the muddy mountainside on his four legs than most of the men, who were weighted down with Kevlar and assault weapons, were able to do.

And then they saw it—the entrance to a mine shaft.

Kenzie held Gizmo back, while Belcourt moved silently forward, crouching near the forest floor. He nodded, made his way back to them.

"They're in there."

Word passed quickly through the LEOs on the mountainside, somehow reaching the throng of townspeople who had gathered below, the buzz of whispers like a breeze.

Quickly and silently, McBride's men and SWAT moved into position surrounding the mine shaft's entrance, careful to stay clear of it.

McBride stood off to the side, out of the line of fire, a bullhorn in hand. "John Charles Ready, this is Chief Deputy US Marshal Zach McBride. I know you're in there, and I know you have Lexi Jewell."

Nothing.

McBride shouted again.

This time, Austin heard it—Lexi's voice. It was faint and sounded far away. She was ... singing.

It took Hawke stepping into Austin's path to hold him back. "We're here. We'll help her. Just wait."

Wait? Fuck that!

McBride knelt down, used the bullhorn again. "Ms. Jewell, is Ready with you?"

The singing stopped. Lexi called back, Austin catching only one word: dead.

Ready was dead?

McBride shouted back. "Did you say he's dead? Are you able to walk out to us?"

She was singing again.

Austin didn't like that at all. He'd seen people act this way when they were badly wounded and deeply in shock, their minds taking them to a different place to help them cope with pain and fear.

Hang on, Lexi.

With a few quiet words, McBride had two of his men move closer to the entrance, one with a flashlight, one with a tricked-out AR-15. They looked inside, clearly suspecting a trap of some sort.

No one opened fire.

They turned back to McBride, shook their heads.

Austin walked over to McBride. "If you need someone to do recon, I volunteer."

"You do realize Ready could have forced her to say he was dead. He could be sitting back there somewhere with his rifle aimed at the entrance."

"Is he also forcing her to sing? I think she's hurt. You heard Trooper Stewart. He heard a gunshot. She could be bleeding out. Let me go in and find out what's going on. If he *is* dead, then we can focus on getting her to safety."

And, God, Austin hoped with all his heart that the bastard *was* dead.

"Okay, but we have to be smart about this," McBride said. "I don't want you just running in there."

"Running into a mine shaft? Are you crazy?" He turned to Belcourt and Hawke and started removing all non-essentials from his duty belt. "Did anyone bring rope? I need an anchor."

Belcourt gave him a nod. "On it."

Hawke reached for his hand mic. "I'm calling for dispatch to tone out the Team."

Austin shrugged out of his pack, dug out his waist and chest harnesses, and put them on, turning to Hawke for a quick safety check. Then he grabbed his helmet and headlamp and tied into the rope that Belcourt had gotten from someone.

It felt good finally to be able to *do* something.

By the time he was ready to go, Belcourt had anchored the other end of the rope to a tree, feeding it through his fancy brake plate. "Belay is on."

Austin moved to the entrance of the mine shaft, his semi-auto in hand. "Lexi, can you hear me? I'm coming in for you."

She was still singing. *"The blackbirds and thrushes sang in the green bushes/The wood doves and larks seemed to mourn for the maid."*

He crouched down and moved carefully through the entrance.

The light from his headlamp illuminated the space, but Austin didn't see her. He didn't see Ready for that matter either. Bats, guano, tree roots.

"Lexi?" He moved slowly forward, Belcourt feeding him slack.

Her singing stopped. "Austin? Jack said you were here. I'm down here. There was a cave-in. Jack says Ready's dead."

"Who's Jack?"

"He helped me."

Austin could tell from her voice that she was in shock. He reached for his hand mic. "Fifty-six-twenty to McBride. Have paramedics standing by."

He took another step, saw that the ground fell away some twenty feet ahead of him, a collapsed ventilation shaft opening up before him.

But where the hell was Lexi?

She screamed.

"Lexi?" He jerked at the rope, hurried forward, stopping when he saw her.

Jesus God!

His stomach dropped to the ground, his knees almost buckling.

She sat on what was left of a mangled rail line, a few wooden ties and a twisted bit of iron all that kept her from falling into the shaft, which was so deep that the light from Austin's headlamp didn't reach the bottom.

He holstered his weapon, jerked his gaze back to Lexi. She looked around, as if she'd only just discovered where she was.

His headlamp.

She'd been in total dark until he'd come along, unable to see the actual extent of the danger she was facing. But if she passed out now, she would die.

He willed the fear out of his voice, tried to calm her. "I'm right here, Lexi. Look at me. Look at me!"

She looked up, the terror on her tear-stained face tugging at him. "Austin?"

There were blood and dirt on her forehead and a bulge on her shin that could only come from a displaced fracture. She was hurt and in shock.

"We're going to get you out of here, but I need more gear." He wouldn't leave her. "Fifty-six-twenty to McBride."

McBride responded. "Fifty-six-twenty, go ahead."

"No sign of Ready. Lexi is suspended over a drop that must be at least eighty yards deep. I can't see the bottom. She's injured, in shock, and hanging on by a few beams of rotted wood. I'm going to rap down and tie her into the rope."

He needed to move fast, or Lexi would die.

"*Her cheeks blushed like roses, her arms full of posies/She strayed in the meadows and, weeping, she said/My heart it is aching, my poor heart is breaking/For Jimmy will be slain in the wars I'm afraid.*"

Lexi kept singing like Jack had told her, but it was getting harder— harder to think, to concentrate. Her fingers were numb from holding so tightly to the iron rail. Sometimes, she was sure she was dreaming, her thoughts detached, as if all of this were happening to someone else.

"Stay with me, Lexi."

Lexi's head snapped up at the sound of Austin's voice. But where was Jack? "You scared Jack away."

"Talk to her, Hawke," Austin said, standing near the edge now, about to step off. "Don't let her drift off."

He started down.

"Scared who away?" Eric asked.

"Cousin Jack. He told me to keep singing."

"Oh. Right. Well, we're here now. The whole town is out there." Eric's head appeared above her. He was lying on his belly, looking down at her. "They've gathered along the road. They made it hard for the ambulance to get through. They're all pulling for you."

Lexi swallowed. "Really?"

Had she been dreaming? How long had she been here?

"Your dad is giving the cops hell. He's shouting at everyone, asking them why no one is doing anything to help his little girl."

"My father is here?" That put a lump in her throat.

"Yes, he is. Kendra's there with him, yelling at him to calm down."

Lexi could just imagine that.

"How do you feel?"

"My leg hurts." That was an understatement. "I feel … strange."

"I need you to stay awake, okay? Sing if you have to. It looks like you have a nasty break, but we're going to take good care of you."

She started singing again, watching as Austin rappelled toward her. A few more minutes, and he was even with her, just beyond her feet.

"Stay where you are, Lexi. Don't try to get to me. I'll come to you."

She kept singing, the words helping her to hold on. *"As I was a-walking for my recreation/A-down by the gardens I silently strayed."*

Austin moved quickly across the rock, avoiding any contact with the mangled shelf of wood and iron that had saved her life.

"Hang on just a little longer." Eric's voice was soothing. "Taylor, the rope is getting caught on—"

"I see it."

And then Austin was there, hanging from the rope beside her, his headlamp blinding her. "I'm here, Lexi, but don't move just yet. I'm going to get you out of here, but I need to get you into a harness first and get your weight on the rope. Just sit still. You're doing great."

She started to tell him there was no way she could put on a climbing harness, but then he took out a long strip of nylon webbing.

"I'm making an emergency webbing harness." He sounded so calm as he went to work, wrapping the strap around each thigh, passing it between her legs twice, then encircling her waist several times.

"That's a fancy trick," she heard herself say.

He clipped it off with a carabiner, attached her to the D-ring of his harness, then reached up and peeled her hands from the iron rail. "I've got you now, sweetheart."

Eric's voice came from above him. "Scarlet FD to McBride. He's got her harnessed and clipped in."

"You came for me." Still, she didn't dare move.

"Of course, I did. We're going to stay here for now." He pulled a small square of shiny silver something from his gear belt, unfolding what turned out to be an emergency blanket and wrapping it around her shoulders and head as best he could. "Rescue One is here. The Team will set up ropes and send down a litter. I'll ride up with you."

"I thought … I thought I was going to die here."

Warm lips pressed a kiss against her cheek. "No way."

She sank against him, her head resting against his chest, and drifted off until pain jerked her awake again. She knew when Megs got there, heard Austin ask someone to send down a med kit with morphine, saw Eric and Megs lowering a litter down to her.

"This is going to help with the pain," Austin said.

She felt the prick of a needle, warmth sliding into her, pain and fear melting away.

When she opened her eyes again, she was lying in the litter, immobilized by an inflatable body cast, Eric and Megs at her head and feet, Austin perched above her on the litter. "Let's get her out of here."

And then they were moving upward, the litter swinging slightly.

Hands reached out, guided the litter over the edge and onto solid ground. Megs, Eric, and Austin stepped off one at a time, the confined space illuminated by a half-dozen headlamps.

"The bats," she heard herself say.

"What about them?" Austin asked.

"They're gone."

"I believe they've flown off to more private accommodations," Megs said.

"Jack is gone, too."

"Who?" Megs asked.

"He taught me that song. He had a funny hat with a candle on it."

Then Conrad, Jesse, and Sasha appeared. Together with Megs, Eric, and Austin, they lifted the litter and carried her out of the mine and into twilight.

It was the most beautiful thing Lexi had ever seen—the forest, the fresh air, the sunset turning the sky above the pine trees a bright shade of pink.

Cheers went up all around her.

"Let's construct the evac anchor and let the paramedics work on her," Megs said.

They set the litter down, Austin staying beside her, taking her hand in his.

"You'll be at the hospital soon," he said.

She turned her head, saw a crowd gathered on the mountainside below. She recognized most of them. Rose was there. Cheyenne was there, too, with Austin's parents. Rain and Lark. Mrs. Beech. Sandrine and her husband. Frank from the gas station. Izzy from the sandwich shop. The rest of the Team. The guy with the bushy beard who ran the marijuana store.

The whole town really had turned out.

"I want to see her!" Her father appeared at her side, knelt down next to her, reached out to touch her cheek. "Damn, Lexi girl, you gave me a fright."

Why were there tears in his eyes?

"I'm okay," she managed to say.

She started to sing again, her mind drifting.

From far away, she heard her father's voice.

"Her mother sang that song to her when she was a baby. I didn't know she remembered it." He bent down, kissed her forehead—the first time he'd ever done that. "Where are those damned paramedics?"

But it wasn't her mother who'd taught her the song.

"Cousin Jack…" She couldn't keep her eyes open. "He taught me the song."

Eric spoke somewhere nearby. "She keeps talking about Jack. From the way she describes him, he sounds like a knocker."

A knocker? Of course! Jack was a knocker.

The last thing Lexi heard before she lost consciousness was her father thanking Austin and Megs and the rest of the Team.

Chapter Twenty-Three

Austin helped paramedics load Lexi in the ambulance, stepping aside so that her father could ride with her. "I'll see you at the hospital."

Her father nodded. "Thanks."

The doors closed, and the ambulance headed down the access road, passing dozens of parked cars.

Megs walked over to him, still wearing her helmet and harness.

"She's going to be okay—thanks to you." She patted him on the arm in a grandmotherly way, then hiked back up the hillside.

Austin followed her to where McBride and the rest of the Team had gathered, discussing what to do next—how best to retrieve Ready's body and whether they should do it now or wait until morning.

McBride saw him and stuck out his hand. "Good work. Thanks for your help. What's this about the other person she saw in there?"

"I think she hallucinated a knocker."

"A knocker?"

Austin did not have time for this. He needed to get to the hospital. Still, McBride had let him go after her, so he bit back his impatience and explained.

"Most of the people who live in Scarlet Springs are descended from Cornish miners. They brought the legend of the tommyknockers with them. Some people say knockers are the spirits of dead miners. Others think they're like fairies or leprechauns. In the old days, miners used to toss them their crusts, believing that the knockers would warn them if there was going to be a cave-in."

McBride's brow furrowed. "She says she saw one?"

"She was in shock in total darkness. I think her mind must have conjured this Jack fellow up to help her stay awake. She grew up with the legend, so…"

What other explanation could there be?

The boss man came up behind Austin. "Your shift is over, Taylor. Get yourself cleaned up, get something to eat, and go be with Lexi."

Relieved, Austin reached for his hand mic. "Fifty-six-twenty, end of shift."

"Fifty-six-twenty, good night. Twenty-forty-eight."

Eight-forty-eight PM already.

These three hours had taken a dozen years off his life.

He hiked down the hill to his vehicle and found Hawke waiting for him.

"Can I catch a ride back to town with you?"

They headed down the highway, neither of them speaking for a time.

"What do you think?" Hawke asked at last. "Do you think she saw a knocker?"

Austin glared at him. "Have you heard anything about Bear or Winona?"

Hawke nodded. "Bear is conscious. It looks like Ready quit living in that cave after his encounter with you and moved in with Bear, forcing Bear to help him. The bastard had burned his hand on the dye pack and was having trouble taking care of himself. Bear didn't know he was a fugitive."

"Does Bear even understand what a fugitive is?" Austin doubted it.

"No clue." Hawke went on. "Bear said he saw Ready kill that doe. He took the fawn back to his cabin. When Ready threatened to kill and eat the fawn, too, Bear brought it to town."

"That's when Lexi and I ran into him."

These are bad times, dark times. The End Times.

Bear had been trying in his own weird and completely ineffective way to let Austin know that something was wrong. If he'd just come out and told Austin…

Damn it.

"Why did Ready go to the wildlife sanctuary?"

"His burns got infected. He told Bear he needed medicine but couldn't go to a hospital and asked him where he could get help."

"So Bear took him to Winona." That sounded like Bear.

"Ready forced Winona to treat him, then drew up a syringe of ketamine for her and Bear. He didn't want anyone to call the police until he'd gotten far away, so he injected them."

"That's when Lexi walked in."

"Ready probably thought he needed a hostage to ensure his getaway, thanks to that call. So he took her. But he didn't check to make sure there was gas in Winona's car. He'd have been hell and gone with Lexi if not for that."

Jesus.

"Thanks for backing me up and helping me get down to her. If she'd lost consciousness… If I had lost her…"

"I was glad to help." Hawke glanced over at him, the two of them making eye contact for a moment. "Seeing her down there scared the shit out of me, too."

Lexi awoke in the recovery room, sound and light crashing in on her. There was an oxygen tube beneath her nose and a couple of IVs dripping into her arm.

What had happened?

"Hey, there. I'm Janice. I'm your nurse. Are you feeling any pain?"

"No."

"You were in surgery for about two hours. The doctor had to put a plate and some screws in your tibia. They gave you a nerve block, so that will help keep your discomfort under control for a while."

She'd broken her leg?

And then she remembered.

Ready. The cave-in. The oppressive darkness. The chasm below her.

Adrenaline brought her fully awake, chased the sluggishness from her mind.

But she remembered other things, too. Austin risking himself to come for her, clipping her to his harness, holding her in the dark. The Team working as fast as they could, lifting her out on the litter, carrying her out of the mine. The crowd on the hillside cheering to see she was safe. So many people.

And her father…

Tears gathered in her eyes, blurred her vision.

"We're also treating you for rabies—something we do anytime a person comes as close as you did to bats. You've had the first injections already, so there are just three to go." The nurse bent over her, patted her arm. "You sure had a rough day."

Yes, she had. But Austin, her friends on the Team, the people of Scarlet, even her father—they'd been there for her.

And Cousin Jack…

Who was he? Where had he come from?

From the way she described him, he sounds like a knocker.

Had she seen a real knocker?

"Your dad and stepmom are in the waiting room. Once we get a room assignment for you, we'll move you upstairs, and you can see them. The doc wants to keep you overnight."

"Okay." Not that it was really up to Lexi at this point.

She drifted off again and awoke in a hospital room.

Her father was sitting beside her. He hadn't shaved. His hair was a mess, his eyes bloodshot, but, damn, was she ever glad to see him. "How's my girl?"

Just those words put a lump in her throat. "I'm okay."

"The doctor says you're going to be just fine once this heals. You're going to be stuck with that boot for six weeks or so. That's not too bad, is it?"

Compared to dying in a dank mine shaft? "No."

"I got your card. Thanks." He seemed to struggle for words.

Her Father's Day card. She'd forgotten about it.

"I'm sorry for whatever I said this morning." He cleared his throat. "I didn't mean it. That was rum talking, not me."

"I know." Still, the apology felt good.

"Hey, Lexi." Kendra sat in a chair near the window. Wearing a T-shirt and jeans and not a stitch of makeup, she got to her feet and walked hesitantly toward the bed, as if she wasn't sure she was welcome. She reached out, patted Lexi's hand, and Lexi could see she'd been crying. "You sure did give us a scare."

"Sorry."

"It's not your fault." Her dad cleared his throat. "I want you to know I quit drinking. For real this time."

"You … you did?" That was news.

"I made God a promise. If He got you out of that damned mine alive and in one piece, I wouldn't touch the bottle again—except on special occasions."

She frowned at that last part. "You'll have to keep your word."

"Exactly," said Kendra, pointedly.

"Austin is out in the hall. I promised him I'd let him know when you were awake—if you feel like seeing him, that is." Her dad grinned.

"Quit teasing the poor girl, Bob," Kendra said. "You know she does."

Austin must have been right outside the door. He poked his head in and walked over to her, bending down to kiss her cheek. "Hey. How do you feel?"

He'd been home and had a shower, his jaw clean-shaven.

"A bit loopy. They gave me a nerve block or something. I can't feel my leg."

"Good." He smiled, but the smile didn't quite reach his eyes.

She reached up, cupped his jaw. "Thank you. Thank you for coming down there after me. I was so afraid."

She stopped there, unable to say more, the aftermath of terror still sharp.

"You weren't the only one." He took her hand, kissed it, warm fingers stroking hers. "When I saw you down there … I've never been that afraid in my life. Jesus."

"You didn't act like you were afraid."

"No? Well, just watch. Come February, I'll be up for an Oscar."

"The whole town was there."

He nodded. "I'd say only about half of it. They closed Knockers, then reopened to celebrate after you were safe. Joe came up with a new drink in your honor, and the first round was on the house for Team members and law enforcement. Or so I was told. I wasn't there."

"Really?" That was so sweet.

"We care about our own in this town."

A rush of warmth passed through her at those words.

"Do you want to know what he named the drink?" Austin asked.

Uh-oh. "Okay. Sure. Tell me."

"The Sexy Lexi."

Lexi smiled. "That nickname is going to haunt me for the rest of my life."

"Blame Hawke."

"Puh-lease! I know it wasn't just Eric."

"What? You think I had anything to do with that?" His look of feigned innocence was comical. "Okay, guilty as charged."

She had to know. "Did they find him? Did they find Ready?"

Austin nodded. "He was at the bottom of the shaft."

"What about Jack? He stayed with me. He taught me that song. If not for him…" She could see from the looks on their faces that they didn't believe Jack was real. "I just imagined him, didn't I?"

"Yeah." Austin gave her hand a gentle squeeze. "The mind does amazing things to protect us."

"He seemed so real."

Her father smiled. "Your mother used to sing 'The Blackbirds and the Thrushes' when she rocked you to sleep. I can't believe you remembered it. It's an old mining song that was popular in these parts. Whoever Jack might have been, whether he was real or not, your mama was with you in there. That's what I believe."

"If I was only remembering a song Mom taught me, then why didn't I hallucinate my mother?" None of it made any sense to her.

Austin shrugged. "No idea."

She remembered the black emptiness beneath her. "How far was it to the bottom?"

"Are you sure you want to know?"

She nodded.

"It was a good hundred twenty yards."

The thought made her stomach flip, made it hard to breathe.

Austin kissed her forehead, stroked her hair. "I wish you hadn't asked."

"So do I." Then she remembered she had something to tell him. "Austin, I … What you said the other night …"

"I meant every word."

Why was this so freaking hard?

"I … I love you. I do. I love you."

He pressed her hand to his lips, gave her a soft smile. "So you finally admit it."

Austin called Sutherland late Sunday night to ask for Monday and Friday off. That gave him five days to take care of Lexi, who was recovering from surgery and learning how to manage on crutches and who would need to come back to the trauma center on Tuesday for her second rabies treatment. As it turned out, however, Bob Jewell had moved all of her stuff back into her room at the inn. When she was discharged just before noon on Monday, she went back to the inn.

A part of Austin was angry about it. After all, Lexi had intended to move in with *him*. But he could see that Bob was trying to make up for what he'd done to drive his daughter away. Austin didn't want to get in the way of that.

It was Tuesday evening, after Lexi had lost sleep to nightmares, that Austin made a decision. He brought Mack and moved in with her.

Bob didn't object when Austin showed up with his backpack, an excited puppy, a dog crate, bowls, kibble, and an assortment of dog toys. "You know the way. I'm betting you've slept in her room before."

"No, Bob, I have not."

"Seriously?"

"Seriously."

Bob's eyes narrowed. "Then where did you go? Don't try to fool me. I know you were having sex with my daughter."

Lexi's voice came from her bedroom. "You two are *not* having this conversation!"

Austin lowered his voice, smiled, whatever was left of the teenage boy in him getting a thrill out of finally being able to rub it in her father's face. "We went anywhere we could. I had an inflatable mattress in the back of my Ford."

"Well, damn." Bob shook his head, then looked down at Mack. "Keep the dog out of the kitchen and away from guests."

"Yes, sir."

Britta flew home Wednesday, so Austin volunteered to pick her up, filling her in and answering her questions on the way back to Scarlet.

"Did they ever find the bastard's body?" she asked.

Austin nodded. "The Team stayed around that night and searched for him. That shaft was a good hundred twenty yards deep. He was at the bottom."

What he didn't tell Britta—what he hadn't told Lexi or her father—was that the protruding support beams that had caught and saved Lexi had collapsed during the evacuation, rotted wood finally giving out and falling more than three hundred feet and landing in pieces.

"Is it true that a knocker saved her?"

He told her what Lexi had seen and what he'd observed. "Some people believe the knocker was real. Lexi's description is pretty detailed, from his dialect to the candle on his hat. A group of them have already been up to the mine to toss in some pastry crusts as a thank you. I believe she was in deep shock and hallucinating."

"Wow." For a time, Britta was silent, clearly thinking about this. "Thank you for saving my sister's life, but please don't dump her again. You broke her heart last time. Do it again, and I'll bust both of your knees."

He decided right then that Britta and Cheyenne should be kept apart.

After Britta arrived, he didn't get much time alone with Lexi. While she and Britta talked and did sister stuff, he helped her dad with the yard work, made a few meals to share with the family, did his share of dishes, played checkers with her old man—and enjoyed it. He watched as the four of them—Lexi, Britta, their father, and Kendra—made hesitant steps toward one another, their attempts to forge closer ties touching to witness.

He would never take his own family for granted again.

At night, he slept beside Lexi, getting her pain pills, helping her get comfortable, and holding her when the nightmares closed in.

He had a little help from Mack on that last one. The puppy seemed to know before Austin when she was having a bad dream and would whimper and slather Lexi with puppy kisses.

"You're a rescue dog of a different sort, boy," he told Mack at four in the morning on Thursday. "But you're *not* sleeping between us. She's *my* woman."

"Are you seriously fighting with a puppy—over me?" Lexi gave a little laugh, looking tousled and beautiful despite the dark circles beneath her eyes.

"If that puppy had his way, I wouldn't be able to do this." Austin drew her against him, kissed her forehead, held her tight. "Go back to sleep. We've got you."

Lexi was sitting on the sofa, her leg propped up on pillows, talking with Britta and waiting for Austin to get back from Food Mart Thursday afternoon, when her father walked into the room with a couple of photo albums under his arm.

He sat, put them on the coffee table. "I … Well, I thought you two might want to see these. They're from the early years."

Lexi and Britta gaped at him, then looked at each other. Lexi hadn't known the albums existed, and she could tell from Britta's expression that her sister hadn't either. "We'd love to see them."

He moved a chair over, he and Britta arranging themselves near the sofa so they could all see the pages. "I started dating your mother in my first year of high school. She was the most beautiful thing I'd ever seen."

Slowly, a story Lexi and Britta had never heard unfolded in images they'd never seen of a mother they barely remembered, her face so like theirs. Their parents had fallen in love, then skipped college to take over the inn from their mother's aging parents.

"The inn came from mom's side of the family?" Britta asked.

That was a revelation.

Lexi studied each photo, a bittersweet ache behind her breastbone. A wedding in the garden outside among the aspens, which had been little saplings back then. Their mother with a wreath of roses in her red hair. Their father with a mullet, his face handsome and young. A honeymoon in Cancun. Month-by-month photos of their mother during her pregnancies, first with Lexi and then with Britta. A photo of their father sitting on their mother's hospital bed, holding Lexi on his lap, while their mother cradled newborn Britta, both of them happy.

First birthdays, second birthdays, third birthdays. The seasons and years moving by so quickly. Picnics. Halloween. An Easter egg hunt with matching pink dresses. A trip to Disneyland that neither Lexi nor Britta could recall.

"Mickey Mouse scared the hell out of both of you." Her father chuckled, pointing to a photo of the two of them crying while someone in a Mickey Mouse costume bent down to say hello.

He ran his finger over a photo of their mother holding them both on her lap beside a Christmas tree. "That was our last Christmas with her."

Lexi looked at the smiling, happy faces in the photo—a moment from a life she'd completely forgotten, a life that was about to change forever.

"The day she died…" Her father's voice broke, his words trailing off.

But they knew the story. They'd gotten it from newspapers.

Lexi reached out, touched his hand. "Dad, you don't have to—

"A drunk driver heading up the canyon tried to pass another driver. He hit your mother head-on coming around a curve. Her car… Her car went over the edge of the embankment, rolled down into the canyon."

Lexi's vision blurred, his words stirring dormant grief inside her.

"I drove down. The Team was called out. It seemed to me they were just standing around when they ought to be doing what they could to save her life." He coughed, cleared his throat. "The fire department had to cut her body out of the car. It took almost all night. The coroner said she'd died instantly in the crash, but I always thought someone could have done CPR or something if they had just gotten to her sooner."

He shut the photo album, set it gently on the coffee table. "Kendra's right when she said some part of me died. God, when I told you girls … It broke my heart. You didn't understand."

Lexi remembered that day.

"The inn had been your mother's pride and joy. I threw myself into making sure it survived. As long as I was working, I didn't have to feel."

Lexi thought she understood. He'd used work in the same way he'd been using alcohol—to numb himself.

But Britta looked angry, her face flushed, tears spilling down her cheeks. "You threw yourself into taking care of a business, but not your daughters, *her* daughters? Wow. That's screwed up, Dad. Mom loved us more than she loved this place."

His face crumpled. "When I looked at you two, I saw her."

He wiped the tears away with his sleeve as if he were ashamed of them, then took a breath and cleared his throat. "I've spent the past few years thinking my life was over, that I had nothing but the inn. The love of my life was gone. My daughters were far away and didn't want anything to do with me. My fault, I'll grant you. My wife was angry all the time. Hell, that's probably my fault, too. But when I heard Lexi had been abducted and had fallen down that mine … I don't want to lose you girls, too."

He coughed again, swallowed hard. "I know I haven't been the father you deserve, the father your mother would have wanted me to be, but if you give me a chance, I'd like to make it up to you."

"Oh, Dad." Lexi reached for her father.

Britta did the same.

And for the first time she could remember, he wrapped his arms around both of them and held them tight.

Chapter Twenty-Four

Austin had volunteered to drive Lexi to the orthopedic surgeon in Boulder on Friday afternoon, so he called Hawke that morning to ask whether he could drive into Denver to pick up Vic at the airport.

"Who is this guy anyway?" Hawke asked.

It took Austin a minute. Hawke thought Vic was a *man*?

Okay, this was going to be fun. "Vic is that friend from Chicago who bought the two of them tickets to the Adele concert and who's doing everything possible to make sure Lexi goes back to Illinois."

"Are you sure you don't want me to lose him in a ditch somewhere?"

"Nah, man." Austin fought to keep the amusement out of his voice. "Hey, I can handle the competition. Besides, if Lexi stays, it needs to be because she wants to live here, not because we murdered her friend."

He was serious about that last part. If she decided to go back to Chicago, he would have to let her go—and give her time to change her mind.

He hadn't brought up the issue with her. They hadn't talked about it even once. He didn't want to press her to make a decision, didn't want to do anything to drive her away. He'd said he'd give her time and, damn it, he would, even if it killed him.

"Yeah, okay, I see your point." There was a moment of silence. "We just finished helping the city handle a controlled burn, so I'm smoky and sweaty. But who cares? I can duck out a little early today and pick this guy up. What does he look like?"

Oh, about five-four, thick dark hair, big brown eyes, a sweet face and even sweeter curves.

Hey, Austin loved Lexi with all his heart, but that didn't mean he was blind.

"No clue." He bit his lip. "Just make a sign that says 'Vic Woodley.'"

"Woodley?" Hawke gave a snort. "The dude probably sips chardonnay, waxes his chest, and buffs his nails."

Austin was biting the insides of his cheeks now. He gave Hawke Vic's flight info. "Hey, man, I really appreciate this."

"Yeah, well, that's two you owe me, though I think uncuffing you from your bed ought to count double."

"You just had to bring that up, didn't you?" The bastard.

"Yeah."

Austin got off the phone to find Lexi watching him.

"What's so funny?"

He cleared his throat, wiped the grin off his face. "Oh, nothing. Hawke is just a real dumb shit sometimes."

"Can he pick Vic up?"

"Oh, yeah. No problem there."

Oh, how Austin wished he could be a fly on the wall at Denver International Airport. He would just love to see Hawke's face when he realized Vic was a woman—a gorgeous woman at that. Lexi had shown Austin photos from her iPhone last night when she'd had trouble falling back asleep.

"Are you ready to go?" Austin grabbed his keys.

Lexi adjusted her crutches, then got to her feet. "I'm finally starting to get the hang of these things."

"I'm coming, too." Britta breezed in with her handbag, in the act of putting on lipstick. "I want to hit the shops on Pearl Street."

Austin opened the back door for them and saw Bob and Kendra sitting on the bench under the aspens—and holding hands. Though Kendra hadn't yet moved back in with her husband, Austin was pretty sure the two of them would make a go of it again. What had happened to Lexi seemed to have cut through their bullshit.

They got to their feet and walked toward the house, hand in hand.

"How long you kids planning on being out?" her father asked.

"I don't know—a couple of hours." Lexi stopped, turned on her crutches to face her dad. "It's an hour to Boulder and back again, plus they want to take X-rays. I have no idea how long we'll have to wait. Brit's going to shop."

"So a couple of hours then?"

Kendra leaned in, lowered her. "We're good, honey. You can't last that long."

Bob grinned, and the two of them hurried into the inn.

Lexi shared a horrified glance with her sister, mortification on both their faces, then looked up at Austin. "Please get me as far away from here as you can."

Lexi was sitting in the kitchen, her right leg elevated on a chair, when Eric's truck pulled up. It was funny to think that she hadn't really been looking forward to Vic's arrival because of the time she'd lose with Austin. But things had changed.

Austin was staying here with her, so she wouldn't be losing time with him at all. Now, she couldn't wait to see her friend.

She reached for her crutches and got to her feet in time for Eric to appear in the doorway, two suitcases in his hands.

Austin opened the door for him. "Need help with that?"

"No, thanks, *buddy*." Eric glared at Austin, still wearing his Scarlet Springs Fire Department T-shirt, streaks of soot on one cheek. "Just show me where you want them."

"I said I can handle it myself." Vic was right behind him, wearing a breezy tank dress in black crepe, strappy black heels on her feet, an irritated frown on her face.

Kendra stood. "She's upstairs in room seven."

"I know the way." Eric disappeared toward the elevator.

"Oh, my God. Look at you!" Vic stepped forward, gave Lexi a warm hug. Lexi had already told her the whole story over the phone, so she didn't need to explain. "Does it hurt? You should probably sit down. Don't you think you should sit down?"

Lexi laughed. "I'm fine. The doctor says I'm healing well."

She introduced Vic to her father, Kendra, Britta, and finally Austin.

Vic shook his hand, smiled sweetly. "I've heard *so* much about you."

Austin grinned. "I just bet you have."

Okay, so this was getting awkward.

Lexi cut it short. "Is anyone hungry? What do you say we head to Knockers?"

Britta said she'd stay home with their dad and Kendra. Eric insisted he needed to go home and take a shower.

"See you later, Vic*toria*." He glared at Austin again and walked out the door.

"What was that about?" Lexi asked Vic.

"I'll tell you later," Vic whispered.

Austin drove Lexi and Vic the short distance to Knockers, Vic staring out at their surroundings.

"You never told me how beautiful it is here." There was an accusing tone to her voice, as if Lexi had tried to keep that secret.

"Well, it *is* Colorado."

It was Lexi's first time at the pub since her ordeal. When she stepped inside, a hush fell over the room, and the band quit playing. And then the place erupted in cheers.

A hard lump formed in Lexi's throat, tears threatening to ruin her mascara.

These people cared about her. She'd been away for twelve years, hadn't given them a passing thought, and still they cared about her.

She blinked back the tears, glanced around, the room a sea of smiling faces, so many of them familiar. Megs and most of the Team members were there, too. They sat together near the climbing wall as usual.

Rain hurried up to Lexi, gave her a gentle hug. "Welcome back! God, it's good to see you safe and getting around. You're Joe's guest, so order whatever you want."

"Thanks. That's so sweet of him." She glanced over Rain's shoulder, saw Joe waving to her from behind the bar, a smile on his face.

"Wow." Vic glanced around. "Everyone really *does* know you here."

With Austin's help, Lexi threaded her way through the tables to a place Megs had saved for her.

"How are you feeling?"

"I'm doing a lot better, thanks to all of you."

These people—her friends—had helped save her life.

Remembering her manners, Lexi introduced Vic to Megs, Mitch, Harrison, Sasha, Malachi, Nicole, Kenzie, Chaska and Winona.

"Those two on the rock wall are Creed Herrera and Jesse Moretti."

But Vic wasn't listening. She was still staring at Chaska.

Lexi leaned over, whispered in her ear. "You might want to close your mouth."

Vic's jaw snapped shut. "You didn't tell me the men here were all so … *hot.*"

Lexi shrugged. "It's Colorado."

They had finished their meals by the time Hawke walked in.

Austin knew with one glance that his buddy was still pissed off, and he was pretty sure he knew why. He got up from the table, pressed a kiss to Lexi's cheek. "I'm going to find out what's up with Hawke."

He met Hawke in the center of the pub. "Want to play a game of pool?"

Hawke glared at him but followed him to the back corner. They claimed a table, Austin racking the balls, while Hawke picked out two cues.

"You let me believe she was a guy."

Guilty as charged. "What's so bad about that? What happened?"

"Thanks to you, I made an ass of myself."

Austin couldn't stop himself. "You don't usually need my help for that."

"Funny." Hawke took the break shot, balls racing over green felt, a solid dropping into a side pocket. "So I get there, and I see that *Vic's* flight had gotten in thirty minutes early. I figure he's waiting somewhere in the terminal, so I page him."

"Are we calling our shots?" Austin stepped aside as Hawke circled the table.

"Six ball, side." Hawke shot again, missed.

"So you paged him."

"Meantime, I head to the little coffee shop to grab a bottle of water, and this incredibly hot chick gets in line behind me. I smile and say hi, making sure she sees the Scarlet FD logo on my T-shirt. And do you know what she says to me?"

"Nine, side." Austin took his shot, made the ball, then circled the table to line up the next one. "What did she say?"

"She leans in, looks me straight in the eyes, and whispers, 'Firemen are my favorite color.' Jesus!"

Austin bent down. "Fifteen, corner."

This time, he missed.

"So I'm thinking, great, this woman and I have a connection. I tell her I'm waiting for someone. She says she's waiting, too. So we sit, and I'm wishing I could ditch this Vic dude I'm picking up and take her out for a drink."

"So far I don't see how you made an ass of yourself."

Hawke bent down, lined up his shot. "Two, corner pocket."

He sank it. "I start telling her how I came to pick up some guy for my good friend who almost died in a mine shaft and how this asshole has flown out from Chicago to lure my friend away from her boyfriend, a guy who happens to be my best friend."

Ah. Okay. Austin understood now. "Do you usually go into that kind of detail with strangers at the airport?"

"I thought we had a connection, man." Hawke circled the table again, his gaze meeting Austin's. "So she gets this funny look on her face and asks me the name of the guy I'm picking up. I show her my sign. She turns beet red, glares at me, tells me that's her name. Then she calls me a jerk and stomps off on those sassy little heels of hers, dragging her luggage behind her."

Austin was glad Hawke was busy lining up a shot and couldn't see the grin on his face. "Did you go after her?"

"Of course, I went after her. Six and three, side." He made the six, but the three spiraled off.

Austin stepped up, studied the table.

"I know she's Lexi's friend, but the woman is cold. I apologized, but she wasn't interested. She probably would have taken a cab or walked all the way here if she could have. She finally agreed to go with me, but she wouldn't let me help her with her baggage. She sat there, angry as hell, all the way back from Denver. She's probably sitting over there right now telling Lexi how you and I joked about dumping 'her friend Vic' in a ditch."

Austin bent down. "Twelve, corner. You told her that, too? And, hey, that was *you*. Did you tell her what I said about being able to handle the competition and all that?"

Eric shook his head. "I forgot."

Austin took his shot, missed.

Austin stood upright. He could see Lexi and Vic, heads bent together, Vic saying something, an expression of outrage on her face. "Shit."

Hawke came to stand beside him, his gaze on Vic. "Tell me about it."

"Then he says to me, 'I told my buddy we should just dump this guy in a ditch somewhere.' I'm starting to get suspicious, so I ask him the name of the guy he's supposed to pick up. He pulls this piece of paper out of his pocket, unfolds it—and it has *my* name on it."

Lexi fought not to laugh, took a sip of her sweet and fruity Sexy Lexi. Hey, she had to try it, right? "It was just a misunderstanding."

"I'm not angry because he thought I was a guy. That's kind of funny. What ticked me off was hearing that he and Austin are conspiring to keep you here."

"They were just joking. The three of us have been friends since we were little. They don't want me to leave Scarlet any more than you want me to leave Chicago. Besides, Austin loves me, and Eric is his best friend. He doesn't want to see Austin hurt."

"I know he's a firefighter and he's your friend, but I think he's a jerk." Vic had clearly made up her mind. "Is he still looking this way?"

Maybe Vic didn't dislike Eric quite as much as she wanted to believe.

Lexi glanced over to where Austin and Eric were playing pool. "He's taking a shot now, but he was looking this way just a moment ago."

Bear walked up to the table, hat in hand, Winona beside him.

"Bear has something important he needs to say." Winona waited patiently beside him, while Bear fidgeted with his hat, at a loss for words now that he wasn't preaching. "What did you want to tell her?"

"Sorry, Lexi," Bear said after a moment. "I didn't know he was such a bad man. I said to him, 'Do not participate in the unfruitful deeds of darkness. Ill-gotten treasures have no lasting value,' but he didn't listen. Are you mad at me?"

"No, Bear. I'm not mad at you."

"You're not?" He looked confused by this.

Lexi got to her feet—or, really, her foot. Using one crutch for balance, she kissed Bear on his whiskery cheek. "It wasn't your fault. He was an evil man. I never blamed you. I'm just glad you're okay."

"See?" Winona smiled up at him. "I told you she wasn't mad at you."

Bear took a moment to absorb all of this. Then his eyes went wide, and a grin lit up his face. He stood up tall and proud. "For if you forgive other people when they sin against you, your heavenly Father will also forgive you!"

"Come on, buddy. Save the sermon till after you've had some dinner." Winona led Bear toward a table, smiling at Lexi over her shoulder.

Lexi sat and found Vic staring after them.

"Who was that?"

"That's Bear. He lives somewhere west of town in the mountains—no one really knows where. He comes down to preach and ask for food or spare change."

"What happened to him?" Vic was still watching him, her voice soft with compassion. "He doesn't seem like he's all there."

"No one knows why he is the way he is. The town just takes care of him."

Vic smiled. "So far Scarlet Springs is not at all what I imagined it would be."

Lexi had to know. "What did you expect?"

"Going off what you've told me, I figured it was a tiny town where there's nothing to do but wish you were someplace else."

Lexi couldn't blame her for having that impression. "That's pretty much how I felt about it for most of my life."

That's not how she felt now.

"It's beautiful here, and the people—they really care about you."

"I know." The crazy thing was she cared about them, too. She cared far more than she had realized.

They talked for a while about the things Vic might want to see—Rocky Mountain National Park, Estes Park, the mining museum, the Continental Divide. Then Austin and Eric rejoined them.

"Who won?" Lexi asked.

"Hawke crushed me." Austin sat beside her. "How do you feel? I don't want to wear you out."

She hated to admit it, but she was fading. "I'm ready to go when you are."

Vic looked surprised by the thought of leaving so soon. "What time is it?"

Eric glanced at his watch. "Eight-thirty-five."

"I might stay for a while, if that's okay."

Lexi didn't mind. "The inn is just a few blocks away."

"I'll make sure she gets back safely." Eric looked over at Vic. "Victoria and I need to start over anyway. We didn't get off on the best foot."

That much was true.

With Austin holding one arm, Lexi got up from the table, but she hadn't taken a single step when a hush fell over the room.

Rain appeared holding a tray with four shot glasses on it, each one filled with amber liquid. "Before you go, Joe wants to make a toast. It's the good stuff."

"A toast?" Lexi, Austin, Eric, Vic each took a glass.

Then Joe stepped out from behind the bar, his long dark hair up in a bun.

"Who's that?" Vic whispered.

"That's Caribou Joe—Joe Moffat," Lexi whispered back. "He owns this place. His grandparents owned the Caribou Mine where most of our grandparents worked."

"We came close to losing one of ours this week," Joe said. "Lexi's been away for a long time, but we all remember her. Hell, the very rock in these mountains remembers her. It's been a couple of decades since anyone has seen a knocker, but when Lexi needed them, they were there for her. So let's remember them tonight."

His words put a lump in Lexi's throat.

Joe raised his glass. "To the knockers!"

"To the knockers!"

Lexi raised her glass, whispered her own toast. "Thank you, Jack."

And then she drank.

Chapter Twenty-Five

On Saturday, Austin kissed a sleeping Lexi goodbye, passed her father and Kendra at the breakfast table, and went back to work. He drove to the county building, climbers already hitting the crags in Boulder Canyon, hoping to get their fix of vertical before the sun heated the rocks. He parked his Tahoe and walked inside to clock in and check his mailbox. He had just stamped his time card when Sutherland opened the door to his office.

What was he doing here on a Saturday? He wore street clothes, not a uniform, a cup of coffee in his hand.

"Taylor, we need to talk."

Damn.

When your boss put it like that, it was never good news.

Austin followed Sutherland into his office, shut the door behind him, pretty sure he knew what this was about. "I should have disclosed to McBride that Lexi and I are involved. He asked whether I knew the area and—"

"Shut up, and sit down. This isn't about that."

It wasn't?

Austin sat.

"I got a call from the county attorney on Monday. He says you found Bear homesteading on the Haley property and came to him with this information, hoping to find some way to circumvent county statutes."

Well, shit.

"Yes, sir."

"Why didn't you come to me?"

"If I'd come to you, you'd have had to act. As the head of this department, you are answerable to the county commissioners. From the moment I told you, you would have faced the responsibility of evicting Bear. I was hoping to find a way to keep Bear in his cabin before putting you and him through all of that turmoil."

Sutherland nodded. "The Colorado Homestead Act."

"The Colorado Homestead Act?"

"It's a law that was passed before Colorado became a state. It protects homesteaders from creditors and others who want to lay claim to their land. Basically, it says that if you've lived on a piece of land for five years and improved that land, it belongs to you outright. Every mortgage in the state includes language exempting the property from the act. Otherwise, some savvy person might live in a house for five years, fix it up, and then decide they don't have to repay their loan."

Austin took all of this in. "So, because Bear has been up there forever, an argument could be made that it's legally *his* land."

"Exactly. We don't want that legal precedent, so we're not going to try to evict him. That's our story, anyway, and we're sticking to it."

Relief washed through Austin. "That's a load off my mind."

He did not want to be the guy who made Bear homeless.

"If you had come to me from the beginning, you wouldn't have had to worry."

Austin stared at his boss. "You knew?"

"Of course, I knew. There are a handful of people in county government who know where Bear lives. We've kept this quiet ever since we bought the property. If the public found out, some would want him evicted. Others would decide to build their own cabins on public land. What a damned mess that would be."

Yes, it would."

"Like you, we don't see how we serve the public good by making him homeless. I've personally asked him to take firewood only from the south side of the creek where the forest is too dense and we're trying to thin them anyway. He keeps to that."

"How long has he been there?"

"No one really knows. Bear is a man of mystery."

"Have you told Hatfield?"

Sutherland nodded. "He and I had this little conversation a few days ago. He didn't know you'd gone to the county attorney, who, by the way, thinks you ought to be given a formal reprimand for going outside the chain of command."

A formal reprimand. He hadn't seen that coming. It would go in his permanent file and probably make it impossible for him to get a raise this year. Still, he could accept that. At least his conscience was clear.

"I wanted to do what was best for Bear."

"I see that. You're one of the best I've ever worked with, Taylor. It's not just your college degree and your outdoor skills. You know the land. You know the flora, the fauna. You're good with people. You bring real passion to the job. This is what you're meant to be doing. So please don't do anything that forces me to bust your ass."

"I apologize, sir. It won't happen again. Is there something you need me to sign?"

"What? No! The county attorney can shove it. I'm not giving you a reprimand. This is as far as it goes. But next time, Taylor, trust me."

Austin smiled. "You got it."

*L*exi spent Saturday riding in the backseat of her dad's Outback, her leg propped up on the seat next to her, while Britta drove her and Vic to see the sights. They took her on a tour of the mining museum, then drove to Estes Park and into Rocky Mountain National Park, where Lexi watched her friend stare wide-eyed at the sea of jagged mountain tops from Rainbow Curve, high on Trail Ridge Road.

"How can this be real?" she whispered.

On Sunday, Lexi went to the trauma center for her third rabies shot. And then it was time for Britta to leave for the airport. She'd booked a shuttle ride to Denver, so they said their farewells at the inn.

It was a measure of how much things had changed that Lexi and Britta were in tears when she said goodbye. "I'll be back for Christmas, Dad, I promise."

"Thanks for coming, baby girl. It's been good to see you."

Lexi hugged her sister tight. "Thanks for being here for me."

Brit hugged her right back. "Are you kidding? Some asshole almost gets my sister killed? Where else would I be?" She dropped her voice to a whisper. "Just between us, I have a feeling you won't be leaving Colorado anytime soon."

It wasn't just between them, however. Vic knew.

Lexi hadn't said anything to her, but she knew just the same.

She didn't bring it up right away. She waited until she and Lexi were upstairs in her guestroom, Lexi on the chaise longue where she could prop up her leg and Vic in the chair near the window. "You know, I can give your Adele ticket to someone else."

Lexi felt relief that Vic had brought it up. "That's probably a good idea. I'm not sure I'd be comfortable traveling with my leg and—"

"It's just the two of us here, Lexi. You're feeling torn up trying to decide whether to stay here or come back to Chicago. From where I sit, it's a no-brainer. Stay."

And just like that—tears again. What was wrong with her lately?

"I thought you'd be upset. You had an ulterior motive for coming here, remember? You're supposed to make sure I *don't* stay."

Vic handed her a box of tissues. "You've got an incredibly hot man who loves you enough to go down a mine shaft after you. You've got your friends on the rescue team and at the wildlife sanctuary. You've got an entire town that cares what happens to you. You know that's not how it is in Chicago."

"You stood by me."

"That's what true friends do." Vic smiled. "Besides, who says I'm not upset? I'm sad that my best friend is going to be living in this amazing place, while I sit at a desk in Chicago waiting for the weekend so I can sit in my condo alone and binge Netflix."

Lexi laughed, wiping the tears from her eyes. "You could always move here. You may have noticed the men."

Or one particular man.

"Oh, yes, I did. It *is* tempting." Vic looked out the window, then turned her gaze back to Lexi. There were tears in *her* eyes now. "The truth is I'd be the worst friend ever if I tried to take you away from all of this so that I didn't have to miss you."

"Thanks, Vic."

They both sniffed.

"So, when are you going to tell Austin?"

Lexi had given this a lot of thought. "When the time is right."

"So ... what are we going to do this afternoon?" Vic dabbed her eyes. "I am *not* going to spend my last day in Colorado sitting in this room, no matter how comfortable or quaint or cute it is."

Lexi had an idea. "Want a tour of our historic firehouse?"

Vic gaped at her in open-mouthed outrage. "Oh, you are evil!"

She'd always had a weakness for firefighters.

"Now it's my turn to be a good friend." She pulled out her phone and called Eric.

"Harrison Conrad. Sasha Dillon. Dave Hatfield. Eric Hawke. Creed Herrera ..."

Austin sat with Lexi in the ops room waiting while Megs took roll, his hair still wet from his shower. Everyone was here tonight, including Gabe Rossiter, his four-year-old daughter asleep on his lap. They had all come to hear Lexi's official report—and to give her a little surprise in gratitude for her work.

She sat beside him, her crutches propped up against the table, a folder of printed documents sitting before her. "First, I want to thank all of you for what you did to save my life. I wouldn't be here today without you."

"You're welcome."

"Happy to help."

"That's what we do."

Then she launched into her report, passing documents around, explaining how she'd conducted the audit and describing the tricks that Breece had used to hide his fraud from them. "He started out with small amounts, probably afraid he'd get caught. But when that didn't happen, he got bolder."

She was confident, her explanations easy to understand, her answers clear and concise. Austin had never really seen this side of Lexi before, the professional side. Sure, he'd seen her working, but he hadn't really known what she was doing. He certainly hadn't understood how much an audit entailed.

She came to the punch line. "In all, he stole seventy-two thousand six hundred dollars from this organization."

"What? Jesus!" Rossiter looked like he might faint. "When you said embezzlement, I was thinking maybe ten grand."

"This is my fault." Megs looked around at the group. "If my resignation will help in any way—to appease donors, for example—"

"No *way* are you resigning." Austin wouldn't have it.

Neither would anyone else. They shouted out their support for Megs, everyone talking at once so that no one could hear anything. When they'd quieted down, Lexi spoke again.

"It's not your fault, and I don't think your resignation will help anything." Lexi drew a document out of the folder, handed it to Megs. "You're the face of this organization and a well-respected member of the climbing community. I think the Team needs you now more than ever."

"What's this?"

"It's an overview of a possible PR approach to managing this crisis. A friend of mine was in town this weekend. Some of you met her." She looked pointedly at Hawke.

Hawke frowned, shifted in his chair.

Lexi explained. "She works for a PR firm in Chicago. I picked her brain last night. Megs, you're at the heart of the plan."

Megs read through it, nodding, then handed it to Ahearn. "I suppose it can't hurt to give it a try."

"Do the rest of us get to know, or is this classified?" Moretti asked.

Lexi smiled. "The plan calls for a straight-up acknowledgment of what has happened, combined with the release of information documenting how many hours you collectively volunteer each year, how many lives you save, the expense involved in running an all-volunteer organization of this kind, and so on. Show the world the value of what you do, and my bet is that the public will rally around you."

"Where is that bastard?" Rossiter asked.

"If I knew, I wouldn't be sitting here," Austin muttered under his breath.

"I hear you," Hawke agreed.

"There's a warrant out for his arrest, but he's made himself scarce," Megs answered. "I guess he doesn't relish the idea of going to prison."

"They'll find him," Moretti said. "And when they do…"

Lexi closed her folder. "That's all I have for you. If you need me to explain anything in more detail, let me know. This report should make things easy for the district attorney. In the meantime, I'm happy to help you start implementing the PR plan."

A chorus of "Thanks, Lexi" moved through the room.

"We've got something for you." Megs took a yellow Team T-shirt out of her backpack and passed it across the table to Lexi.

Everyone laughed.

Lexi pushed it back. "Thanks, but you already gave me one. I don't want to use up Team resources when things are tight."

"Aren't you a peach?" Megs smiled. "I wish the rest of you had *her* attitude."

"Way to make us look bad, Jewell," Sasha joked.

Megs pushed the T-shirt back over to Lexi. "Look at it."

Austin couldn't keep the grin off his face. "You don't have a T-shirt like this."

Lexi unfolded it, held it up.

The front was the same, but the back…

She turned it around. "Oh!"

There on the back was her last name in big, black letters: JEWELL.

She turned to Austin. "Did you know about this?"

"Of course. Hey, I can keep a secret—even from you."

"We took a vote. In gratitude for the important work you've done for us, we've made you a supporting member," Megs explained. "Whether you stay in Scarlet or head back to your life in Chicago, you'll still be part of the Team."

"Damn it!" Lexi pressed the heels of her hands to her eyes. "You're going to make me cry."

Austin rested a hand against her back in silent support, laughing with the others. But there was a knot in his chest. Would she stay here with him, with the people who cared about her, or would she go back to the city?

*L*exi lifted herself into the front seat of Eric's Chevy Silverado, then handed Austin her handbag and crutches, which he stuck behind her seat.

Her father stepped out of the back door. "Hey, where's your Tahoe? Isn't that Hawke's truck?"

"Tonight's the only night of the year when firefighters get to *start* fires and blow stuff up, so he's busy having the time of his life. He let me borrow it while I get some engine work done."

Oh, Austin was smooth! But then he'd always been the better fibber.

"Where are the two of you headed?" Her father walked toward them.

He was going to look. She knew he was going to look.

Austin walked around to the driver's side. "I thought we'd drive up to Caribou ad watch the fireworks from there."

"That'll give you a nice view." Her father peered into the truck's bed. "No air mattress."

He'd done it. He'd looked.

"Dad! I'm a grownup now."

"I was just checking." He chuckled to himself, then turned around and walked back toward the house. "Have a good time."

Lexi buckled her seatbelt. "I told you he'd look. Where did you hide it?"

Austin grinned. "It's in the toolbox along with the air pump."

They drove up the highway, sunset painting the sky above the Indian Peaks in pinks and oranges, the day's heat giving way to a cool breeze. Lexi reached over, rested her hand on Austin's thigh, a sense of contentment washing through her, mingling with anticipation.

She had a surprise for him.

They talked about a little of everything as they drove. Austin had written eight tickets to people carrying open containers of alcohol today—a record. The injured beaver Winona had been trying to save was responding to antibiotics. New donations to the Team had passed $30,000 yesterday. Sasha was leaving tomorrow to compete in an international sports climbing competition.

It took all of ten minutes to reach the turnoff. Caribou, now a ghost town, sat right at 10,000 feet elevation—just below timberline. It had once been a thriving mining town of 3,000. Now only a few stone buildings and a cemetery were left to tell the world that people had once made their lives here, worked here, died here.

Austin turned onto the dirt road that would take them to their secret spot—a secluded meadow overlooking Scarlet Springs. He took his right hand off the wheel, threaded his fingers through hers. "Do you realize it was twelve years ago tonight?"

"Yes." Lexi had thought about that all day. That's the reason she'd waited till tonight to tell him. She liked the symmetry of it. Or maybe Rose was rubbing off on her. "Strange, isn't it?"

"I made the biggest mistake of my life that night."

She squeezed his hand. "We both made mistakes."

"I didn't bring that up to pressure you, by the way."

She gave him a smile. "I'm not feeling pressured."

He parked where they had always parked, then left her in the cab while he got out the air mattress and inflated it—a process that took almost as long as the drive. "This foot pump is a lot better than that old bicycle pump I used to use."

Lexi had forgotten about that. "I can't believe we used to do this all the time."

When the mattress was fully inflated, Austin put the pump in the toolbox and settled the mattress in the pickup's bed. Then he hopped to the ground and opened Lexi's door. "It's probably easiest if I just carry you and lift you over the side."

"Don't drop me." She wrapped her arms around Austin's neck.

"Not a chance." He scooped her into his arms and lifted her out of the truck, holding her for a moment and pressing a kiss to her nose. "I kind of like this."

"So do I." Why had she ever thought she could live without this man?

He carried her to the back, holding her steady while she climbed over the side and sat on the air mattress. Then he leaped up onto the tailgate and sat beside her.

To the west, the sun had set, the horizon bright pink.

"The fireworks will be starting soon." His lips curved in a slow smile. "Then again, we didn't really come here for that, did we?"

He leaned over to kiss her, but she stopped him.

"There's something I've been meaning to tell you." She could see by the subtle shift in his expression that her words had made him instantly wary.

"Okay."

She came out with it. "When I get this boot off, I'm going back to Chicago—and I'm really hoping you'll come with me."

He closed his eyes, his brow furrowed. "That's your decision?"

She'd meant to tease him, not torment him. "I can't very well load all my furniture into a moving van by myself. I need you to lift the heavy things."

His eyes snapped open. "What?"

She reached up, cupped his jaw. "I'm moving back to Scarlet for good."

The hope and relief in his eyes made her heart melt. "Are you sure?"

God, yes, she was sure.

"You know that little house on the corner of First and Valley View?"

"That Victorian cottage with the iron fence that we all thought was haunted?"

"I bought it." She was so excited finally to be able to tell him this. "I closed on it Friday. It's going to be my office—Jewell and Associates. I'm opening my own CPA firm. Brit has already designed the logo. It needs a lot of fixing up, but when it's restored, it will be adorable."

But she was going too fast for him.

He ran a thumb down her cheek, his eyes looking intently into hers. "You're really staying?"

"Yes. I am." She tried to explain. "I spent my childhood wanting to run away from this place without really knowing why. I think my mother's death was so painful that it tore my family apart, and I just wanted to be somewhere I didn't feel ... so *hurt*."

"It's a lot to lose your mother—and your father—when you're only four."

She swallowed the lump in her throat. "This past month, I've come to see everything differently—my family, the town. When I was tied up in litigation in Chicago, all of my friends except Vic turned away from me. But when I was trapped in that mine shaft, you were all there for me—the whole town. It didn't matter that I'd been gone for twelve years. Joe even closed the pub."

"Don't forget that he also named a drink after you. How many drinks are named after you in Chicago?"

That made her laugh. "People here love me—especially you."

"Especially me." He leaned down, brushed his lips over hers.

"I love you, Austin. I don't want to live without you."

"That is the best damned news I've heard in twelve years." He kissed her hard this time, slow and deep, pushing her back onto the mattress.

And the sky above them burst into color.

Also by Pamela Clare

Romantic Suspense

I-Team Series

Extreme Exposure (Book 1)

Heaven Can't Wait (Book 1.5)

Hard Evidence (Book 2)

Unlawful Contact (Book 3)

Naked Edge (Book 4)

Breaking Point (Book 5)

Skin Deep: An I-Team After Hours Novella (Book 5.5)

First Strike: The Prequel to Striking Distance (Book 5.9)

Striking Distance (Book 6)

Soul Deep: An I-Team After Hours Novella (Book 6.5)

Seduction Game (Book 7)

Dead by Midnight: An I-Team Christmas (Book 7.5)

Historical Romance

Kenleigh-Blakewell Family Saga

Sweet Release (Book 1)

Carnal Gift (Book 2)

Ride the Fire (Book 3)

MacKinnon's Rangers series

Surrender (Book I)

Untamed (Book 2)

Defiant (Book 3)

Upon A Winter's Night: A MacKinnon's Rangers Christmas Novella (Book 3.5)

About The Author

USA Today best-selling author Pamela Clare began her writing career as a columnist and investigative reporter and eventually became the first woman editor-in-chief of two different newspapers. Along the way, she and her team won numerous state and national honors, including the National Journalism Award for Public Service. In 2011, Clare was awarded the Keeper of the Flame Lifetime Achievement Award. A single mother with two sons, she writes historical romance and contemporary romantic suspense at the foot of the beautiful Rocky Mountains. To learn more about her or her books, visit her website at www.pamelaclare.com. You can keep up with her on Goodreads, on Facebook, or search for @Pamela_Clare on Twitter to follow her there.